ALMOST

KARENA LAPLACE

AUTHOR
ACADEMY elite

Copyright © 2018 by Karena LaPlace
All rights reserved.

Printed in the United State of America

Published by Author Academy Elite
P.O. Box 43, Powell, OH 43035

www.AuthorAcademyElite.com

Edited by Natalie Hanemann and Kendra Koger
Cover artwork by Augusto Silva at BlesseD'Signs

Paperback ISBN: 978-1-64085-220-4

Hardcover ISBN: 978-1-64085-221-1

Library of Congress Control Number: 2018933874

Dedication

To Ann Johnson, the sweetest and funniest mother ever. Thank you for giving me life.

To James LaPlace, my match, my sweetheart, my husband. You brighten my days and nights.

To Aija, my joyful songbird, my daughter. Your very presence causes my heart to leap for joy.

To Joshua, my miracle, my energetic and inquisitive baby boy. You are my answered prayer.

To DarKel, my nephew. I love you!

To my inner circle, my siblings. Thanks for life lessons, genuine love, and always looking out for your little sister.

In loving memory of Walter Johnson, Sr. I am who I am in God because you were my father.

CONTENTS

PROLOGUE

PAUL

The day began just like any other mid-May afternoon in the twin cities of Champaign-Urbana, Illinois. But any activity related to the infamous Chameleon would prove to be anything but typical.

Teachers across town were preparing to dismiss for the weekend. I sat in my patrol car at a local elementary school, the humidity a damp blanket hugging my skin. My radar gun was extended to ensure that motorists complied with the twenty-mile-per-hour speed zone. The urban, soulful sounds of Common, Nelly, and Toni Braxton were programmed in my cell phone and shuffle-played through my car speakers. That was before dispatch interrupted.

"We have a potential 10-29F. Assailant reported running from The Healthy Women's Clinic toward Peachtree and Pine. Any nearby officers?"

"Go ahead with the description, Rose." I scanned the area for anyone looking suspicious, my radar gun now on the passenger seat.

"The assailant is a white male, approximately seventy years old, about five feet ten inches, 170 pounds, has white hair, gray eyes. He's wearing a pinstriped, navy blue suit, white shirt, red tie."

"10-8." Easing out of the school zone, I flicked on my lights, but not the siren. I didn't want to alert the accused of my presence. My heart pounded at the thought that this could be him. This would be the biggest break, in the biggest case, in the history of cases that this state had ever known.

Why else would a seventy-year-old man be running from a women's clinic? Random thoughts crowded my mind like a thousand-piece puzzle. Holding my breath for several seconds before exhaling helped to still my thoughts. I understood that if I handled this pursuit just right, and apprehended this criminal, I would accomplish what many of my own colleagues swore to me was impossible.

I hovered over the steering wheel as I cruised through the upscale subdivision reported by dispatch. The speedometer steadied at ten miles per hour. I stopped when I saw a woman with salt-and-pepper hair fixated on me and watering her newspaper instead of a nearby bed of flowers. I lowered the passenger window and motioned her over. She dropped the hose and scampered through her well-manicured lawn.

"How might I assist you, officer?"

While she was still speaking, I spotted the blur of navy dash between two houses up the street.

"I'm sorry, ma'am," I yelled while flooring the gas pedal.

Then, between two houses, farther down the street, I saw the navy blur again. In a single motion, I slammed the car into park and jumped out. From my holster, I removed the Taser instead of the gun. We needed this one alive. As I crept from one house to the next, I had to remember to swallow. The crashing sound of metal hitting the concrete came from behind another home, and my body reacted before my mind could process it. I moved from one backyard to the next, thankful none of them were enclosed. When I reached the source of the noise, I found a restaurant-sized barbecue grill broken into pieces on a patio. Not a person in sight.

With my arms extended and locked, I held the yellow and black Taser like a gun. I blinked away the sweat that trickled from my hairline and surveyed rows of houses. All I saw were peaceful pastures of backyard green. I eased to the front of the houses. Nothing out of the ordinary. Fighting feelings of defeat, I snapped my Taser back into the holster and observed the neighborhood, wishing I had my sunglasses. Down the street I saw a young couple taking a jog. An older woman walking a well-groomed Yorkshire terrier. All around, I saw moderate activity. But no one who resembled the accused.

When Officer Hernandez screeched to a stop alongside me and parked in the opposite direction, I didn't bother to look at him.

"Looking a little spooked there, Officer Reese. I heard the dispatcher's description. Are you afraid of a senior citizen?"

"Naw, man. It's just that . . . I think it's the Chameleon."

"Well, why didn't you say something before now? There you go. Tryin' to take all the glory for yourself. I'm calling for backup."

Minutes after Officer Hernandez hung up with dispatch, more than a dozen police cars swarmed the neighborhood, blocking every entrance and exit point.

Tasers drawn, blue uniforms swarmed the neighborhood like bees on a mission. Every inch of open land was searched. Front and rear yards. Areas with an overabundance of trees. Homeowners were questioned through cracked doors and encouraged to stay in their homes until the search was over. In just under a half hour, the entire subdivision had been searched. But the Chameleon had not been located. The search was called off.

"He could be hiding in someone's home or garage." I stood next to Chief Lewis as we watched squad cars pull away.

"He very well might be, Paul, but we can't search inside every home. You know that. Maybe next time, son." My boss started off toward his unmarked car.

"If it's okay with you, I'm just going to drive through the neighborhood a few more times."

"If that's what you need to do, I won't interfere. All I ask is that you remember your training."

"You got it, Chief."

I watched him drive off. Something in my gut told me the Chameleon was still in the neighborhood. Watching. I could feel it. I sat in the car, engine running. Waiting.

People emerged from their homes like a great exodus was about to take place. Neighbors congregated and shared what they knew. I drove through the neighborhood, looking up and down streets before I parked again. I glanced into the rearview mirror every so often. A school bus full of children pulled up a block away. Then two neighbors scurried toward me.

"Good afternoon, officer." A fifty-something-year-old man adjusted his black wire-rimmed glasses and tucked his shirt into his khaki shorts.

"Good afternoon, gentlemen." I looked past them into the distance. "What can I do for you?"

"We couldn't help but notice all the commotion in our normally quiet neighborhood. We're a little concerned. Wondering if you could give us some insight about what's happening 'round here," said the other neighbor, whose round belly made his shirt look too small. His large reading glasses rested on his balding head. He leaned against the squad car, pausing every couple words to catch his breath before he spoke again. "What are your names?"

The taller guy answered. "I'm Bob, and this here is Harry."

I offered them a firm handshake.

"Well, Bob and Harry, we have a seventy-year-old suspect on the loose. He was last seen running from the clinic around the corner and into this subdivision."

"He must be pretty dangerous since your entire police force was just here looking for him." Bob clearly was fishing for information.

"Yeah, it looked like something from the movies. Are we safe? Should I consider putting my house on the market?" Harry's chuckle conflicted with his eye contact and wrinkled forehead.

"Gentlemen, I don't know that I, personally, would go so far as to sell my house over something like—"

I peered down the road. Two blocks away, I watched as more children marched off the bus and crossed the street.

"Well, I'll be." There in plain sight walked a white-haired, old man wearing a navy-blue suit and surrounded by about ten children who were gathered at the street corner. The stop sign on the bus remained extended. I thrust the gearshift into drive, and smashed the gas pedal. Bob and Harry looked like they were tap dancing when I glanced into the rearview mirror.

Keeping a safe distance between me and the bus, I made it to the corner in seconds. In this moment, all I saw was the Chameleon. I charged toward him without even shutting the car door. When he noticed me approaching, he raced toward me, knocking several children to the ground. My hand grazed his sleeve as we ran full speed right past each other, in opposite directions. I continued falling forward even though my mind told my body to stop and pivot. By the time I got back on track, it had cost me a few feet of distance.

As a former all-American running back for both my high school and college football teams, few could catch me on the field. Fewer could catch me off. *So how in the world is this geriatric outrunning me?* With fifteen feet between us, he shifted his motor into second gear. So I leaned in and pressed forward harder too. But somehow the distance between us was growing. I felt like I was breathing fire through my nostrils. I'm twenty-five years old, run an average of six miles per day, and my double shot of espresso, chiseled physique is proof of that. But this situation was making me doubt who I was.

I could feel my muscles burning as I pursued him on an incline. He turned to look at me. Suddenly, out of nowhere, Bob and Harry appeared—fast walking, hands swinging, and eyes bulging. The Chameleon turned back around, and *bam!* Walloped right into them. An assortment of smacking sounds filled the air as all three hit the pavement. I heard a snapping sound, like a twig.

Bob's eyes rolled back in his head as he grabbed his hand. "I think something broke!"

Harry's head had hit the concrete. Now he laid unconscious. Both of their glasses were mangled in the street.

As I arrived at the spectacle, the Chameleon was positioning himself to take off. I dove atop of him and pinned him to the ground.

"You, sir, are under arrest. You have the right to remain silent," I managed while catching my breath.

The metal handcuffs were hot to the touch. I enjoyed the clicking sounds they made as I tightened them around his wrists.

"Bob, do you think you can pull your buddy out of the street and onto the sidewalk so he won't get run over by a vehicle?" I said.

"Oh, yeah, yeah. I can do that."

"I can see he's breathing. Let me get this one into the car, then I'll call an ambulance for you two."

As Bob bent down, I noticed his right hand was swollen to twice the size of his left, but he carefully placed his arms under Harry's and pulled him a few inches out of the street and onto the sidewalk. Before I called the station to alert them that I had apprehended the suspect, I called an ambulance.

"Rose! Are you there?"

"Unit 2372. Go ahead."

"10-15 on the seventy-year-old suspect."

"Excellent work, officer. Bring him in."

"On my way."

The old man sat in the back without making a sound. I made eye contact with him through the rearview mirror.

The man smiled. "You know, if those two hadn't been in my path, you would have never caught me, right?"

I would never admit to this, but it was a fact. I did what any young man trying to preserve his ego would do in a situation like this. I changed the subject.

"Who are you?"

"You have me handcuffed in the back of your squad car, and you don't know who I am? Let me out of this car!"

"I don't know your legal name, but you are known as the Chameleon."

"I've been told."

"You've been told by whom?"

"By your kind. Officers of the law," the man said evenly, looking out the car window.

I felt a prick of annoyance at his demeanor. "So, tell me. Why would you knock out a doctor, assume his identity, and hurt his patients?"

"I was just handling all those assigned to me."

"Who assigned them to you?"

"The better question is, why are you so interested in me, Mr. Officer Paul Reese, of 1223 Eagle Way Drive, Champaign, Illinois? On the police force for exactly one year, four months, one week, and three days. Husband for two years, nine months, three weeks, and five days to a very pretty wife named Jenesis Marie."

I silenced all my sensibility, and before I knew it, I was parking along the side of the road. I jumped out and flung open the back door. I caught a glimpse of my fist trembling as I struggled to keep it from making contact with the Chameleon's face, "If you even so much as think about visiting my wife in her dreams, I will hunt you down and execute my own personalized justice on you."

"Now, now, Officer Reese, you're supposed to be the one who upholds the law. You see how easy it is to break it for a cause you believe in? You and I are similar."

"I am nothing like you." I adjusted my uniform, slammed his door, and returned to my seat before merging into traffic.

"You don't even know me." The Chameleon maintained a steady, respectable tone.

"I know enough about you to know that we're nothing alike. You're a career criminal who preys on innocent people in the worst ways."

"Officer Reese. Sir. You know nothing."

"Okay. Well, tell me who you are and why you do what you do. And how in the world do you know where I live?"

"I will tell you who I am, and why I do what I do, but first, let's talk about the five cases that you and your partner chose to investigate that are related to me."

"What five cases?"

"Oh, you know exactly what five cases I'm talking about. But I'll explain since you want to play coy. There are 489 cases attributed to me, but only 425 of those cases are actually mine. I know this for sure because I put a special mark on all of mine."

"You're admitting to branding your victims!"

"Some may look at it as a type of branding, but that's not really what it is. It's just for identification purposes."

"Pathetic." I could feel my nostrils flare as I regretted glancing at the Chameleon in the rearview mirror.

The Chameleon, looking bored, said, "Of those 489 cases, you and your partner, Officer Jeff Hughes"—he paused, looked through the bars that separated us, and then at the clock—"who happens to be at the high school right now doing some community outreach, selected five local cases to build your investigation around. You two selected these cases because you wanted to sit down with the victims, look into their eyes, and see if you could better understand me through them. If I may be so bold, it's a great batch."

"I'll ask again, how do you know this information? Have you been snooping around the station? Wait! No. You've partnered with some of the officers, haven't you? There is no way you could know this classified information otherwise. Unless, of course, you have some eyes, ears, or wiretaps at the station. Many of my colleagues say you're former CIA. But you don't fit CIA." I caught him smirking so I decided to try a different approach.

"Come on. How did you get into the station? Was it Johnson? Sergeant Stevens? No, wait. I'm willing to bet it was Officer Prince. The money you're stealing from these clinics, are you splitting it with them?"

"You and your partner selected five of my all-time favorites for your investigation. Let's see, you chose Maria."

I tried another tactic. Two things I know about narcissists: they love to talk about themselves in a positive way, and they love for other people to talk about them.

"So, who did you previously work for? Your reputation as an expert master of disguise precedes you. I hear you're the best of the best. That's how you've evaded us or escaped capture all these years. Huh. How do you do it?"

"And then you have Nancy. You were able to find Tamika. Though she was an easy one to find. Now, Abbarane and Beatriz were a little more hesitant before you could get them to comply, but your perseverance in persuading them both really paid off for you, huh?"

"Do you understand that you have some serious charges brought against you? The severity of your crimes is no casual matter. You're looking at two life sentences just in this region alone. Similar crimes were reported in St. Louis, Chicago, and other smaller nearby communities. Been traveling a little, have you?"

"They're all my favorites, really. But Abbarane is definitely at the top of my list." The white-haired criminal sat in the back of my squad car reminiscing about his favorites. "God . . . it was God who told me to do it."

"Now, that's enough, old man!" A sour taste filled my mouth. "It's bad enough that you have favorite victims, but to blame God for your sick behavior is just too much. Take some personal responsibility."

"But you haven't even heard what I have to say, and you're already passing judgment on me."

"I've been investigating you for four months now, and one thing I know for sure. You're really twisted, old man."

"Every person I—uh—how do you all phrase it in your reports? Oh yes, violated. Every person that I 'violated' was done so with perfection."

I paused at a red light. I couldn't resist the urge to turn and look him in his eyes. "What kind of a sick pervert are you?"

"I helped them. Every one of them is better because of what I've done. The world would be a darker, emptier, more grief-stricken place had I not done all that I have for those people."

I was speechless.

"I have, at one time or another, tracked every single person that I encountered at a clinic. I like to keep tabs on them. Especially my favorites."

"What is your problem?"

"Abby."

"Who is Abby?"

"Abbarane. I call her Abby for short."

"Abbarane is your problem?"

"No, she is *not* my problem. She is my favorite."

"Just be quiet, now. We'll get your statement down at the station."

"Oh, where was I?" The Chameleon acted deaf to my instructions. "Oh, yes . . ."

"Oh, no!" Rush-hour traffic caused the speedometer to rest at fifteen miles per hour.

"Abby was only fifteen at the time."

"Sick. Just sick."

"Listen. Abby, even at just fifteen, was stunning to look at."

"You old geezer! Do you remember your right to remain silent? Why don't you do that! Preferably until we get to the station."

"Many a young men at her school were captivated by her beauty and personality. She was popular among all her peers—girls and boys alike. That's how she ended up as a sophomore snagging the attention of that handsome boyfriend and popular senior class president, seventeen-year-old, Chad Evans. They dated for several months."

"How do you know all of this?"

"Oh, Paul, they don't call me the Chameleon for nothing."

"You know what? It really doesn't matter how you know what you know. With all the charges against you, you will never see the light of day again. Right now, I'm just satisfied that I have done the impossible by capturing you once and for all."

"Have you captured me? Once and for all?"

1

THE CEREMONY

PAUL

FOUR MONTHS EARLIER

It was nice to receive affirmation. Not ever receiving it from my father, I craved it elsewhere. It was the chief whose arm was wrapped around my shoulders. I never knew my father; he left before I was born. My mother worked two jobs and did the best she could to raise my older brother and me. Because neither my brother nor I had strong male figures to model after, I was attracted to law enforcement from an early age. My brother, Mark, chose the opposite side of the law, embracing drugs and a life of crime.

The chief and I stood tall and entered the large, crowded room where the ceremony honoring me and four other officers for outstanding accomplishments was about to begin. In this, my rookie year, I had solved an ongoing, thirty-year-old case.

I was the only rookie in the history of this ceremony to be presented with this prestigious award. There were officers on the force for thirty plus years who had never received this honor. Officers from across the state of Illinois came to celebrate the capture of five criminals in milestone cases. I'm guessing most came to celebrate the apprehension of the criminal I was responsible for locking away.

The chief and I were escorted onto a stage with the other award recipients and their chiefs. The officers-only ceremony began. Each chief presented the case that their specific officer had solved and explained its significance. Each recipient received a thunderous applause. They announced my name last.

"Officers," Chief Lewis said into the microphone as the chatter diminished to a hush, "we have honored and celebrated the accomplishments of four officers sitting here today for remarkable service to our departments and communities. I stand here today as the proud chief of our final recipient."

Pressing the clicker he held in his hand, he advanced the presentation slide on the display screens behind us. A large number appeared.

"Five hundred and seventy-seven," he said, moving from behind the podium and scanning the audience. "That's the total number of officers, detectives, and FBI agents who have worked this case over the last thirty years. Many of you in this room right now have, at some point in your career, probably worked on this case."

He advanced the slide to show another large number. In a more solemn voice, he spoke slightly louder than a whisper into the cordless microphone. "Twenty-nine"—he sighed—"is the number of victims Roger Washington raped, tortured, and killed."

The next screen showed four numbers arranged one over the other, "Ten, ten, nine, and—" He paused before saying the final number. "One."

"The first ten represents the number of women Roger Washington murdered in the first decade of his killing spree. The second ten represents the number of victims Roger Washington killed during the second decade. The nine represents the number of women Roger Washington killed during this present decade. But, the one . . . the one represents the one woman who will *not* become Roger Washington's thirtieth victim during his thirtieth year of madness. This monster has killed too many daughters, sisters, mothers, friends, and wives."

Moving to pick up a plaque from the table, Chief Lewis advanced the slide before putting the clicker down. "But this zero . . . this zero represents how many more victims Roger Washington will ever be able to touch again thanks to the wit, wisdom, and just plain ol' gut instincts of this young man right here. Please join me in celebrating Officer—Rookie Officer—Paul Reese."

I smiled wide and stood along with the entire room.

Chief Lewis smiled at me and said, "Officer Reese, why don't you tell the room how you went about capturing Washington."

I moved to the podium and cleared my throat, suddenly feeling self-conscious. I gave some background information into the case that helped me leading up to the day of capture. "I saw a peeping Tom peering through an apartment window at two a.m. When I questioned him, he claimed he was the groundskeeper. He had no priors when I ran his license, and everything checked out, so I let him go. But my gut told me something about Roger wasn't as squeaky-clean as it appeared. A week later he was back, peeking through the same window. When I approached him, this time he took off running. Upon capturing him, I discovered he had a camera on him. In it were some very disturbing images." I cleared my throat again. "Now, he's behind bars for the rest of his life, and the world is a little bit safer." The applause resembled rolling thunder.

Afterward, I was greeted with firm handshakes and congratulations from the officers gathered in the room. Many gathered together in groups of two or three to eat skewers of grilled chicken and shrimp hors d'oeuvres, an assortment of fruit, and desserts. Some stayed to shake each recipients' hand, but the line of officers and detectives waiting to shake my hand curved around the room. My hands were sweaty and cold. Some officers took the time to tell me their stories of near captures, or gory details of scenes left behind by the perpetrator, and some asked more specific questions about how I did it. Officers from my division hung around to greet me last.

"How does this work?" Jeff has always been the light-hearted one of the bunch. "I'm your partner who labored and taught you everything you know for the last eleven months. I take two sick days, you go off on a hunch, and you get a lifetime of glory." A belch escaped me when he lifted me off the floor in a bear hug. "I'm proud to be your partner, man."

My other colleagues congratulated me in a cordial manner. I felt my smile fade after the last officer shook my hand. Why did all this feel like a drug, and now my supply was out. The recognition felt good. I craved more.

I went home that evening to my wife and handed her the plaque.

Jenesis kissed my cheek while drying her hands on a dish towel. "What's this?"

I didn't respond, but instead focused my eyes on her, and watched as she silently read the engraved words.

"Oh honey, this is an incredible honor. I knew this was a pretty big deal, but looking at the size of this thing, it seems like I underestimated just how significant a role you played in all of this. I am so proud of you." Jenesis leaned in close. Her hair smelled of a perfect blend of fresh dryer sheets, citrus, strawberries, and summertime. She leaned in, pressed her chest against mine, and traced my ear ever so slightly with a finger before she wrapped her arms around my neck. My right knee buckled. She leaned in, ever so close, to give me a kiss on the lips, but then turned her head before bursting into laughter. She had me.

"You tease, you!"

Her legs came from under her as I picked her up like a groom carrying his bride over a threshold. Before I eased her onto our king-sized bed, replete with a dozen blue and gold throw pillows, I thought I heard her whisper against my neck something about wanting to make a baby.

The next day was my day off. By the time I rolled out of bed, Jenesis had been gone for three hours. I staggered into the bathroom to freshen up just enough to go relax on the sectional sofa in the great room. I'm not a big TV watcher, but this was how I planned to relax today.

I surfed through the channels. The local midday news caught my attention. Reporting live: a union protest that was getting heated. The news reporter interviewed people from both sides of the issue. I sat up when I saw the name of a woman being interviewed. Sarah Davis shook her fist and raised her voice as she spoke to reporters about the need for unions to remain intact and not be dismantled, as the politicians were pushing for. Though she appeared on screen for only seconds, I continued to stare blankly at the television. I wasn't a betting man, but I was willing to wager that this was *The* Sarah Davis.

Two days later I stood outside of Chief Lewis's office.

"Hey, Chief"—I knocked and peeked my head inside—"have a minute?"

Never looking up while shuffling through some papers on his desk, he replied, "That's all I can spare, Reese. What's up?"

"I can come back when you have more time, if you—?"

"Here it is." The chief popped out of his chair holding a sheet of paper up like his life depended on it. "I knew it was here somewhere. Whew. Without this paper here, a real humdinger could have gotten off on a technicality." He took a relief stretch and then rested his hand on my shoulder. "How can I help you, Reese?"

"Well, Chief, I was watching the news the other day and ran across a Sarah Davis who was being interviewed."

"And?"

"Well, I know Sarah Davis is a very common name, but I'm almost certain it was *the* Sarah Davis."

"Reese, excuse my ignorance, but, who is Sarah Davis again?"

"Chief, Sarah Davis is the woman that Roger Washington was planning to make victim number thirty."

"Oh! *Sa-rah Da-vis*." He articulated the syllables in her name as if I had not said it correctly.

"Yes, sir, Sarah Davis."

"What about her, Reese? What was she on the news for?"

"Oh, nothing pertaining to the case. She was demonstrating for unions or something like that."

"Okay. Where are you going with all of this?"

"Well, I was wondering if you—or someone—was planning to tell Miss Sarah Davis that she was the intended victim number thirty for Roger Washington."

He leaned back in his chair, and rested his head in his interlocked fingers. "Well, Paul, he's been in custody a few months. How do you know that no one has told her?"

"The report indicates that she was never informed by anyone of our findings."

"Huh. You said you saw her on the news protesting, did you?"

"Yeah, the day before yesterday."

"You know, during the day shift, they brought in a group of protesters from both sides who got out of hand over on campus by the football stadium. A physical altercation erupted resulting in injuries requiring visits to the hospital. Maybe they brought her in. You may want to check that out and get back to me about this."

"I'll get right on it."

On the internal database, I clicked on the inmate's tab and then clicked on *today*.

"Okay, let's do this alphabetically by last name. D. Davis, Adam. Davis, Charles. Davis, Lynette." I kept scrolling down the list. "Davis, Sarah. Date of birth is May 23, 1987."

I left my chair spinning as I hiked back to the chief's office. I leaned against the door frame. "Chief!"

He jumped a little. I glanced down a moment and waited.

"You know, Reese, it's not too bright to startle a man who carries a loaded gun."

He turned his chair to face me.

"She's here. Sarah Davis was booked earlier today. Can I talk to her?"

He scratched his balding head. "Have you ever done anything like this before?"

"Like what?"

"Broke news to someone that a serial killer had an extensive plan to make them their next victim?"

"Uh, no, I haven't." I wondered what was so hard about telling someone their life had just been saved.

"Maybe I should go in with you. I've been here for thirty-four years, and these things never get easier. You might want to see which psychiatrist is on call this evening. We'll need one."

The holding officers had removed Sarah Davis away from her group of co-protesters and placed her in an interrogation room.

We entered the room. Me, the psychiatrist, and Chief Lewis.

Slouched back in her seat, she sat with her legs bouncing and her fingernails tapping the table. She addressed us first.

"I don't know what you folks think you're doing, but I didn't hurt nobody." The red in her cheeks matched her fiery hair. "I have been through this process more than twenty times, and this has never been part of the routine. Why's today so special?" She crossed her arms and leaned into the table.

"Miss Davis, I'm Chief Lewis. This is Officer Reese. And this is Dr. Langley."

"Do I look like I need a doctor?" She tilted her head. "Okay, now you're freakin' me out."

"Miss Davis," I interrupted, "we're not here to talk to you about your protesting activities."

"Well, genius, I figured that much. What I haven't figured out is what you *are* here to talk to me about. I'm listening."

I had to tamp down my irritation because I knew the news I was about to share with her would be chilling. "There really is no easy way to say this."

"Just spit out already, big-bad-man-with-a-gun. Spit. It. Out. Good grief."

"Miss Davis," Chief chimed back in. "Officer Reese here discovered a plot to murder you."

"Oh, is that all? When you have been a loud mouth protester in so many rallies that kinda comes with the territory. It's not the first death threat I've received, and it won't be the last." She walked her small frame to the door and paused. "Are you folks going to let me go now, or what?"

"Miss Davis, sit down!" Chief stood in front of the door. "Now, this has nothing at all to do with your life as a protester."

"Well, then, what does this have to do with?" Her eyebrows drew closer together.

The piercing silence in the room grew.

"Miss Davis, are you familiar with the Roger Washington case?" Chief leaned on the edge of the table in front of her.

"No, I don't think so. Wait, is he that crazy psychopath who killed all those women over like thirty-five years or something before you cops decided to leave the donut shops and actually do your job?"

The chief didn't respond but the look he gave her let her know she was crossing the line of showing proper respect to a police chief.

"I still don't see what any of this has to do with me." She stretched and yawned.

"Miss Davis, do you know how many victims got away from Roger Washington once he abducted them?"

"Um, should I know this?"

"None. And do you know the average length of time Roger Washington studied his victims before he abducted them?"

"I really don't know the answer to this. I don't know . . . Do I need a lawyer? I want you to know that I know I have rights, you know. So, don't be trying to tie me up into no mess that I didn't have nothing to do with in the first place. I want a lawyer."

"He studied his victims for an average of ten and a half months before successfully abducting, torturing, raping, and killing them."

"I want a lawyer. I'm not saying anything else."

"Miss Davis, you don't need a lawyer for what we're here to discuss with you today." As he motioned, I handed him a manila envelope. He set several pictures on the table in front of Sarah. "Miss Davis, is this you?"

She rubbed her eye and studied the pictures.

"Yeah, these are all of me, but I don't understand where you got these from. Have y'all been spying on me?"

"Miss Davis!" I interjected. "I am the officer who captured the serial killer Roger Washington. When I found him, these pictures and hundreds more just like these were taped on his bedroom wall. All the pictures were of you. He had been watching your every move for exactly ten months and one week. Miss Davis, you were about to be—"

"Miss Davis, what Officer Reese is saying here is that he stopped a very disturbed man from hurting you, and making you his thirtieth victim in thirty years."

Her eyes didn't blink and her gaze didn't break as she viewed the display set before her. The many pictures captured her in both private and public moments. Gasping for air, her mouth moved but no words escaped. She zoned in on one picture that had been taken from inside her apartment. Her mouth widened as she gasped for more air. Taking in shorter, quicker breaths, panic filled her eyes. A single teardrop rolled down her cheek.

"Miss Davis," Dr. Langley said in a calm voice. "I need you to sit back and take slow, deep breaths. Here, breathe with me. Slowly in-hale. Ex-hale. Again, really slowly now. In-hale. Hold it. Ex-hale. Now again. In-hale. Hold it. Ex-hale."

Though her breathing normalized, her tears were streaming down her cheeks.

"Oh my. Oh my. So, where is he now?"

"He's being held at a maximum-security prison far from here while he awaits trial." I handed her a box of tissues.

"How close was he to-to-to maybe abducting me?"

"We can't answer that with certainty, but according to his pattern he was ready to do so within a day or two," I answered.

Her nose narrowed as she breathed in. She closed her eyes as she allowed air to escape through the oval she created with her lips. Staring at a blank wall, and with slumped shoulders, she said, "I want to stay here. Right here in jail with all you police officers."

She sat up and looked me in the eye. "But especially with you, Officer Reese. I'm not leaving. I'm telling you. I'm not leaving."

Dr. Langley scooted her chair closer, and her calm voice filled the room. "Why don't you want to leave jail, Miss Davis?"

"Are you kidding me?" Sarah pursed her lips, and she looked at me and Chief, wide-eyed. "This is supposed to be a doctor?"

She scooted her chair closer to the doctor. "Lady, open up your eyes. Here in jail, I have twenty-four-hour police protection, surveillance, ammunition, you name it. This here is the safest place for me. I tell you, Chief"—she walked over and sandwiched her pint-size frame in between the chief and me—"Officer Reese, I am not leaving this place! I'm telling you now, I will act a fool if anybody tries to make me leave."

"Miss Davis." Dr. Langley's voice had lost its soft, gentle tone.

"Lady, Miss Davis is my mother. My name is Sarah, okay? And what do you want?"

"It was nice meeting you, Sarah," Chief interrupted, shook her hand, and opened the door.

"Yes, Sarah." When I put my hand out to shake hers, she buried her face in my chest and threw her arms around my waist, squeezing my lungs until I felt light-headed.

"Okay." I managed to free my arm from her embraced and tapped her head with a finger.

Releasing her embrace, tears began streaming again. "Officer Reese," she said in a childlike tone, "thank you so much for saving my life. I am *very* grateful."

"Y-you are welcome," a lump emerged in my throat.

I left her standing with her arms limp like wet noodles. She watched as I joined the chief in the hall. The sound of the door clanked shut.

"You know, studies show that the reason women fair better in their health is because they aren't afraid to cry." Chief patted my back.

"She's a unique young woman. A real piece of work. But, special somehow."

"Yeah, she's real special, all right. In all my years, I never met anyone who refused to leave the county jail. Maybe institutionalized prisoners. But never someone in county jail."

"But I understand where she's coming from."

"Yeah, I do too. I really hope Dr. Langley can help her. That can really do a number on a person's mind."

2

THE NEXT CASE

PAUL

A week had passed since the ceremony. In our weekly staff meeting, Chief was briefing everyone about some current issues, guidelines, updates, and procedures. He was about to assign cases, first, to volunteers, then to voluntolds.

"Smith and Braggs, along with Hernandez and Jones, have volunteered to work the drug sting operation over on Ninth Street with narcotics. Perry and Wilson volunteered to work the Operation Ten-Ten case. You two can see me after this for more details. Holland and Shultz agreed to take on the newly reopened case of *Operation Missing Twins*. Everyone else will receive standard traffic and city zone assignments. But we have one case we still need some partners to volunteer for."

The chief bent down and picked up a boxful of papers and set it on the long, brown table next to the podium.

"This next case," the chief said in his strong command-ing voice, "is classified as an ongoing unsolved mystery.

This case, I want you to understand before volunteering, is going to take some commitment and a lot of hard work. Many have tried to work this case, and everyone has given up instead of seeing it through to the end. There are over fifty boxes of evidence on these forty-four years' worth of case files."

I admit, my interest was piqued, but I was trying not to get ahead of myself.

"Please, Chief, don't tell us this is *Operation Almost* again," yelled Sergeant Stevens, who'd been on the force for seventeen years.

An outburst of grumbling, side chatter, and snickering filled the room.

"Yeah, Chief, I'm with the sergeant on this. Please not *Operation Almost!*" yelled Officer Lopez.

A female voice rang out from the back of the room. "Chief, do you really want to go through the disappointment of *almost* catching this guy before he slips away . . . again?"

"Well—" The chief scratched his head. "This joker just struck again six days ago over at the Lafayette Clinic. So as long as he keeps doing what he does best, we must not become apathetic just because we have not fine-tuned our skills as detectives and officers enough to catch a man in his late sixties, early seventies. You all are young, strong, and have sharp minds. Surely a pair of you young chaps can take down an old worn-out criminal. Unless you're scared of failing."

"Chief." I raised my hand. "My partner and I will take the—uhh . . . *Operation Almost* case. 'Cause we ain't scared."

"We will?" Jeff's nose and top lip met as he shifted in his seat.

I elbowed his side.

"Oh right, yeah, we want *this* case."

"Look at Reese! Mr. Big Time. Always wanting to prove himself." Officer Prince, whom the ladies swore was a good representation of his last name, glared at me from across the room.

"He won't last a month on this case!" The taunting came from every direction.

"Man, you have no idea what you are getting yourself into."

"Retract! Retract while you still have a chance to preserve your dignity. This is way out of your league." Officer Bond had been the last detective to work this case.

"And your pay grade," someone I couldn't see added.

"Well,"—I could no longer accommodate the negativity—"many of you gave me a hard time when I volunteered to assist detectives with the *Operation Red Ladies* case too. I was a rookie then. But I proved you all wrong. I'm a little older, and a little wiser, with more experience now, and me and my partner here, will prove you all wrong again, but thanks for all the support. We really appreciate it."

"Reese, trust us on this one. This case is nothing like what happened with Roger Washington in the *Red Ladies* case. This case will forever change your life," Sergeant Stevens said.

"And if you ever want to make detective, then you just need to forget about this case," someone else said from the back.

"Thank you all, again, for your overwhelming support. But, I—we—have made up our minds. We are taking this case. And that's that." I stood up to leave.

"Okay, well, it's settled. I expect everyone to become familiar with your assignments. Everyone who has volunteered for a case, please remain seated. Everyone else, head back to work. Thank you." Chief Lewis stood and gathered up the folders in front of him.

Several hours later, during our seven o'clock shift change, I showered, changed into street clothes, and was gathering things from my locker.

"Jeff, you're always talking about a fiancée, but I'm beginning to think she's a figment of your imagination."

"Naw, man. She's real. She's not just real—but, she's real fine too." Grinning, Jeff closed his locker. "Have a pleasant evening. I sure will. With my fiancée!"

"Bye."

The locker room door closed behind him. I couldn't understand how we had been partners for more than a year and I had never met his supposed fiancée. It was a little odd.

As I closed my locker, I heard several officers debating outside the door. It was the same bunch who objected to me taking this assignment.

As I made to leave, Officers Bond and Prince blocked the door.

"You sure this is something you want to do?" Johnson stood in front of my locker.

"You can still retract," Bond said matter-of-factly.

"This case will turn your world upside down. You really want that for yourself and that pretty wife of yours?" I could smell the cinnamon from Lopez's gum.

"G'on and tell the chief you changed your mind," someone behind me said.

"I don't understand what the big deal is about me taking this on."

"Just trust us, Reese. Leave the *Operation Almost* case alone. You have no idea what you're getting yourself into." Sergeant Stevens was more demanding than suggesting.

"Fellas." I grabbed my duffel bag off the wooden bench. "Thanks for all of your concern, but I got this. Not only do I have this, but if I don't capture the Chameleon once and for all, then I'll volunteer for parking duty for a year. That's how confident I am in my abilities to do what none of you could. Since we're all being so vocal, why don't you just admit it? That's what this is all about. I keep making all of you look like you're just eating donuts and sleeping on the job. I'm here to serve, protect, and make a difference. And if that makes you all uncomfortable, sounds like a personal problem to me."

My shoulders brushed against Bond's and Prince's as I left everyone standing in silence. Slushing through the dirty gray February snow as I made my way through the parking lot, I could hear rhythmic sounds of rubber soles gushing in slush and glanced over my shoulder. It was Officer Johnson. I pressed the trunk button on my key fob, heard it click open, and tossed in my bag. When I attempted to close the driver's door of my Camaro, Officer Johnson stood between me and the door.

"Once you believe no one will be able to capture him, including you, then come back to see one of us. We won't hold all the junk you just said about us against you." His top lip curled and what seemed like slow motion, and he shut my door.

By the time I arrived home, my head was throbbing. Only by pressing my thumb and forefinger against my temples did some of the tension in my head subside. I sat on a barstool and semi-watched as Jenesis finish preparing dinner.

"Paul, honey, are you okay? You look a little sick." She placed the back of her hand against my forehead.

"I just don't get it, Jen. I don't know if it's jealousy, or if I'm about to find out that Sergeant Stevens, Lopez, Prince, Johnson, Mint, Bond, White, and who knows who else, are all illegally involved in this *Operation Almost* case. I mean, they were pretty much demanding that I abandon it. I never experienced any of this with the Roger Washington case. I got a funny feeling they're all somehow tangled up in this one. Like they're afraid I'll uncover some dirt on them. But all this makes me want to solve it now more than ever."

"Maybe they don't like being shown up by some new, confident, young cop."

"Well, it's a little late for that. I was that same guy with the last case, but most of them seemed genuinely happy for me back then. I can't figure this out."

Jenesis turned to finish chopping the fresh garlic, which she then added to a ramekin of melted butter. "What does *Operation Almost* stand for?"

"The way the chief explained it was that for the last forty-four years, many officers and detectives have worked this case. In each instance, they would write in their final report that they "almost" had the guy. They would have him in custody, and somehow, he'd get away."

"Wait. Something's not right."

"That's what I've been saying."

"You're saying that only a few officers had him in their custody?"

"I'm saying, according to what I've been told, every single officer, detective, and investigator for the last forty-four years—every single one—has written in their report that he was in custody, they *almost* had him, but he mysteriously got away."

"Wow, how does that happen? What's wrong with the cops in Chambana?"

"Either this man is a gifted magician or he's got something on these cops. Unfortunately, I believe I'm about to uncover a major dirty operation run from the inside by a bunch of crooked cops."

She stopped cooking, cupped my ears with her hands, and stared into my eyes. "If that's true, then I don't want you to take this case. You and Jeffrey may be in over your heads on this one."

"Now you're starting to sound like them."

She placed a pitcher of her perfectly sweetened, mouth puckering, can-never-drink-just-one-glass lemonade before me.

"It's enough that I worry about you on the streets. I don't want to worry about you in the locker room, too, Paul." The pitch in her voice rose a few octaves. "Besides, the doctor said stress is not good for couples attempting to conceive."

"I'm not getting support from too many other places. I would like to at least have the support of my wife." I lowered my voice—tone and volume.

"Well, you got it. You just betta not get yourself hurt is all I'm saying."

Wearing oven mitts, she eased a pan of bubbling lasagna in front of me. The smell of her homemade garlic twisty bread caused my mouth to salivate before she placed them next to the lasagna. "Dinner is served."

"See, this is one of the many reasons I married you." My mouth burst with flavor. Eyes closed, when I pulled back my fork, I could feel cheese dangling from each corner of my mouth. "Your lasagna takes me places I've never been before."

"Oh, is that right? You married me because I'm a good cook?" Jenesis' hands rested on her hips as a smirk rested on her face.

"No, no, baby, that's not what I meant." I stuffed more lasagna in my mouth. As she walked away, I grabbed her by her curves and pulled her into my lap. "I absolutely love everything about you, and that's why I married you. But, your cooking, girl, puts a spell on me."

Her smirk was replaced by a full-faced smile. She stood. "Hold up. I forgot the salad. We need our veggies too. And you forgot to say grace, Mister."

"Now Jenesis, you know I don't say grace."

3

THE FILES

PAUL

Jeff and I took the elevator to the basement of the station where evidence and files were stored. The dim lights, damp feel, and musty smell reminded me of staged training rooms back in the academy.

"Hey, Cheddar." I stood in front of the cut-out window of his glassed-in space. "How's life treating you in the castle these days?"

"Same ole, same ole. Not much action happening down here like I s'pose you fellas are seeing out there in the streets. But I'm not complaining none. With this bad knee, and problems with my back, it's like I always say . . ." And in unison he and his work companion, a parakeet, said, "a man's castle is what he makes it."

Charles "Cheddar" Randolph was a former cop who'd been with the police department longer than anyone else, and had no interest in retirement. He walked with a limp and grimaced often due to a traumatic leg injury obtained in the line of duty, and as such, everyone knew he would make them get their own files.

"What can I do for you fellas today?" Cheddar asked.

"We need the files for *Operation Almost*," Jeff said.

Cheddar clinched his lips and shook his head. "When are they gonna stop with this nonsense?"

"Nonsense. Nonsense," the parakeet, Buddy, repeated.

"What nonsense would that be?" I asked.

"Who put you up to this? If someone thinks they're going to make me retire by sending you down here for the *Operation Almost* files, you let them know it's gonna take more than that to get me outta here." He buzzed the metal door. "Come on in here."

"Cheddar, we volunteered to take the *Operation Almost* case. That's the only reason we came down here." The tone of Jeff's voice was calm. "We didn't mean to upset you."

"Oh, you didn't upset me. This case will upset you before it ever upsets me. I don't know why they won't give this a rest already. I've been here for forty-five years and nobody has ever come close to solving this case. Y'all capture him. He gets away every time. End of story. Every year or two you have some young suckers who think they'll be the ones to crack the coveted *Operation Almost* case, only to walk away with their tails tucked between their legs." Cheddar let Buddy nibble on his finger. "I don't care that you wanted the case, I'm just not getting a single box. That's why I buzzed you in. The two of you can carry the fifty-plus boxes to wherever you feel necessary. There's a dolly over there. Cases are in alphabetical order. Have at it."

"Have at it," Buddy chirped. Jeff broke off a piece of bread Cheddar always kept in a plastic baggie on his desk, and fed it to the bird.

There were fifty-seven boxes in all for the *Operation Almost* case. An hour and a half later and a combination of twenty-one trips using the elevator, we had all the boxes stacked in a large conference room we'd reserved.

We collapsed in the plush executive chairs. "Lunch?" I felt bad that I had dragged Jeff into this mess.

"Let's go." He led the way out of the room.

"Black Dog. My treat."

The nourishment of the barbeque from this favorite downtown restaurant gave us the energy we needed to begin the journey down this very long road.

"How about you work with the most recent cases, and I'll work with the older cases, then we can meet somewhere in the middle?" Jeff suggested.

"Sounds good. If something extraordinary stands out in any file, we'll let the other know."

Jeff grabbed a box with the year 1976 written on it. He took out several files and plopped them on the table. We studied our files in silence for several minutes.

I looked up. "I just realized that I don't know what this *Operation Almost* case is even about. I mean, are we dealing with a mass murderer, a thief, a drug dealer, a terrorist? What's this guy's story?"

"I thought you knew all of that when you volunteered us."

"No sir. I just volunteered our services because you know how I love a challenge."

"Well . . ." He pointed at me like he was in charge. "Now we know what to start looking for in all these boxes."

"What's that?"

"We need to identify what this old man did for so many years that's got everybody walking around here like they have a permanent wedgie."

I felt better knowing my partner was okay with what I'd gotten us involved with.

With our notepads and pens besides us, we resumed studying the files.

"What?" Jeff said loudly some minutes later. He started digging rapidly in his right ear with his index finger. He did this when either nervous or excited.

"What did you find?"

"It says here that the perpetrator is going around pretending to be a doctor. No, a surgeon. An abortion surgeon!"

"What?"

"Let's see. It says he's been given the code name Chameleon by our predecessors. Why? Because . . . he is some sort of master of disguise. No one knows his real name."

"Abortion surgeon imposter? Master of disguise? I'm scared to ask, but what exactly is he doing as an abortion . . . surgeon . . . imposter?"

Jeff shuffled through some more papers. "Oh, here's something. It reads: 'June 19, 1976: The Chameleon entered Able Clinic at approximately 9:15 a.m. through one of the two entrances. All nurses and receptionists were extremely busy, so they could not verify which door the Chameleon entered. At 9:30 a.m. Dr. Mann, the only surgeon working at Able Clinic, was scheduled to perform an abortion with Nurse Sumner acting as his assistant."

I was trying to paint a picture in my mind of this criminal's actions. "Okay, keep reading."

"Nurse Sumner set up all of the surgical tools, which she had previously personally sterilized. She waited for Dr. Mann to enter the surgical room where the patient was already positioned on the table. According to Nurse Sumner, Dr. Mann entered the surgical room wearing typical surgical attire consisting of his surgical gown, scrubs, hat, mask, shoes, and gloves. He was also wearing his glasses. Nurse Sumner did not notice anything unusual about Dr. Mann, though she did notice that the air vent in the surgical room was much louder than normal. She remembered Dr. Mann having to raise his voice in order for her to hear what tools he needed next."

"So, the regular doctor, Dr. Mann, is covered from head to toe in surgical garb. And there's a loud ventilation system that's not typically so loud." I grabbed a pen and notepad and starting jotting notes as Jeff continued to read the old police report.

"After Dr. Mann completed the abortion, with the assistance of Nurse Sumner, he left the surgical room to clean himself up and to prepare for the next scheduled patient. Nurse Sumner was responsible for helping the patient off the table and into the recovery room. She then handed the patient off to Nurse Hill who assisted the woman with getting dressed, and then gave her the recovery orders from the doctor."

"Okay. I haven't heard anything out of the ordinary yet."

"Nurse Sumner was responsible for cleaning and prepping the surgical room for the next patient. During the process of cleaning the surgical room, Nurse Sumner entered the mop closet only to find Dr. Mann unresponsive and curled up on the floor."

"That's strange. Why was he in there? And how did he get there in such a short span of time?"

"Hang on, let me finish reading the report." Jeff read aloud, "Nurse Sumner checked Dr. Mann's pulse and called for the other nurses to assist. They were able to pull Dr. Mann out of the closet and determined that he had been given something that caused him to fall into a deep, unresponsive sleep. Chloroform. Nurse Sumner found this particularly bizarre because less than two minutes had elapsed between the time she had worked with Dr. Mann and the time when he left to take a shower and change his dirty surgical clothing."

"Exactly!"

"Oh, this is interesting." Jeff eyes shifted left to right. "Nurse Sumner indicated that Dr. Mann's surgical scrubs were blood-stained, but when she examined Dr. Mann lying unresponsive on the mop closet's floor, his scrubs were clean.

"Wait. How much time did you say had lapsed?" I was trying to get down every pertinent detail.

"Two minutes."

"Nurse Sumner stated this was strange because the doctor couldn't change clothes that fast. And Dr. Mann always showered in between surgeries, and prior to putting on clean scrubs."

I looked over my notes.

Jeff kept reading. "When Dr. Mann finally came to, he had no recollection of performing an abortion on the morning of June 19, 1976. The last thing he remembered was walking down the hallway toward the surgical room and tying his mask behind his head as he prepared himself for the first procedure of the day. Two receptionists, Eve

Maples and Cheryl Sims, saw Dr. Mann exit the clinic through the side door at the exact time Nurse Sumner found him in the mop closet and began to yell for help. The two receptionists identified both the man leaving the clinic as Dr. Mann and the man found unresponsive on the floor as being Dr. Mann."

"Whoa. Hold up. So, not one, but two receptionists said they saw Dr. Mann leaving the clinic? Right as Nurse Sumner was calling for help? Help with Dr. Mann, who was passed out on the floor of the mop closet?"

Jeff stood. His face twisted as he stared at the police report. "This is crazy, man."

"Was Dr. Mann a twin? Does the report identify a motive? Is there a real Dr. Mann and an imposter? I need to make the connection with the Chameleon. Let's piece this thing together. This . . . this Chameleon . . . did he assault the patient in some way? Why go through the trouble of impersonating this particular surgeon? And the eye witness accounts . . . These nurses worked with the man every day. Two receptionists were adamant that both men were Dr. Mann. Nothing alerted the nurse that the doctor doing the procedure was not who they believed him to be. Is that what the report said? Heck, I'm more confused now than before you started reading."

Jeff read through the follow-up pages to the initial report. "Oh, here it is: 'June 20, 1976: Nurse Sumner phoned the patient who was allegedly operated on by the Chameleon to check her health status. Patient said she was feeling wonderful, and had no complications from the surgery as far as she could tell. Officer Todd Martin witnessed the phone call.'"

"Okay, so somehow, this master of disguise was the one who worked on the patient."

Jeff read an additional follow-up report. "July 2, 1976: Nurse Sumner phoned patient again to verify the patient's health status. Patient claimed to feel better than ever before. She had none of the bleeding she was told to expect. Officer Robert Hansen witnessed the phone call this time."

"So, they didn't bring the patient back into the clinic to examine her?" This time I stood and paced the room.

As Jeff continued to read through the report, he summarized the findings. "The police agency collectively decided not to disclose to the patient, or to the public, that there was a possibility that she'd been operated on by an imposter instead of Dr. Mann, since there was no apparent harm done to the patient, seeing as how Nurse Sumner never left the operating room while the procedure was taking place. Also, Dr. Mann felt that the negative publicity could shut his clinic down. He aggressively suggested to the police department that since he had no injuries, he personally did not want to press charges. He was, however, shaken up and afraid that if this happened before, it was possible that it could happen again. He requested some police protection, which he received for two weeks."

I studied my notes. "So, I guess the million-dollar question is: what did he do to the patient? And why wouldn't the clinic call the patient back in to examine her." I stood and started making notes on the whiteboard.

"If Nurse Sumner thought he was the real Dr. Mann, had she really been paying attention? Also, you have to remember, this was 1976. Malpractice laws were lax back then. It sounds like the doctor's wishes were more important than the patient's well-being." Jeff closed the file folder.

We decided to organize the files in chronological order. Most of them contained the same basic information, which was bewildering. Woman goes into an abortion clinic for abortion. Nurse assists doctor with abortion. Doctor performs abortion. At least, this is what the nurse believes—and what the patient believes—is taking place. Only it's not the doctor working on the patient. It's a person who is pretending to be a doctor. Patient leaves clinic believing she had terminated her pregnancy. Patient contacts clinic months later informing clinic they took her money, but did not perform abortion. Clinic refunds money out of fear of lawsuit. Patient never pursues lawsuit due to shame, guilt, and exposure. Occasionally, doctor is found dazed and confused moments after he supposedly had just performed an abortion. Paranoia sets in. Respectable doctors are looked at suspiciously by nurses and receptionist every day thereafter. Repeat. It doesn't appear to matter which abortion clinic, which doctor, which city, which year—over the last forty years. These reports are all reading basically the same."

We read through seventeen cases prior to our shift ending. We learned the Chameleon always used chloroform or some form of sleep agent to cause the true surgeon to become unresponsive before hiding them in a secluded location and assuming his identity. The patient never appeared to be harmed. The Chameleon always used a combination of all the surgical tools. In many cases, it's mentioned that the sound coming from the air vents was loud, causing the Chameleon's voice to become hard to hear. The Chameleon always exited the building without confrontation. Once the Chameleon exited the building, all cash taken for that day's abortions exited with him. Cash is often the preferred method of payment in these clinics so the patient can maintain anonymity.

Before leaving for the night, I created several diagrams across the whiteboard to keep track of all the details. We were so intrigued researching this criminal that we didn't realize it was twenty minutes past our shift. We ended the day with more questions than we had answers.

The next morning, even after a restless night's sleep, I arrived at work a half hour early.

I ransacked some files, wondering if there were some statistics on this case somewhere. Finding nothing, I headed down to the file room to see if Cheddar could help.

"Mornin', Cheddar. Was wondering if the *Operation Almost* case had any statistics on it. Like how many victims, how many clinics, doctors impersonated?"

Cheddar paused to let Buddy finish the bread Cheddar was holding before he responded. "Yeah, all that information is in one of those fifty-seven boxes y'all took upstairs."

"Well, it'll take us another forty-four years just to find those statistics in all those boxes. Would you happen to have them saved on the computer somewhere?"

"Yeah, they're saved on the computer. Why don't I buzz you in and you come in here and find it on the computer yourself."

"No problem, Cheddar, thanks."

I was in no way familiar with this database. An old DOS system, it was the original system used at the police station. Cheddar insisted that they keep it because it was the only one he knew how to use. I was struggling with just the big box white cursor on an empty black screen, when Cheddar looked over my shoulder.

"Move."

A minute later, he'd located the information I needed and printed it off.

Jeff was already situated with files, coffee, and bagels when I made it back upstairs.

"I just got these statistics from Cheddar. It says that the Chameleon is suspected of leaving behind a total of 469 victims in which he pretended to perform 469 procedures on in this region over the last 40 plus years. There were a total of 28 doctors over this same timeframe. Those are the ones who reported it. Eighty nurses gave statements. Investigations revealed there were some days he'd stay at a clinic for multiple abortions. Other times, he visited the same clinic days, weeks, months, and even years later, repeating his same criminal behavior. This man is a professional at what he does. How else does someone so active in his criminal activity evade the law for so long? We need to find out where the other officers fell short."

"Whoa, hold up! This file that I read to you yesterday has a page I missed. It says that the victim, when they followed up with her six months later, reported that an abortion had not been performed, and that it became evident around her seventh month of pregnancy. She delivered December 19, 1976. Looks like the victim threatened to sue the clinic for negligence and a refund. They willingly gave her a refund and offered an apology, which she accepted. The Chameleon made off with fifteen hundred dollars in cash. That was the cash taken in for all abortions for that day. God only knows what he did to the patients. We certainly know it wasn't what they paid for."

I grabbed a dry erase marker and wrote down all the possibilities of motives behind the Chameleon's actions. "What do you think, right wing extremist? Former doctor? Religious freak? Former abortionist full of regret? Former CIA nut with a head injury? Magician? Hollywood make-up artist flexing his skills? Pervert? Med school drop-out? Strapped for cash? If his motive is to rob these abortion clinics of their cash, why not just rob and go? If he looks identical to the doctor, perfect way to get away with it. But why go through the trouble of assaulting women on an operating table? What's his motive?"

Jeff took a sip of his coffee. "He sounds like a pervert wrapped up in a thief."

After two weeks of going through the case histories and police reports, taking notes, creating diagrams, crunching numbers, speculating about motives, and studying patterns and trends, we narrowed it down to the five cases we wanted to thoroughly pursue to try and understand the mind of the Chameleon, as opposed to doing surface research on a larger number of cases. That had already been done and proved unsuccessful.

I sat back and twiddled a pencil between two fingers. "It's been interesting reading through these 'almost' files, and I'm gathering a lot of data, but I don't feel like anything I've read so far will help us capture the Chameleon and bring him to justice once and for all. We need to approach the investigation with fresh eyes and ears, not be swayed by what we've read."

"Why don't we have an intern pull the information for these five cases and then set up a time to conduct fresh interviews?"

"Let's grab some lunch, and I'll ask Tom on our way out." I stacked the papers in front of me, then started to get up.

Jeff hurled an empty soda bottle in my direction, which I instinctively caught before it hit my head. Without missing a beat, Jeff said, "I've been wanting to try Kofushion, the sushi restaurant that has dollar sushi once a week. Are you game?"

"Let's do it."

Jeff paused and shifted from foot to foot. "By the way, my schedule is booked next month with middle school and high school presentations. Would it be a problem if I can't join you for some of the victim interviews? I should be able to reschedule most of the presentations, if any interfere."

"Naw, I should be able to handle it solo. I'll fill you in on the details."

A week later we typed the address of the first interview into the GPS anchored to the dashboard and headed toward an upscale neighborhood containing the most expensive homes in all of Champaign-Urbana. Extravagant fountains and exotic gardens greeted us as we turned into the secluded subdivision. Until now, neither of us knew our city contained such lavish homes. Jeff spotted a Hennessey Venom GT in a driveway and informed me that it went from zero to 186 miles per hour in thirteen seconds.

We pulled into the circle drive of a beautiful mansion. At the nine-foot-tall, solid Mahogany front door, Jeff's finger danced between the buttons labeled Doorbell and Intercom before settling on pressing the doorbell. I had a feeling the next hour would be one I wouldn't soon forget.

INTERVIEW #1

BEATRIZ BARROS

"Hello, welcome, I am Mrs. Barros."

Each officer shook my hand as they introduced themselves.

"Follow me, please." The two officers towered over me as I led them through my home. This interview was just another reason for me to have my hair professionally styled and curled. I chose a sweet and expensive perfume. I thought it complemented my white pants, which my personal assistant Josephine had perfectly creased. I attempted to mask my nervous energy as I straightened my silk blouse. I looked back and observed the officers' eyes scanning our home's high ceilings, imported woodwork, and fancy staircases. My shoes made a tapping sound as I walked across the shiny hardwood floors.

I led them past several rooms before I opened French doors leading to the office where my husband was already seated behind the desk. He stood to shake the officers' hands and introduced himself. Though he was a foot taller than me, he looked small compared to the officers on either side of him. At sixty, he was still handsome, dressed in a white polo shirt and khaki pants I'd bought him. He kept a Cuban cigar in his mouth, only removing it to speak.

"Will the smoke bother you, gentlemen?"

"No sir," Officer Hughes said. "I like the smell of a good Cuban cigar."

"Please, have a seat." I motioned toward two chairs in front of my husband's desk. I sat in a wingback that had been placed next to the desk just moments before they arrived.

"Thank you." Officer Reese sat down and placed a black leather notepad on his lap.

"Well . . ." My husband exhaled a cloud of smoke. "How can we help you?"

"Ma'am, we have some questions regarding the circumstances surrounding your visit to a clinic on March 18, 1995," Officer Hughes said.

"Well, what are your questions?" My husband's voice was stern. He knew exactly what this was pertaining to. We'd discussed the matter the moment the intern arranged this interview. It was a subject he did not like talking about. In fact, he had refused to discuss it since the last time law enforcement had questioned me many years ago.

"It's okay, honey." I rubbed my husband's hand.

"On March 18, 1995, did you visit a clinic by the name of Healthy Women's Health Center?" Officer Hughes asked.

"Yes, sir, I did." I lowered my head and twirled my pearl bracelet.

"When you visited the clinic, did you go alone?"

"No. Not alone. Anthony came with me." I could feel tears welling in my eyes.

"What was the purpose of your visit?"

"Now that's going too far!" my husband boomed, his Brazilian accent heavy with anger. "Why don't you get to your questions about this . . . this . . . Chameleon character? You stop harassing my wife about why she was there. Besides, I know for a fact that her health information is protected under a HIPPO law or something like that."

Anthony's entire face was the color of the candy-apple red blush I dabbed on my cheeks.

"That's the HIPAA law, but it's okay. That doesn't apply here." Officer Hughes adjusted in his seat.

I stood and walked to stand near my husband. "Honey—" I leaned in and whispered into his ear, "Why don't you take the dogs out for fresh air?" I kissed him on the cheek.

"Okay, dear, but I won't be gone long. And I will have my cell phone if you need anything. Anything." He stood, folded his arms, and stared at the officers before finally removing himself from what had become a tense situation.

After my husband left, I returned to my seat, crossed my ankles, and rested my interlocked hands in my lap. "Now, where were we?"

"Yes, ma'am." Officer Hughes cleared his throat. "What was your purpose for going to the clinic?"

"All the other times that detectives came and interviewed me, I just answered their questions as quickly as I could. If I am going to answer your questions today, I want to give you the whole story. Is that okay with you?"

"Absolutely, ma'am. All we ask is that you tell us the truth."

"I only speak truth, Officer Hughes."

"Yes, ma'am."

I closed my eyes and tried to brace myself for the emotional roller coaster I knew was ahead.

"Please, take your time," Officer Reese said.

"My husband and I immigrated from Brazil to America in 1982. We wanted to make a better life for ourselves. We came to America with two suitcases and two young children. My husband's uncle started a furniture business in New York that was soon thriving. Lots of customers. Back orders. He needed a manager he could trust. Someone who would make sure employees weren't taking shortcuts. My husband was that someone. Manager that is. His uncle taught Anthony to make quality furniture. We did really well. Made lots of money that first year and half."

Officer Reese was busy jotting notes.

My head felt like a heavy weight was resting on it as memories came flooding back.

"Then, my husband's uncle had a heart attack at the factory. Died right there. No one else in the family knew how to run the business. At that time, we spoke almost no English. The business failed. Closed. Before long, we had run out of the money we'd saved. Anthony and I took whatever jobs were available. None paid very much. Our English was still not too good back then. Because we had two small babies, we had a hard time keeping jobs. Babies get sick. We took them to the doctor. It costs too much to pay someone to watch the babies. We had more bills than money. Just when we'd saved a little money to catch up on our bills, we learned we were having another baby."

Officer Reese took a break from writing and cracked his knuckles.

"I was able to get public assistance to help out with some of our medical expenses, but we still incurred lots of bills from the delivery. We got financial assistance for utilities here and there. Food vouchers helped at times. But we fell behind on rent and other bills. It wasn't long before we were evicted. That's when we moved here to Champaign. Moved in with my aunt and her husband. Her husband was a professor at the University of Illinois. He was the breadwinner for their family—and he was generous. We stayed until we got back on our feet. That took a few months. Then, we rented a tiny, two-bedroom house. We stayed there for a while." My mouth felt dry.

"Would you care for something to drink?"

"No, ma'am," they answered in unison.

"I'll be just one moment." I left them to their own small talk and came back with glass of iced tea with lots of ice. I sat it on a coaster on Anthony's desk.

"We had three more children over the course of . . . What was it?" I scanned the room trying to remember. "About seven or eight years. My husband and I along with six children in a two-bedroom bungalow. It seemed that house was getting smaller and smaller. It was a very difficult time.

"The older children started school, but the younger ones were still at home all day. Too young for school. Babysitters cost too much. I could no longer work with so many babies at home. Sometimes my husband worked three jobs.

"Too many days and nights he would only get two hours of sleep. It really wore on his body and health. He got sick. One time, do you know they thought they would have to amputate his right foot?" I looked at both officers and took a swig of tea.

"He worked hard. His feet would bleed something terrible. He was diabetic and we didn't know. His right foot got infected and then gangrene set in. They performed emergency surgery to remove the poison from his foot, but due to repeat infections, it took him a year to fully recuperate. I was home nursing him to health, so neither of us were working for a little while. Bills piled up. High. We received disconnection notices. We couldn't pay the hospital bills." A lone tear slipped down my cheek.

"Our children were made fun of at school because they wore shoes and clothes with holes in them. It was bad. Bad times." Officer Reese held out a box of tissues from the desk. Though I wiped away the liquid relic of my sorrow, my voice still tremored with remembered pain.

"Sometimes, my oldest daughter would sneak her free school lunch into her book bag to share with her siblings once she got home. I don't know what I would have done without that one.

"While Anthony was still recovering, I got two jobs. Had to. We got caught up on some bills, but never all of them. I got on birth control pills; we didn't want to bring another child into this world to suffer. The clinic gave them to me for free. I took them faithfully every day . . . for a while. They made me feel sick. So, eventually, I stopped."

Another swallow of tea washed away words trying lodge in my throat.

"I would come home from two jobs and the house would be a mess. I'd hear babies screaming when I walked through the front door. I didn't blame Anthony. My dear husband was still in no shape to properly care for them. My aunt and her husband were now caring for his elderly parents and had their own problems to worry about. I quit my full-time job and worked only part time most evenings. During the day, I'd care for my husband and take care of three children all under age five. It was difficult times. Financially. But even worse, emotionally and physically for me. Our children suffered terribly."

Thoughts of how they'd suffered during those years caused tears to flood my eyes. A big, round, wet spot formed on my white trousers. My tissue was streaked with black mascara, tan make-up, and candy-apple red blush.

"It was never easy trying to explain to the children why we had no water. Or lights. Or heat. Or why we had to move . . . again.

"When our oldest child turned sixteen, she decided to get a part-time job to help with some of the bills. By then, we had how many more children . . . ?" I asked aloud, not expecting an answer. "Let's see. We had one more child. So, a total of seven."

I grabbed for my tea. A mouthful of sugar that had settled at the bottom made my lips pucker. "So, we struggled with nine mouths to feed. Too many. Not enough food."

I leaned forward and asked, "Have you ever looked into the eyes of a hungry child you couldn't feed, Officer Reese?"

He cracked a few more of his knuckles. "No, ma'am. I can't say that I have."

"Well, just be glad you can't. It's the most painful sight in the whole world."

"And, as if seven weren't enough, in January of 1995, I found out I was pregnant again. Number eight! We talked for weeks, trying to figure out what was best for our already struggling family. Through much heartache and many tears, we agreed together to do the only thing we thought was right for our entire family. Now you have to understand!" I don't know why I felt the need to justify to strangers what I was about to say next. "This was not something we wanted to do, but was what we felt we had to do back then. We felt stuck.

"I'll tell you what didn't help our situation. When we finally went to the free clinic in late February to verify the pregnancy, the doctor who examined me handed us a brochure and encouraged us to seriously consider it. We saw the brochure as the answer we needed. It silenced any remaining doubts we felt."

Officer Reese stopped writing and joined Officer Hughes in observing me.

"I'll never forget, it was a frigid February night. We hadn't paid our electric and gas bills, so we didn't have heat. Again. We lit the fireplace and all nine of us were huddled around it in blankets trying to keep warm. It was sad to see the children's teeth chattering like that. Some were coughing. Everyone had a runny nose. It was hard for me, as their mother, to watch that. Pregnancy had me emotional. I couldn't stop crying. I felt worthless. Seeing my children suffering, not having the basic necessities like heat, pushed me to the breaking point. I ran to the bathroom in tears. My husband followed. But I couldn't be consoled. I didn't want to be."

This time I chomped on a piece of ice as dryness tried to occupy my throat.

"In that single moment, we decided together that we had to call the number on the brochure. So, first thing the next morning, we called Healthy Women's Health Center. Here's what's interesting. We couldn't get any assistance from friends or family to help us pay our bills, but when we told them why we needed the money this time, they were more than happy to give it to us."

"Will you please state for the record what procedure you had done?" Officer Reese asked.

"I didn't have any procedure done."

He started writing in his notebook again.

My husband returned from taking our toy poodles on a walk. They were well-groomed and looked like show dogs. Big, blown-out mane covered their faces and upper bodies. They were shaved close to the skin on the back half of their bodies, right down to the fluffy balls of fur around their ankles.

Anthony eased into his chair with his now extinguished cigar in hand. Everyone remained seated. The only sound was the clicking clock. I twisted and adjusted many diamond rings and it calmed me to trace my fingers across a fresh, smooth coat of red nail polish.

Officers Hughes and Reese watched my husband as he tapped grayish-white ash off the end of his cigar and into the glass ashtray. He picked up his white marble cigarette lighter and relit the tip of his cigar. Smiling, he exhaled and leaned back in his chair, eyes closed.

"Everyone is quiet. I guess that means you gentlemen have all you need, then, huh?"

"No, sir. We don't," Officer Hughes answered.

"Our files tell us . . ." Officer Reese shuffled through pages in his notepad. "Oh, yes, that you were present at the clinic when everything happened."

My husband, eyes locked on the end of his cigar, nodded.

"Perhaps you can tell us what happened at the clinic," Officer Hughes said.

"Not my fondest memory, gentlemen."

"Go ahead, honey."

"I went into the clinic with my wife the day of the appointment. We wanted to get some basic information and find out what the procedure would entail. We met with a nurse who explained how long it would take, what to expect during and after, and what it would cost. The doctor came in. He answered one, maybe two questions. He seemed to be in a hurry, didn't stay longer than a minute or two. They did tests on Beatriz. We came back the next day for the abortion."

Anthony paced around his office, never letting go of the cigar. "Gentlemen, the day of the abortion, I took my wife to the clinic, paid the money, and sat in the waiting room for the whole ordeal to just be over and done with."

My heart ached for my husband as he recounted the details.

"I looked at magazines and newspapers. I had a million thoughts running through my mind. I looked out of the clinic window and noticed the doctor we'd met the day before dressed in a nice black, Italian suit. He got into an even nicer Mercedes. Just sped off. I didn't think much about him leaving. But I remember I felt sick to my stomach. Knowing that it was our money helping him to pay for that shiny new car."

When Anthony sat down, it looked as if he'd aged a decade in a minute.

"That felt like the longest day of my life as I waited for her. The thought crossed my mind several times, to just go in there and stop it. Instead, I just kept waiting." He smoothed out his mustache with his finger and thumb.

"Finally, the nurse helped my wife out to the waiting room. I took the recovery orders from her, helped Beatriz to the bus stop, and we went home. I didn't notice anything unusual. But then, I didn't know what was normal about a place like that to begin with. Sorry, fellas, but that's all I got for you." He lowered his cigar. Exhaled more smoke.

The officers continued to write notes in their little notepads even after Anthony finished speaking.

"And you, Mrs. Barros? What can you tell me about the day you went to the clinic?" Officer Hughes rubbed his finger in his ear rapidly.

"It was the worst day of my entire life. I try not to remember that day because it reminds me of just how low I had fallen in life." I spoke over the ticking clock sitting on the desk.

"We met with the nurse the day before the procedure, like my husband said, and she explained everything to us. She said the doctor was simply going to remove a blob of tissue. Yes. A blob of tissue." My wet eyes locked with my husband's before he looked away.

"I was three months along. The next day, I believe they gave me local anesthetic and some other medication because I was not out all the way, but I wasn't 100 percent with it either. I remember a tugging sensation. What I remember more than anything was the loud sound of the suction machine the doctor was using on me. Sometimes, I can still hear it! Do you know, to this day, I have to leave home whenever housekeeping vacuums. The sound brings back painful memories."

My nails made flickering sounds as I removed small particles of dirt from underneath them.

"I didn't want to watch, so as I laid on the table, I closed my eyes, and tried to convince myself I wasn't really there. I was a little out of it when the nurse helped me off the table into a wheelchair and settled me in the recovery room. I stayed there for a little while and they took my vital signs. When she saw I was able to stand on my own, she helped me walk out to the waiting room. She gave Anthony the recovery orders. We left and took the bus home. I never wanted to see a place like that again. Even though the orders said it was important to come back to make sure the procedure had gone as planned, I could never bear going back. So, I never did. I cried myself to sleep every night after that." My shoulders tensed up, burning.

"Mrs. Barros, did you notice anything about the doctor that was different the second day from the first day you saw him for the consultation? Anything, even what you might consider insignificant. Was there any change in his appearance? Voice? Eye color?" Officer Hughes leaned in, but I refused to make eye contact.

"You mean, was he a different person?"

"Yes. But I mean anything."

"He looked exactly like the doctor my husband and I saw the day before. Had same black hair. Same medium build. Same height. Same brown eyes. And the same clean-shaven face when he came into my room to perform the procedure. He didn't do much talking. In fact, now that I think back"—I made eye contact with Officer Hughes—"I guess it was a little odd because I don't remember him talking to me or the nurse at all. No. I'm mistaken. He did ask her for surgical tools. I just remember him coming into the room, putting on his mask, and then putting on big, surgical glasses that had a bright light on it. They put an IV in my arm, so I was a little out of it. I don't know. Maybe they were talking."

"Did he say anything to you before he left the room?"

"No. Nothing I recall."

"Did he do anything after the surgery that stands out in your mind?"

"You know, now that I think back . . . I didn't think much of it then, but . . . yeah . . . he came to my bedside after he was done working on me and rubbed my hand. Fast. Not long. He cupped my hand between his, smiled, winked at me, and then left the room. I just figured it was his way of saying the procedure had been a success. Maybe it was the Chameleon who cupped my hand and smiled and winked at me, not the doctor. At the consultation the day before, the doctor seemed to be a coldhearted man. He got straight to the point: just one, two, three, four. I'll take the blob of tissue out. You'll experience some cramping. Some bleeding. You'll go home and problem solved. You know what I mean? But the doctor after the abortion had gentle eyes. Maybe I'm thinking too much."

"Mrs. Barros, pardon me, but I'm a little confused." Officer Hughes scooted to the edge of his seat. "When Officer Reese asked you earlier what kind of a procedure you had at the clinic, you said that you didn't have a procedure at all. Now you're saying that you thought the doctor winked at you and smiled and shook your hand because you thought he believed the abortion was successful."

"Officer, I meant exactly what I said earlier. And I mean exactly what I'm saying now. I did go to the clinic to have the procedure. An abortion. But an abortion never happened. I thought that was the whole purpose of your visit today, officers."

"Well, it is. But this is where everything gets tricky. Where we need to piece together the missing information in our investigations. If you say the doctor was the doctor, and the nurse was present, and surgical tools and abortion devices were used on you, what happened? How did you go in for an abortion? Lay on the table? Have a doctor working on you? With a nurse present? Believed it was successful? But no abortion occurred?" Officer Reese asked.

Anthony placed his cigar in the ashtray. He folded his arms, his forehead wrinkled. "What we do know is when we were first interviewed by detectives about a year after this happened, they at least had a motive for this Chameleon's behavior and knew more about him than you two, apparently. They said he was going around to these clinics, obviously not performing these procedures, but instead, he was fondling innocent women. He's some sort of sick pervert. Please tell me you knew that already."

"Yes, sir, we did. But our job is to look at the situation from a fresh perspective. We are trying to see if there is more to the Chameleon than what has been gathered in the past. We are interviewing you first. With our own questions. Later, we will compare notes with those detectives who interviewed you in the past," said Officer Reese. "So, ma'am, if you would, please tell me about when you discovered that an abortion had never taken place."

"My husband and I walked to the nearest bus stop in silence. I was cramping a little bit, just like the nurse said I would, but it was not unbearable. My oldest daughter was home with the younger children. The bus ride home was a foggy memory. When we made it home, I went straight to our bedroom, shut the door, and slept for three days.

"My husband brought me food. He had to make me eat. I only got out of bed to use the bathroom. Later, I discovered I was clinically depressed. I felt like an unfit mother. I felt like a horrible, horrible human being. I believed I had taken the life of my own child. I was having regrets, but it was too late. Guilt and shame were taking over my mind. No one at the clinic ever told me to expect that." I straightened my pearl necklace. "It took about a week before I could look after the smaller children again. I'd get up, fix something to eat, change a few diapers, and then go right back to bed. I did that for about two months."

I glanced over at Anthony, he was sinking into his chair.

"I lost a lot of weight, but my stomach was swollen. I didn't think much of it. I just thought my body was trying to recover. The nurse told me it would take a while for my menstrual cycle to return to normal, and every woman's body operates on its own clock. She even told me I might not get my menstrual cycle again because I was already over forty years old. I might go into menopause, she told me. So, I didn't think much of the fact that I had no period. I had no idea I was five and half months pregnant then."

I grabbed my iced tea, only the ice had melted.

"I blamed my husband. Told him it was his fault. I asked him over and over, 'What kind of real man would let this happen?' Officers, I was never a mean person before that. But I was unhappy and wanted everyone around me to feel what I was feeling. I didn't want to hold any of my children. Not anymore. I felt too unworthy. I was bad off. Sick in the head."

I motioned for Fluffy, our gray poodle who had managed to squeeze through the slightly opened French doors. I placed him in my lap. I brushed strands of Fluffy's fur from my white pants with one hand and cuddled him with the other.

"But early one Sunday morning, I woke up because there was a baby moving inside of me. I would have been about seven months along. I sat up in bed and cried all over again. I had been too paralyzed with guilt, shame, anger, and depression in the months before. I could not recognize then that the abortion had not taken place. All the signs were there, but I'd trusted the nurse when she said the abortion had been a success."

Now a smile escaped my face. "Poor man over there was used to me crying by now, so he was not surprised. I had conditioned him not to touch me, so he didn't move from his side of the bed. I woke him up with kisses all over his face. This was huge! I had not allowed him to kiss me since the day of the abortion or whatever. He sat up and I gave him a big hug. I was sobbing. Then, I started laughing. I think I confused him."

"Yeah, I thought you had completely lost your mind. I had tried to convince her to go to the free clinic to see a therapist for the depression, but she always refused. That morning, I thought she had finally lost it all. Then, when she told me she was still pregnant . . . Well, I really thought she was delusional. Someone at work told me that one of the stages of grief was denial. I just thought she was in denial." Anthony sat up straighter in his chair now.

"I carried seven babies in my body. I knew what it felt like for a baby to move about in my womb. I had no doubt on that Sunday morning that I was still pregnant. I got up out of bed that morning, happy to make a small breakfast for everyone. It wasn't much, but I felt renewed in my spirit. The sun seemed brighter. The air crisper. I felt like I had been given a second chance."

I cuddled and rocked Fluffy. I flashed Anthony a smile, which he returned.

"My stomach grew quickly after that. At the beginning of my eighth month, I had my husband take me to the free clinic where they confirmed that I was thirty-six weeks pregnant. That was the first time in my life I ever saw my husband cry."

"I couldn't believe it was possible. I didn't show it like my wife, but I had a lot of regrets after the supposed abortion. Then, when she started blaming me for letting it happen, I didn't think our marriage, or our life, would ever return to normal after that. When they confirmed that she was still pregnant, I knew that God had given us a second chance. I must admit, I felt relieved. Confused, but relieved."

"Then, on September 18, 1997, I gave birth to an eight pound, four ounce baby boy we named Victor. He seemed to come out of my womb singing. He was a very happy child. His birth restored my life. My peace. Our marriage. My hope, and my joy. So, you see, Officer Hughes and Officer Reese, I don't know who this Chameleon fella is. I don't even care what he did to me on that day—good or bad. What I do know is when I tried to abort my child, regardless of whatever criminal activity this man was up to, he ended up helping me in more ways than I can even begin to explain. So, even if you capture this Chameleon, I will never willingly testify against him." I felt like I could breathe for the first time since this interview started. "This criminal blessed me by being a fraud. Not knowing what he was doing in that abortion room was a blessing. If you capture him, I would actually like to thank him."

"But, ma'am, he violated you in the worst way," Officer Hughes interjected, "and all these years later, he's still doing the same thing to other innocent women."

"Okay, gentleman, I think it's time for you to go now." Anthony quickly stood, opened the office doors, and waited.

"Ma'am, it has been a pleasure meeting you." Officer Reese shook my hand.

Officer Hughes nodded and did the same.

"Sir, here are our business cards. If either of you think of anything else you would like to share with us, please don't hesitate to call."

I led them to the front door and watched as they made their way to the patrol car. Through the intercom, I could hear their fading conversation.

"How in the world can a perverted criminal be seen as a blessing?"

"I guess I can kind of see where she's coming from. But it still doesn't change who the Chameleon is . . . a perverted, old man who preys on innocent young women."

I watched as they pulled out of the driveway and then turned to find my husband watching me from the office doors. I made my way to him and put my arms around his waist. "Let's go find our son and give him a hug."

4

THE CASE OF THE LATE-NIGHT RUN

PAUL

I arrived at work a few minutes before the start of my shift. Jeff met me in the conference room.

"You'll never believe what happened to me this morning. I went through the drive-thru of our favorite little donut shop over there on 10th and Clint Street. I ordered my usual Danish and a medium coffee. When she handed me my coffee, I grabbed it from the top like I always do. But this time . . . all in my lap, scalding . . . hot . . . coffee. Today . . . not off to a good start."

"Man, quit lying, you know you peed on yourself."

"Never that! As a matter of fact, do you see any wet spots on my pants?"

I looked at him.

"Answer the question. This is not rhetorical."

"Naw. I don't see any wet spots on your uniform pants."

"No, you don't!" Jeff eased himself into a chair. Groaning. "The reason for that is I keep extra clothes in my locker. That is something my beautiful girl recommended. I used to give her a hard time about it, telling her than I'm not some elementary school kid who needs to keep a change of clothes on-site. But now, I appreciate her looking out for me." His body relaxed as a smile emerged.

"Jeff, why do you always talk about this girl of yours, but nobody here has ever met her?"

"You'll meet her. Calm down. But she's a mover and a shaker. She works. She has hobbies, friends, a social life, and looks after me. I'll get her here soon enough if she can carve a moment out of her schedule."

"*If* she really exists, then you'd better get her up here so we can meet her. No more excuses. A'ight?"

"Whatever."

"I'm gonna grab a water. I know it's not the gourmet coffee you managed to spill all over yourself, but would you like me to bring you a cup from the break room?"

"Yeah, sure. And can you bring one creamer and three sugars?"

"Yup."

I'd just finish pouring Jeff's coffee and was thinking aloud as I grabbed a stirrer. "Okay, Chameleon. Who are you really? And what's your MO?"

"Well, well, well! If it's not Mr. 'I've Got All the Answers' and 'I Am the Best on the Force' in here talking to himself and turning all crazy. Why don't you just give up this case already? Leave it alone. You'll never catch the Chameleon! You should walk away now." Officer Prince walked toward me, his eyes squinted and his mouth set in a firm line.

I put the coffee cup on the table. "Leave it alone? Walk away? Why? Afraid I might find some dirt on you? Your highness! The more you come at me with these reckless threats, the more I believe you're a dirty cop, somehow assisting this criminal. I'll quit before I walk away. Who do you think you're intimidating? Certainly not me."

As we stood nose-to-nose, Sergeant Stevens entered the room. "What's going on in here?"

"I was just trying to convince Reesie here that he needs to give up the *Operation Almost* case." Officer Prince continued to stare at me without blinking.

"I'm with Prince on this one. Reese, man, you need to have that chat with the chief and let him know you made a huge mistake volunteering for this case. Get off it before you get yourself hurt."

"Now you're threatening me, huh? Get myself hurt? Who is it that's planning on hurting me?"

Jeff came sauntering in. "Fellas, fellas, fellas! I can hear y'all all the way down the hall. We are not about to do this!" He forced his way between me and the two of them and tugged at my arm. "Paul, we have to prepare for our interview with the next victim on the list. No one but you can stop what you're already doing."

"Yeah, you're right." I held my gaze with Officer Prince as I back away and picked up Jeff's coffee. "Here's your coffee. You still have to get your cream and sugar."

"Sure thing. Thanks."

I grabbed my water and we walked back to the conference room.

"So, who are we interviewing today?" Jeff asked.

"Tom arranged for us to interview Mrs. Maria Herrera. However, there was some conflict with her schedule, and he told her that we would call her back to set up a new time."

"No problem." Jeff sat and pulled out his cell phone. He placed it on speaker and dialed the number. He took a deep breath before he pressed the last digit. I was preoccupied looking at Mrs. Herrera's files, but I heard the phone ring twice before someone said, "Hello, Herrera residence, how may I assist you today?"

It was the voice of a little girl, about five or six years old.

"Hello, may I please speak with Mrs. Maria Herrera?" Jeff said.

"I'm sorry," the little girl replied in a sweet yet confident voice, "you have the wrong number," and with that, she hung up the phone.

"Well, that went well." Jeff raised his eyebrows and scratched the back of his head as he held the phone in his hand.

"What just happened?" I asked.

"Apparently, there is no Mrs. Maria Herrera living at the . . . and I quote, 'Herrera residence,' according to the darling little five-year-old who just answered the phone."

"That's cute. Okay. Call again." I was ready to move forward with the investigation.

Jeff dialed the number again, and before the first ring, he pressed the speaker button. Again, we heard the angelic voice, "Good morning, thank you for calling the Herrera residence, how might I assist you?"

"Well, hello there. Is this the Herrera residence?" Jeff asked.

"Yes, it is," the little girl replied in her same sweet voice.

"May I please speak with an adult?" Before she could answer, it sounded as though someone grabbed the phone from her.

"Hello. Who is this?" a woman asked.

"Yes. This is Officer Jeff Hughes from the Champaign Police department."

"Oh, yes, I have been expecting your call. I am really sorry about my granddaughter just now. You have to ask to speak to Nana, because in her precious little mind, my name is not Mrs. Maria Herrera. It's Nana."

"Yes, ma'am, I understand." Jeff frowned and shrugged his shoulders. "So, is this Mrs. Maria Herrera, also known as Nana?" Jeff asked as he glanced at me and snickered under his breath.

"Yes, sir, it is. I'm supposing you want to set up an interview to discuss the continuous tactics of this Chameleon criminal that you all still haven't caught in all these years?"

"Yes, ma'am. We certainly would. Is today still a good day for you?"

"I'll be done watching my granddaughter at one o'clock, so will two work for you, Officer Hughes?"

"Yes, ma'am, two o'clock is good. Now, were you okay with us interviewing you at your home?"

"Oh, no, sir! Not at all!"

"Okay, well, where would you like for us to interview you instead?"

"I don't know . . . How about I come to you? You may not truly be who you say you are. But if I come to the police station and they say they've never heard of you, well, then I'll just fill out a report on you. Besides, I wouldn't want the neighbors to think me or my husband had committed some kind of crime with a police car parked in front of our house and all. Where did you say your station was located?"

"We're at the corner of First Street and University Avenue."

"Oh, yeah, I know where that is. I will see you two at two then."

"Yes, ma'am. We'll see you then." Jeff hung up the phone and grimaced as he used the table to pull himself up from his chair. "Where is her file?"

I handed Jeff her files. "A little paranoid, you think?"

"Let me see what I can find. Here it is: 1973, the Case of the Late-Night Run. Oh, yes," Jeff said looking through the papers. "I remember reading through this one. Poor lady. She has every right to be paranoid after what she's been through."

INTERVIEW #2

MARIA HERRERA

"I have an appointment with two officers," I said to the lady at the reception desk. I pulled my notepad out of my bag and looked at their names. "Officers Jeff Hughes and Paul Reese."

"I'll get them for you now if you want to have a seat over there." The lady offered a friendly smile.

I sat down in the busy station. As I looked around, I started feeling claustrophobic and dizzy. The constant ringing of phones, shuffling of papers, movement of people, back and forth of police officers, and stares of strangers became more than I could tolerate.

"I should have never come here," I whispered into my armpit as I stood.

I'd gathered my things and was walking toward the exit when an officer called out, "Mrs. Herrera?"

"Yes, that's me." I turned around, relieved to hear my name as I did not like to go back on my word.

The officer extended his hand. "I'm Officer Jeff Hughes. Thank you so very much for agreeing to meet with us today."

"You're quite welcome, Officer Jeff."

"Follow me this way if you would, please." He led me past the wooden latch swing door and into the office part of the station, then down a quieter hallway where we stopped at an elevator. He pressed the up button.

"So, how old is your granddaughter? The one who answered the phone."

"My little Maria. She's named after me. Five years old. She'll be six on Sunday." How could he possibly know that talking about little Maria would soothe my anxiety and reverse the panic attack that moments earlier felt inevitable?

"That's a fun age." The elevator door opened. Officer Jeff stood in the hallway with one arm extended inside as he double pumped his four fingers for me to get on first. We stood in silence for a moment with his eyes fixed on my shoes.

"Do you run?"

"Yes. What gave it away? My neon pink running shoes. Or the jogging suit?"

"A combination of both. But I've been known to put some miles on some running shoes. The brand you're wearing is my favorite."

"Yes, they really help with my shin splints and they're kind to my knees. At sixty-five years old, I have to take more precautions to preserve this old body."

"Well, I would've guessed you were at least twenty years younger, so you must be doing something right. This way." He escorted me to a conference room that could comfortably seat five.

"I'm Officer Paul Reese. Thank you for agreeing to meet with us, Mrs. Herrera. We really do appreciate you taking time out of your day to come down here to the station. Can I get you something to drink?" a tall, fit, African-American cop said.

"What do you have?"

"Let's see . . ." He walked to a mini-refrigerator that was tucked in the corner of the room. "We have cranberry-grape juice, soda pop, water, apple juice, ginger ale, and orange juice. And we have some coffee over in one of our other rooms if you'd prefer that instead."

"Um, I'll take a water. No, make that a cranberry-grape juice. Umm, I'm sorry; I should go with the water."

Officer Reese grabbed both a bottle of water and a cranberry-grape juice and handed them both to me. "Please, drink one now and save one for later."

"Thank you." Feeling a little embarrassed about my indecision, I twisted the cap off the water and chugged down half of it.

"Mrs. Herrera," Officer Jeff said, "we asked for this interview because we are trying to capture a man we only know as the Chameleon. As you may already know, he is some master of disguise who is responsible for going into abortion clinics, pretending to be a doctor, acting as if he is performing abortions, and then leaving women pregnant who believe they are no longer. We have a file here that says you were not pleased when you discovered that you were still pregnant after going to a local clinic to have an abortion. Can you tell us what you remember about that day?"

"Going to the clinic to actually have the procedure is a muddled memory. I had just experienced a traumatic event a couple weeks before. I do remember a good friend of mine being there with me. She supported me through the entire process. It's all rather murky to me because I was in and out of the emergency room, hospitals, clinics, and therapists' offices so much back then, they all seemed like the same place to me after a while. I was a real disaster back then. But, after all I had been through . . . well, I'm sure you understand."

I gathered my newly highlighted, honey-blonde-streaked dark hair into a single ponytail and tied it with a hair tie that was on my wrist. This was going to feel like a workout I didn't prefer to do today.

"I remember my friend, the ER nurses, my therapist, and everyone who was familiar with my situation, all giving me the same advice. Every one of them told me, more than asked me, 'You're not planning on keeping the child, are you?' because I suppose rapes that result in pregnancy should be terminated, no questions asked. I'll confess, I was indifferent about the situation."

"Do you remember anything about the day of the abortion?" Officer Jeff leaned toward me. "Or, more specifically, what do you recall about the doctor who performed the abortion?"

"Well, legal abortions were still fairly new back then. In the emergency room, immediately after my assault, it was just way too early for them to determine if I was pregnant. There was no such thing as a morning-after pill back then. I had to wait a couple weeks before a pregnancy test would even detect if I was pregnant. I prayed and prayed that I wasn't."

"So, you were assaulted, went to the emergency room, but it was too early to determine if the assault resulted in a pregnancy?" Officer Jeff recapped what I said as he wrote in his notepad.

"That's right. My therapist prescribed me some anti-anxiety and anti-depressant medication. I thought she provided me with sleeping pills because all I did after the assault was sleep. I couldn't seem to keep my eyelids open for three months straight.

"Then, one day out of the blue, while washing my hair, it hit me. I had not had a period in almost . . . what was it . . . three months. When my mother learned of this, she insisted I see a doctor. That day! They took a urine sample. I got a phone call the next day. The pregnancy test came back positive. I hit my head on the kitchen counter when I blacked out. Thank goodness my friend, Susan had stopped by to return my hair dryer.

"I woke up in an ambulance. They took me to the emergency room. That same afternoon, I was at an abortion clinic. The next day they did the procedure.

"I was still on anti-anxiety and anti-depressant medications at the time of the procedure. So, like I said earlier, it's all a foggy memory really. Susan drove me there, helped fill out the paper work, and waited for me in the waiting room during the whole ordeal.

"On the operating table, I couldn't stop crying and wondering how it was even possible that this was my life. There was a nurse in the room rubbing my forehead and holding my hand during the procedure. I *do* remember the doctor working on me. Oh, and the loud sound of that suction machine. I could never forget that. I don't remember much of what anyone said to me on the day of the abortion. I'm sorry, but I don't recall much about the doctor either. Other than the fact that he was a man, and he wore white like most doctors did back then. Nothing else really stood out about him."

"Did he say anything to you after the procedure was over?" asked Officer Reese.

"I don't recall ever hearing him speak. But, again, I was not completely with it. After the procedure, they monitored me for a little while, and then they released me. Susan took me home and I became practically incapable of taking care of myself. The medication I was on had me abnormally drowsy. All I wanted to do was sleep. Disappear really. Well, sleeping all day and night doesn't pay the bills. I lost my job, and then I was evicted. My parents traveled all the way from Texas to come get me. I was under their supervision and care. There I was, twenty-four years old and helpless.

"My mother, after I was put under a new team of doctors, attempted to wean me off the medications. She said it broke her heart that I had been so independent my whole life and now was so helpless.

"It was my mother who actually discovered that I was still pregnant. I was so bad off . . . she had to bathe me." I felt uncomfortable telling two men such intimate details, but wanted to get the interview over with.

"She looked like she'd seen a ghost. She burst into tears and shot out of the bathroom. Then, as quickly as she'd left, she returned. Never one to beat around the bush, she said, 'You're clearly very pregnant,' and started rubbing my average-sized yet round belly. I argued that was impossible because Susan herself took me to have an abortion. She'd been in daily communication with Susan up until the day she and my father picked me up. And she had the abortion paper work to prove it."

"Mrs. Herrera, we have some questions to ask that might be difficult. Is that alright?" Officer Reese asked.

"I'm okay to continue." I wondered if Officer Reese was okay because beads of sweat had formed on his forehead.

"So, once your mother discovered that you were still pregnant, did you attempt a second abortion?" Officer Jeff asked.

"Oh, no. Based on the date of the rape, we knew that I was just over six months pregnant. Late-term abortions were not legal back then. I had to carry this child full term. It wasn't so bad. I didn't even realize, being so heavily sedated, that I was pregnant for the first six months. I thought, *What's another two and a half months?* It was never a question, I would give the child up for adoption. My mother and father found a well-off couple who had been trying for years to have children, but could not. Minutes after I gave birth, they took him as their own. The adoption process was probably the easiest part of all I had been through." I felt relieved that we were nearing the end of the interview but I had something else I needed to know. "Is it okay if I ask a couple of questions?"

"Yes. Absolutely." Officer Jeff leaned forward and set his pen down.

"I understand that it was wrong for this master of disguise, former CIA operative, or whatever he is, to impersonate a doctor. It was horrible that he infringed upon my rights to do as I pleased with my body. But . . . what about the man that raped me? How is it that after all these years, you haven't put in one-tenth of the effort or manpower to keep him in prison as you have put in to catching this abortion-stopper-doctor-fraud?"

"I thought the man who raped you received a lengthy sentence." Officer Reese started shuffling through some files and notes.

I crossed my arms. "Yeah, he served seventeen years of a twenty-year sentence for what he did to me. But why didn't the courts make him do the other three years? Better yet, why didn't they give him *more* time for what he did to me? Tell me, officers, if you catch this Chameleon, how much time do you think he'll serve?"

"Oh, he'll get a life sentence . . . easily," Officer Reese answered without hesitating.

"All I'm saying is what the Chameleon did was wrong, but what that rapist did was a hundred times more criminal. Why does a rapist get a slap on the wrist, but this Chameleon, you want to put under the jail?"

"Ma'am,"—Officer Jeff glanced at Officer Reese before making eye contact with me— "we understand your frustration. But you are comparing two very different criminals who committed two very different crimes. And violated a vastly different number of people. Laws and sentences vary based on these factors."

Officer Reese asked, "Can you tell us what, if anything, you remember about the day you were sexually assaulted?"

I didn't see how the rape was pertinent to the Chameleon case, but I answered him anyway. "Even though I spent a lot of money and years trying, I can't seem to forget. May 8, 1973, to be exact. It was a beautiful spring night. Perfect weather for a run. I had run this route more than a hundred times over a three-year period.

"I normally got off work at six p.m., but that night I worked for a little extra cash and stayed until eight. I had plans to take a weekend trip to visit some old college friends. The sun was going down, but I thought I'd have time to get back before it was totally dark out.

"I was running the mile and a half trail that was off a nearby park and pond. I knew this path with my eyes closed. As I was running, I tripped over what was later identified as a tree limb. It was intentionally placed on one of the darker areas of the path. I hit the rocks on the trail pretty hard, scraped up my hands and knees. While I was sitting on the ground trying to clean the dirt off my knee wound, he grabbed me beneath both arms and dragged me on the other side of some bushes that were maybe three feet off the trail. Um-hmm . . ." I started feeling like the room was closing in on me, so I took a long drink of water.

"Are you okay with continuing?" Officer Jeff asked.

"Yes, it's just tough remembering these details. But I'm okay. Uh, he grabbed me so fast, I didn't even realize what was happening at first. Then he placed a knife to my throat and told me I better not make a sound. He did right there, behind the bushes, what rapists do. I still screamed, but he had his hand over my mouth. It probably only lasted a few minutes, but it felt like an eternity. When he was done, he ran off into the darkness toward a wooded area. I laid there. Paralyzed from the inside out. I couldn't move or scream. All I could do was cry silently. It wasn't until I realized that he could come back that I found the strength to get up.

"I was hurting in so many ways, emotionally, a busted knee, what I had just experienced…but I made it to my car, which was parked in a small parking lot about three-fourths of a mile away. I got in, drove home, and got straight into the shower. I must have washed myself ten times. It was a really rough night.

"I didn't feel safe, even in my own place. I piled every piece of furniture I owned in front of my door.

"When I didn't show up at work the next day, they called repeatedly, but I didn't answer.

"Susan, we also work together, stopped by during her lunch break to check on me. It was around noon. I planned on not answering, but she knocked until I could no longer ignore it. By the time I got out of bed and made my way to the door, her feisty self was beating on my door with her high heel shoe. I could maneuver some of the furniture to create a path wide enough for her to squeeze in. She was in shock when she saw my place, but she was completely devastated when I explained what had happened to me. I don't know what I would have done without her." I could feel tears surfacing.

Officer Jeff grabbed the box of tissues that was sitting on the window ledge. He placed the box in front of me. "Did you want to take a little break?"

"No, no. Let's finish up." I was careful to dab at my eyes so as not to smear my eye make-up. "I told Susan what happened to me. Blinked. And she had me in her car racing me to the emergency room. A nurse told me that I should have come there right away, not showered, but she understood. They administered the rape kit to get any remaining evidence off me. They were the ones who set up an appointment with me to see a therapist. I told you the rest of the story already."

Officer Reese, flipping through a file, said, "I noticed here that you filed a lawsuit against the abortion clinic, and you were prepared to go the distance. What changed? Why'd you drop it?"

"Oh, that!" I released a combination of a chuckle and a grunt. "I spent years hating both Scott—I eventually learned the rapist's name—and the abortion-stopping-doctor-fraud, whom you all have cleverly named the Chameleon. It took decades. Three to be exact. But I have forgiven the Chameleon for his crimes against me."

"What made you decide to do that? Did you settle out of court?" Officer Jeff asked.

"No. We never settled. The case dragged on for years. The clinic claimed that they were victims of the Chameleon too. I ended up just dropping the case. No one but my family knows the real reason why I dropped the case and forgave the Chameleon. I have actually seen good come out of the Chameleon's involvement, that until recently, I had never seen. And when I say recently, I mean like almost six years ago, recently."

Officer Jeff perked up and sat so close to the edge of his seat I thought he would tip over. "Have you had some contact with the Chameleon?"

"No. At least none that I am aware of."

Officer Jeff relaxed his posture again. "What good could have possibly come out of the Chameleon's involvement?"

"Good? Coming out of such an evil act like rape? That doesn't even sound right, I know. But, yeah . . ."

Officer Reese pulled up his sleeves and leaned back. "What happened almost six years ago that changed how you felt about the Chameleon?"

"Several years after the rape, my father introduced me to a handsome young man. They worked together, and he was from Champaign; this is my father's hometown. We eventually fell in love and got married. We had a beautiful daughter together. Then, years later, my daughter got married and had a daughter of her own, almost six years ago. That's what changed how I felt about the Chameleon." I smiled at the officers and waited for the additional questions I knew would follow.

Officer Reese first looked at me with a blank stare. Then his left eyebrow took on the shape of an inverted *V*. "So, you falling in love, getting married, having a daughter, and then having a granddaughter made you forgive the Chameleon for violating you, defrauding you, and causing you so much pain?" The calm in his voice failed to match the veins popping out on his neck and arms. With his fingertips, he pinched his lips together as if it were the only way he could keep his mouth closed.

"Please help my partner and me see how the Chameleon's involvement in impersonating an abortion doctor, and defrauding you of a sought after, paid, abortion proved to somehow *help* you." He quickly turned back a page of his notepad. "A moment ago you stated, and I quote: 'I have actually seen good come out of the Chameleon's involvement, that until recently, I had never seen. And when I say recently, I mean like almost six years ago, recently.' What exactly did you mean by those two statements?"

My body started feeling stiff and the air in the room seemed to evaporate. I stood and stretched. The partners glanced at each other. I couldn't retrieve the yawn that slipped out with a grand entrance. I sat back down. "I'm sorry about that. I sometimes get a little stiff in my back if I sit too long."

"If you're willing to tell us what you meant by those two statements, then we can call it a day." Officer Jeff sounded as if he were offering me some kind of an appealing deal.

"I have no reservations telling you what I'm about to tell you. It's the best part of everything I've told you up to this point.

"Exactly six years ago, on this upcoming Saturday, my granddaughter Maria was born." I flashed a proud, grandma smile at Officer Reese.

"Like I told your partner here a little earlier, she was named after me. That little girl is my heart. She and I, we're cut from the same cloth, you know? But when she was born two months premature, the doctors gave her only a 10 percent chance of living. The odds were stacked against her."

Officer Reese smiled one of those tight lip smiles that communicated he was following along.

"You see, she was born with three large holes in her heart: one in her aorta, one in her ventricle, and one in her atrial. She required immediate surgery if she was to have a chance at survival. With surgery, they gave her a 10 percent chance to live. She weighed two pounds twelve ounces at birth. The smaller a baby is, the more difficult those little heart parts are to reach. If she had been a full-term baby, minimum seven pounds, with the same three holes, they would've given her about a 45 percent chance of survival following the surgery. Only a small number of doctors in the country had been successful in performing one of these three heart surgeries on premature babies her size. Each individual hole was a task within itself, let alone three."

Officer Reese stopped taking notes, leaned back in his chair. His mouth was still set tight.

"It was difficult to watch that tiny, gray baby through the incubator. She struggled for every single breath. It broke my heart. Eating affected her ability to breathe, so she didn't. Things weren't looking good for her."

Officer Reese fiddled around with his ink pen. The sound of rapid clicking filled the room.

"The doctors informed us that time was not on her side, and we needed to inform them about what we wanted to do regarding surgery. They had a pediatric heart surgeon on staff at the hospital where she was born, but he was honest with us and told us he'd never attempted anything to the degree of what little Maria needed. We had less than forty-eight hours after she was born to decide if we wanted that surgeon to attempt these surgeries on her. We were devastated that our choices included either a zero percent survival for no surgery or a 10 percent survival with surgery. It felt like a lose-lose situation."

"Mrs. Herrera!" Officer Reese swallowed hard, took a breath, and managed to regain a professional tone. "What does any of this . . . about your granddaughter . . . have to do with the Chameleon?"

"I'm trying to tell you." If I came all the way to this station and shared the most horrific details of my life, the least these two could do was allow me the opportunity to tell the best part of my life's story.

Officer Jeff, attempting to smooth things over, interjected, "I'm sure you'll tie it all together for us. You were saying it felt like a lose-lose situation."

"Yes, that's when we, as a family, decided to take matters into our own hands. We did research on premature, cardiothoracic surgeons who had performed all three surgeries that our little Maria needed. We found a handful of doctors who had each performed one of the three surgeries individually. Eventually we found the one premature cardiothoracic surgeon in the country who had successfully operated on all three holes within a single operation. He had a 100 percent success rate on all four of the premature babies he'd performed these surgeries on. They called him the "Doctor with Miracle Fingers." He could reach the tiniest of places and perform the most impossible sutures, stitches, and whatever else is needed in these types of surgeries. We wrote down his name. I'll never forget it: Dr. Joshua Friendenberg."

Officer Reese resumed taking notes.

"There were only three problems. One, baby Maria's condition was getting worse. Her doctors attempted to convince us to have the surgery right then and there, a day ahead of the initial deadline. We, for obvious reasons, only wanted Dr. Friendenberg to operate on her. Our second problem was that we lived here in Champaign, and he was in California. Our third issue was, according to his nurse, Dr. Friendenberg was booked solid for a month. Only he could give the okay, and no one could reach him at the moment. Time was not on our side, and we didn't know if he would even agree to take on little Maria's case.

"Dr. Friendenberg was our only hope. Little Maria's team of doctors, nurses, and social workers were great in accommodating our wishes. They were relentless in their race against the clock to secure a surgery with Dr. Friendenberg per our pleas. Everything fell into place. Can you believe that doctor emptied his schedule to get my sweet grandbaby in? We were cleared with the insurance company to move forward. They were able to secure an emergency medical helicopter from here to California.

Within a ten-hour period, baby Maria and my daughter were landing at the hospital in California. Her dad flew out later that night and met them there. The rest of us stayed and prayed. We called everyone we knew. Started a prayer chain."

Officer Reese stopped taking notes again and resumed clicking his pen.

"After the rape. I must admit, I stopped believing in God. But I was willing to give it another try if it meant saving my granddaughter's life. So, for the first time in thirty-five years, I began to pray again. I begged and pleaded with God. I made bargains with Him. I was desperate."

A crackling sound came from the water bottle as I finished it off.

"We got a call that they had stabilized little Maria and were prepping her for surgery. We got another call as they wheeled her off. The surgery took seven and a half hours. It felt like forever."

Someone knocked on the door. Officer Reese jumped up and cracked it open. I could hear a man asking how much longer we were going to be because someone else had reserved the room for three o'clock.

Officer Reese looked at his cell phone. "Oh, wow, I didn't realize it was so late. Sorry Chief, we'll wrap it up now."

The officers began gathering their things. "We can finish this over in the big conference room where we have all the boxes stored," Officer Jeff whispered to Officer Reese, as if I couldn't hear his every word.

"Mrs. Herrera, can you spare us a few more minutes of your time today?" Officer Reese asked as he walked toward the door.

"Absolutely, I was just getting to the best part."

I followed them into the hallway. Officer Jeff led the way into a much larger conference room with files all over the table. "Please excuse the mess. We normally don't meet in here."

"Sure."

Officer Reese, wasting no time, asked, "Now, you were saying something about getting around to the best part. How so?"

"So, I went and researched this Dr. Joshua Friendenberg on the Internet. I discovered he was a remarkable man. Learning more about the doctor who could potentially save the life of my grandchild really helped my anxiety subside. He graduated at the top of his class and received some very prestigious awards in the medical field for his research and medical breakthroughs related to premature pediatric cardiothoracic surgery."

I broke the safety tab on my can of juice and took a swallow.

"Was this doctor the Chameleon?" Officer Reese asked.

Officer Jeff kicked him under the table.

Misty bits of a purple shower hit Officer Reese in the face as I fought a losing battle to hold in my laughter. "I'm so sorry."

Officer Reese, with a stoic face, stood.

"But to answer your question, no. I don't think so. But the next day, we received news that the surgery had been successful." I couldn't control my smile. "Huh. It was the first time in more than thirty years that I thanked God for answering a prayer. I know that it's wrong now, but I felt like God owed me one for what He allowed happen to me."

Officer Reese sat down after retrieving some paper towels from the other side of the table.

"Little Maria remained in California under the supervision of Dr. Friendenberg and his team for four and a half months. Her parents stayed in one of those houses funded from donations. When it was time for her to come home, her other grandma and I drove to California to pick them all up. Having her fly on an airplane was cautioned against due to all the germs.

"Once there, I refused to leave without personally thanking the man who saved my grandbaby's life. A small gesture, I felt was necessary from me. Little Maria had already been released from the hospital. I thought I could just go there and shake his hand and be on my way. Do you gentlemen know how difficult it is to meet a surgeon of his caliber when you're not one of his patients? Geez. You would've thought I was trying to meet the President of the United States."

The officers exchanged a gentle smile with me.

"My daughter had to accompany me back to the hospital. After waiting in a lobby for over two hours, she spotted him getting off an elevator and shot over to him. She explained that her mother had driven all the way from Illinois and refused to leave without thanking him in person. There are no words on this earth that can explain the feeling that came over me when we shook hands. I felt embarrassed, because when I looked in the doctor's eyes, my mouth opened, but no words came out.

"He just smiled, holding my hand. Waiting on me." I snickered, reliving that memory.

"Poor fella. I had a death grip on his hand. My daughter was like, 'Okay, Mom, the doc's very busy and really needs his hands for his profession. If you have something you would like to say, now is the time.' All I could say was, 'When is your birthday?' His lips formed an upside-down *U*, but he answered. I hugged him again. Tighter and longer." I nibbled on my bottom lip to keep from choking up.

"I've never seen my daughter's face turn pinker. Still, I made her take pictures of me and the doctor with her phone. Then, I made her stand next to the doctor as I took pictures of them. Such a nice young man. Never made me feel bad for the way I was behaving. I thanked him, kissed him on the cheek. My daughter pulled me away so he could leave. I cried and laughed all the way to the car . . . because I knew it. Just knew it."

"You knew what?" Officer Reese asked.

How do I explain this? I smiled.

"You know what, Mrs. Herrera, thank you for your time today." Officer Reese stood and extended his hand to me.

"Wait a minute," Officer Jeff said. "Why did you ask the doctor about his birthday?"

"Oh, I'm sorry. You two still don't get it. I asked him his date of birth because that would confirm the truth that I knew in my heart."

"And what truth was that?" Officer Jeff asked.

"That he was my biological son."

The room grew silent. Their eyes shifted like someone attempting to read movie credits that were moving too fast. I could almost hear the turbulence of thoughts rambling through the officers' minds as they tried to make sense of all they'd just heard.

"Wait, wait one minute. Wait!" Officer Reese said. "What did you just say?"

"Which part?"

"The part about—son." Officer Reese dragged his chair from around the table and positioned it in front of me.

"Yes, yes, he's my son."

"Who's your son?" Officer Reese asked.

"Dr. Joshua . . . Friendenberg . . . is my son." I pronounced his name, making sure they understood exactly what I was saying this time. "That's what I've been trying to tell you all along. If my father had never introduced me to a handsome young man. If I had not fallen in love. Gotten married. Had a daughter. Who then had a very sick daughter. I would have never had a reason to discover—or should I say rediscover—Dr. Joshua Friendenberg.

"I always equated the child with its rapist father. To me, they were one in the same. I couldn't fully bond with the child in my womb because he was a reminder of the night that he was conceived. My mother never let me forget. I chose to let go of that part of my past, including the child I gave up for adoption. I had no plans of ever looking for him. Ever! When I told you that it was almost six years ago when I forgave the Chameleon, well, little Maria, and all of this, is the reason why.

The moment I looked Dr. Joshua Friendenberg in the eyes, I had no doubt he was my biological son. Instantaneously, I realized that there was some good that came out of what the Chameleon had done. He interfered with an abortion that allowed a one-of-a-kind, world-renowned, lifesaving, premature, pediatric, cardiothoracic surgeon to be born."

"Wait. This is too much!" Officer Reese said. "Okay, so you look at him, and you just *knew* that he was your son? Yeah. We're gonna need a little something more than that."

I gathered my belongings, tossed the empty water bottle into the trash, and headed toward the door when Officer Jeff blocked me.

"What Officer Reese is trying to say is, do you have anything else you can share with us, or show us that would help us to believe that Dr. Joshua Friendenberg is your biological son?"

If not for the "smoothing things over" efforts of Officer Jeff, I felt no need, otherwise, to share my life's story with people who didn't believe me.

"Yes." Like a gentleman, he held my seat. "But I have to leave within the next fifteen minutes."

"Okay," Officer Jeff said.

"What I didn't tell you is why I couldn't speak when I first met Dr. Joshua Friendenberg. I was in absolute, utter shock at how much he looked just like my father when I was growing up. The resemblance was undeniable. That's why the first thing out of my mouth was to ask him his birthday. He said February 7, 1976. That's the exact date I gave birth to a baby boy. I had my confirmation in that moment. But, like you gentlemen, I wasn't satisfied with my gut instinct. I wanted proof too. I *needed* proof.

"Once back home, I set up a private family meeting with my husband, mom, dad, and brother, Juan. My mother, who was my power of attorney back then, handled the entire adoption process. We agreed to a 'No contact with baby or adoptive parents' type of adoption. My mother said the adoptive parents lived in St. Louis at the time. They had several miscarriages. Only first names were exchanged. The adoptive father's name was James and the mother's name was Anna. He was a physician, and she, a teacher by profession. She planned to stay home and raise the baby. They knew that the baby had been conceived as a result of a violent rape.

"They were Christians and okay with the circumstances surrounding the baby's conception and birth. They were aware that I had attempted an abortion that failed. At the time of the adoption, the adoptive father was thirty-nine years old, and mother was thirty-seven. They had no other children, and were planning to raise him as an only child.

"My mother and I were able to locate an agency that had all the records we needed about the adoption. Everything happened a lot quicker than we expected. Because of the extensive application process, the adoptive agency required that his adoptive parents included more information in the files than what we ever expected. Their phone numbers, addresses, places of employment, character references, driver's license, you name it. It was all in that file. But, the biggest piece of evidence is on this paper right here."

I reached into my bag and pulled out a leather daily planner. I opened the front cover and removed a sheet of paper that was tri-folded. I placed the planner off to the side, brushed a little dust off the table before me, and wiped my sweaty palms on my pants before I unfolded the thin blue paper. I smoothed out the creases, and laid it on the table.

"What's that?" Officer Jeff asked.

"Here, have a look." With both hands, I handed it to him.

His eyes whisked over the paper. "Wow. Yeah. Dr. Joshua Friendenberg is your son."

"Let me have a look at that!" Officer Reese held out his hand.

"Careful!" I said

He read aloud. "Biological mother's maiden name: Maria Chavez, age twenty-four. Biological mother's date of birth, November 17, 1951. Biological father, unknown, child's name given at birth, Joshua. Child's date of birth, February 7, 1976. Adoptive mother's name at time of adoption: Anna Friendenberg. Adoptive father's name at time of adoption: James Friendenberg. Adoptive father's occupation: Physician. Adoptive mother's occupation: Teacher. *Hmmm.*"

Officer Jeff opened a file that he'd had with him since the start of the interview. "All information confirming your identity. Date of birth. Maiden name of Chavez. Is right here."

Officer Reese's face was all kinds of distorted: eyebrows rising and falling, top lip twitching, forehead wrinkling and smoothing out.

We all sat in silence. Officer Jeff rapidly dug his finger in his right ear. Officer Reese resorted to cracking his knuckles.

"Once I had this official document in my hand"—I walked over to Officer Reese and retrieved it—"all doubts were forever put to rest. Dr. Joshua Friendenberg is my biological son."

Now, both of their eyes were focused on me as they leaned in. "It was then that I realized that he did not just have a very bad man's blood running through his veins. He overwhelmingly had my blood running through his veins.

"Can you believe that the very act that occurred to bring him into this world was quite evil, but God rearranged a very evil act to extract more good out of it than my feeble mind could've ever imagined? It was a liberating few days. Knowing that my very own biological son was single-handedly responsible for saving the life of my precious granddaughter was a transforming moment of liberation. The man who raped me, his biological father, in my opinion, is a scumbag. He's the scum of the earth for what he did to me. But I had to humble myself before God and cry out to Him acknowledging that I held God in contempt unjustly because of my limited knowledge and understanding. I experienced a great deal of emotional and psychological healing nearly six years ago when I learned the true identity of my son. I also learned a valuable lesson that has changed my life. I learned that God did not plan rape. But God had a plan for that child's life. That same innocent child that had absolutely nothing to do with the rape. The child was innocent, just like me. The rapist was not! Hindsight. Gotta love it. I realized that I could not have raised Joshua to turn out to be as good as he turned out. No way. Impossible. I was an emotional wreck for too many years after the rape. Couldn't even take care of myself for years after it. But his adoptive parents were exactly what he needed. And he, what they needed. All I can say to that is. Well. God is awesome. No one could have paid me enough to say that back in May of 1975." Anxiety was an afterthought anytime I told this part of my life's story. I placed the paper back into my daily planner, and slid that back into my bag.

"Would you be willing to testify against the Chameleon if we brought him to trial?" Officer Reese asked.

"About the Chameleon? With how my son came back into my life full circle? How he was the answered prayer that saved little Maria's life? What the Chameleon did was a blessing in disguise. I don't know who put the Chameleon up to doing what he did. I don't know how they could've known what they knew. I don't know if it was a fluke. I don't know if he was another sick pervert. I don't have an answer for any of this. But a lot of good came out of the Chameleon pretending to be a doctor and not performing that abortion on me. I almost aborted a life-saving surgeon, and one of the greatest people on earth that I have ever met. As absurd as it may sound to you, I would actually like to thank this . . . Chameleon. So, to answer your question, no, I could not testify against him." I placed my purse and bag together on the table and pulled out my cell phone to look at the time.

The officers glanced at the clock in the back of the room. Fifteen minutes were up. They stood. I followed suit.

Officer Reese extended is hand. "Mrs. Herrera, thank you for agreeing to meet with us today, allowing us to interview you. We appreciate your time." He looked like his wheels were spinning.

"Officer Reese, you're welcome. I hope you find whatever it is you are really looking for." I released his hand.

Officer Jeff opened the door and extended his hand into the hallway. "I will be happy to walk you down to the lobby, Mrs. Herrera."

"You are a fine young man, Officer Jeff. Thank you, and I accept your offer."

"This way, ma'am."

5

A FAMILY

JENESIS

I could always tell when my husband had a stressful day at work. He showed it in his body language. His facial expression and posture exposed him too. While preparing dinner, I glanced into the living room. Paul, with one hand holding up his head, slouched forward on the couch. I washed the onion residue off my hands before drying them on my apron. I made my way into the living room and carved a seat through his police gear scattered about on the couch. I removed the remote control off his lap and pressed the mute button, as I had neither the energy nor the voice to compete with the high volume from the television.

"Honey, are you feeling okay?" Applying a mixture of pressure, my fingertips glided up and down the back of his neck.

He opened his eyes, taking in a deep breath and then releasing it. Normally very articulate, the words, "Yeah,

I'm okay," sound like they had to wrestle their way out through a mouth full of cotton balls.

"Something's got you stressin'. It's all over you."

"It's this *Operation Almost* case. Can't seem to get it off my mind. I'm sorry—" He grabbed my hand and kissed the back of it. "I never wanted to be that person to bring my work home with me. In fact, I really shouldn't. But . . ."

"No need to apologize. That's what I'm here for. If something is stressing you, work or otherwise, you don't have to go at it alone. I won't go back repeating anything. Now what is it about this *Operation Almost* case that's troubling you?"

Crack was the sound that came from his back as he straightened up before leaning sideways into the couch and facing me at an angle.

"This Chameleon criminal makes no sense to me. Most criminals have a pattern. Something that makes them predictable. A flaw. How does this guy look just like every single doctor he's assuming the identity of? Surely they vary in height, and hair, and thickness of body, shape of face. Even if he is former CIA and a master of disguise, there's just no way to make a six-foot-two-inch doctor transform into a five-foot-nine-inch doctor. I'm having the hardest time determining his modus operandi. I mean, is this guy a pro-life extremist? Pervert? Former cop? I can't get into a rhythm for understanding the guy. Normally, I can spot a pattern before anyone else. This Chameleon. He's got me blinded by something. Something I keep missing. I can't quite put my finger on it. I've got to find the missing link!" Paul hesitated for a moment. "Can I ask you something?"

"You can ask me anything."

"I'm just wondering if this is a woman thing," Paul said. "If someone hurt you in some way . . . because of their own hang-ups or shortcomings in life . . . because, they're a criminal, okay? Let's say a thief snatched your purse and cut your arm with a knife. As a result of the knife wound, you go to the hospital for stitches. While at the hospital the doctors discovered that your eyes look a little funny, and they ask to run some tests on you. They discover that you are in the early stages of kidney failure. But because they caught it early, they can reverse the whole condition. Now, the only reason they caught it early was because this psycho cut you with a knife and that placed you before a very competent doctor. If the police caught this criminal and asked you to testify against him when he was placed on trial, would you tell them no because the criminal's tactics helped to save your life? Instead of testifying against him, would you want to thank him?"

"No. Of course not. I would be grateful for the outcome of catching the illness early, but I would not want to thank some psycho criminal for stabbing me."

"Exactly! Thank God I am married to a sane woman." His soft lips puckered up against my forehead before he stood. "What's for dinner?"

"Well, I'm happy to see that you're feeling better, mister. But what is going on?"

"We've interviewed two women who would rather thank a criminal who violated them during an abortion procedure than testify against him. It's ludicrous!"

"I don't understand. Why did these women say they wanted to thank this particular criminal?"

"Because they feel like, even though he could've fondled them while pretending to be an abortion doctor, that the child they tried to abort was born because of him."

"Well, honey, that's a little different from the scenario you gave me."

"How's it different?"

"Well, in the first scenario, the woman had done nothing immoral or debatable as right or wrong. It was all the criminal's fault, even though something good came out of it. In the second scenario, the woman probably struggled with whether to have an abortion or not. You don't know the circumstances surrounding why she chose the abortion. She could've been dealing with guilt, shame, or indecision about it. Someone could've pressured her into it. I mean, there's a lot going on when you start looking at women in those situations. And when this 'criminal' stopped something that could be viewed by some as morally wrong, she probably felt . . . umm, how could I put it? She probably felt like . . . maybe she was given a second chance to get it right? I don't know. It sounds a little strange, but I kinda understand where they might be coming from."

"All I know is a criminal is a criminal. Period. Why do people have to make things so complicated? Please, don't answer that! I'm done. I will figure this out at work. My mind needs to rest. What did you say was for dinner?"

"I didn't say. But we're having my award-winning chili and cornbread."

"I love your chili! Here, have a seat." His hands around my waist guided me to a chair at the dining room table that could seat eight. "I'll get the bowls and everything else."

"Careful! Chili's hot. Use the mitts, Paul. And don't forget the trivet for the pot of chili."

"I got this." And he did. He even lit candles.

"Let's bow our heads and say grace. Would you like to?"

Paul gave me a look. "Now, Jenesis, you know that's not my thing."

"I know. I just thought I'd give it a try in case you changed your mind."

"I'm not changing my mind. So please stop asking."

I waited a moment for the tension to clear before speaking. "I don't see the big deal, Paul. I'm just asking that you take the lead in blessing the food and thanking God for providing it."

"It is a big deal, Jenesis. After all, we're the ones who go to work every day. We're the ones providing for ourselves. I see no God putting food on my table."

"You've gone to church your whole life. We met in church! How could you talk like this?"

"Here we go again! I've told you this a thousand times. I go to church because it puts a smile on my mother's face. It's the only reason I've ever gone to church. It will be the only reason I ever go to church. How or why she trusts in a so-called God who allowed her to struggle with daily needs while raising two boys is beyond me. I never saw a God when my brother and I needed a father. Never saw a God show up when my mother cried herself to sleep at night. Never saw a God when she got sick. I certainly don't see a God now that she's in the early stages of Alzheimer's!"

"I'm sorry for asking. Really, I am. Can we please just enjoy our meal? I put a lot of love into preparing it. Would hate for it to go to waste."

He traced the top of his forehead with his finger and thumb before closing his eyes and applying pressure to the bridge of his nose.

"Sure."

We sat in silence.

Steam rose from his spoon and his tongue traced across his top lip.

"I've told you all about my day." His eyes shifted and locked with mine. "So how did your doctor's appointment go this morning?"

"You remembered?"

"Of course I did."

"Uh. Okay, I guess. My doctor ran more tests on me. She said some of my numbers were off with the blood work. She said since we've being trying for over a year now, we may want to consider using some medicines that can bring my numbers into a more conducive range. But we won't know until these new test results come back."

"Okay, so what do they think the problem could be?"

"Well, we could be infertile."

"But you're young and healthy."

"If my results come back okay, then they'll want to run some tests on you."

"What?"

"Baby, one of us is the reason we're not getting pregnant." I put my spoon down, no longer hungry.

"So, when will you get the results?"

"In the next day or so."

His eyes fluttered as the spoon emerged from his lips. He covered his mouth with a cloth napkin as he chewed. "Regardless of the outcome, Jenesis, just know that I love you. I'm only trying to have a baby because you want one. And I want you to be happy. But know, if it comes down to it being just the two of us for the next seventy-five years, I'll still be a happy man who loves you."

"I know you will. I just want a baby something awful."

"We'll get through this together." My four fingers rested in a tender embrace between his hand before he released it for his other love. "My goodness, this cornbread!"

"Glad you're enjoying it."

"Mind if we take some dinner over to Mom's after we're done here?"

"Don't mind at all. I'll package it for her."

INTERVIEW #3

NANCY SMITH

I watched from my window as Officer Reese arrived. He'd already told me that he'd conduct this interview alone because his partner had a presentation to give. He arrived at my home ahead of schedule, but waited in the car for several minutes before knocking on my townhouse door. Neighbors were bundled up in this frigid February, Midwest weather, walking their dogs, mindful to use their doggie bags to pick up any poop along the way. Both men and women were shoveling snow from the driveways and sidewalks. These were the usual happenings for my neighborhood.

I yanked open the door and planted my hand into his. "Hi there. You must be Officer Reese."

"Yes, I am. Nancy Smith?"

"You got that right." With a nice firm grip I shook his hand up and down before dropping it.

"Come on in." I closed the door before leading him through the living room and into the open dining room area. "We can sit at the table."

I joined him before popping back up. "I'm being rude. May I offer you something to drink?"

"No, thank you. I'm good."

I sat back down, crossed my legs, and bounced my dangling foot. "So, what would you like to know?"

"First, thank you for your time and for inviting me into your home. We've opened up another investigation into the Chameleon case. I believe you're familiar with him."

"Another one? This is like the fourth time someone has interviewed me! Isn't that like . . . incompetence?"

"I know it may seem like that, Mrs. Smith. Is it Mrs. or Miss?"

"Oh, it's Mrs. Smith. My husband is at work. Depending on how long this takes, he may be here before we're done. But I prefer that you call me Nancy, please, Officer Reese."

"Well, Nancy. I know it may seem like incompetence, but we are up against a very clever criminal. As you may have already been told, he's an impersonator. That's why he's been so difficult to apprehend. But all criminals make mistakes eventually. That's part of the reason why new officers and detectives are put on the case. Sometimes, a fresh pair of eyes can see what someone who's been on the case for many years cannot see."

"I understand. So, what do you need from me?"

Officer Reese pulled his small leather-bound notepad from the top pocket in his police uniform. He flipped it open and placed it on the table along with a pen. He pointed to a question written on the paper. "Did you have an abortion at a clinic here in town?"

"No, I did not."

He blinked like he was attempting to clear something from his eye. I decided I would help him out. "I went to the clinic to have an abortion, but it never happened. The man I was seeing at the time took me there and paid for an abortion, but the procedure never happened, and boy, am I glad it didn't."

"Can you slow down for just a moment? Bear with me if I'm not writing as fast as you are talking. But first, please tell me, what do you know about the Chameleon?"

"Well, I've been told that he's gone around to clinics acting like the abortion doctor. But instead of performing an abortion, he's fondling women and taking the money patients are paying for himself. Does that about sum it up?"

"Have you heard anything else about him stealing the money?"

"One of the ladies who worked at a clinic where he's hit said he stole all the abortion money that was in the drawer for that day."

The officer didn't look surprised by this information as he wrote in his notepad.

"Is there anything else you know?"

"Like what, Officer Reese?"

"Okay, so tell me what you remember about the day of the abortion."

"I remember I was quite emotional. I was angry. Sad. I felt manipulated into it. I did not want an abortion. Did you write that down? But I also felt out-numbered in my decision. It was supposed to be a two-day procedure, but I had to go to the clinic three days in a row."

"So, you went there three different days and still walked away pregnant?"

"Exactly."

"Was it the same doctor on day one, two, and three? Did you notice anything strange about him on any of those days?"

"He looked and acted the same on all three days as far as I can remember. I just recall thinking that he—like my mother, boyfriend, and the nurses—was my enemy. I was angry with everyone. Everyone! Because I did not want the abortion in the first place."

"Did anyone go with you to have the abortion?"

"Oh yeah! My mother went on the third day. And my boyfriend went with me on the first two days. He wanted to make sure I went through with it. Eric wasn't taking any chances. He knew I didn't want that abortion. But, of course, he was more concerned with his life than he ever was with mine.

"When we first met, I was twenty years old and had just started the second semester of my junior year in college here at the U of I. I met him while working a part-time job at a local coffee shop on campus. He was a handsome thirty-one-year-old attorney. He worked in one of the local law offices just off campus. He occasionally taught a law class for the university. I never had him as a professor or anything because I was working on my degree in social work. He came into the coffee shop every time I worked. I worked Mondays, Thursdays, and Fridays. I knew exactly how he liked his coffee, and we made small talk whenever he came in. He was flirtatious.

"I got to know him pretty well over the course of several weeks before he finally asked me out. I was hesitant because I knew he was having problems in his marriage. But, being a lawyer, he was very persuasive. He even stopped wearing his wedding band. Told me he had moved out of the house where he and his wife lived, and that he had filed for divorce. According to him, he was staying in a hotel. I asked to see the papers showing he had filed for divorce before I would even agree to go out with him. And . . . well . . . he showed them to me. So, that was the beginning of our relationship.

"It was his chivalry that won me over. He was a complete gentleman. He opened doors for me, pulled out my chair, helped me put on my coat, and all that stuff that makes a woman feel like a lady. I had never been treated so well by a guy. I loved every bit of it. He sent roses to my job, and even had some delivered to two of my classes, right before finals' week. He won me over pretty quickly with his consistency.

"I had an apartment off campus that I shared with one roommate, Roxie. She spent most of her time at her boyfriend's apartment. So, Eric and I spent a lot of time at my apartment. Alone. He spent nights with me. Brought his work there to prepare for cases while I studied.

"We had a physical relationship. Seems he couldn't keep his hands off me. Ever. He told me the divorce with his soon-to-be ex-wife was almost final and he wanted to marry me after I graduated from college. But he didn't want marriage to interfere with me getting my degree.

"He never wanted me to visit his office or call. Back then, beepers and pagers were pretty popular. Do you even know what a beeper or pager is, Officer Reese?"

"Yeah." He chuckled. "I've seen one on the Internet, but never actually touched one."

"Youngins! Anyway, I called his pager if I wanted to talk to him, and he would call me back whenever he could. Most of the time he called right back if he wasn't in court or preparing for a case. He told me he was trying to make partner, and they frowned upon their new attorneys mixing work with pleasure or family life. I didn't want to be the cause of him not making partner, so I never visited his law office."

The older, more mature me could only shake my head as I recounted the details of this relationship.

"For my birthday, he bought me this great pair of diamond earrings. Let me tell you, up to that point, I had never owned a diamond anything. I was angry with him on Valentine's Day, because he had made all these big arrangements for us to go out of town to a fancy restaurant. I was right there when he called in a reservation a month in advance. He reminded me the day before Valentine's Day that I needed to be ready by five o'clock because we had reservations at six thirty and it would take a little over an hour to get there. I rushed home from my last class that ended at three and took my time getting ready. I'd bought a new dress and shoes. Five o'clock came around, and he wasn't there. I knew something wasn't right. He was always on time. In fact, he would often lecture me about my lack of punctuality. How I needed to improve to compete in the real world."

I walked over to the recliner where my brownish-orange leather purse sat. I dragged my purse back to the chair I'd been sitting in and then flopped it onto my lap, digging through it as if my life depended on it. I couldn't break my focus until I found it.

Officer Reese just watched, his eyes getting wide.

"Yes! Here you are." I pulled out a package of gum. "At the doctor's urging, I started chewing nicotine gum. I've been without a cigarette for nine weeks, but all this talk about my past lover. Well, let's just say, I don't want to relapse." I popped a piece into my mouth.

"When Eric didn't show up at five o'clock, I was a little concerned. By 5:15, I was on pins and needles. So. What did I do? I paged him. When he didn't return my page, I became a little nervous. I paged him a dozen times after that. By 5:45, I was a nervous wreck.

"All I could imagine was that something terrible had happened. I thought maybe he had been in a car accident or something. I called the two local hospitals and asked if there had been an accident involving an Eric Dade.

"I tried to figure out what else it could be. Nothing was making sense to me. I went from being scared for his life to being skeptical about what was really going on. By the time six thirty rolled around, I got the wise idea to call the restaurant. I called and asked if the reservation for Mr. Eric Dade, party of two, had been canceled. The hostess said no, that as a matter of fact, he had just arrived with his wife a few minutes earlier. I asked if she was sure. She said they check ID at that particular restaurant because people will say anything to get in. She had personally looked at his identification, and it was, according to her, Mr. Eric Dade and his wife."

A fruit fly was hovering over the fruit bowl, and I kept swatting at it and missing.

"Let me tell you, Mister Officer Reese, I . . . was . . . livid! I just held the phone in disbelief. The hostess was still talking, but I hung up the phone. I had never been so angry in all my life. I cried myself to sleep that night.

"The next day was Sunday. I had no desire to do anything. I was angry and depressed at the same time. But angry more than anything.

"Around two o'clock, guess who came a'knocking at my door? I wasn't getting out of bed for anyone. So he kept knocking. Roxie was there and she let him in. He came into my room, all apologetic. I asked what happened. I knew the truth but wanted to see if he would be honest. He said his daughter had gotten sick. Had a high fever. Was vomiting. And he and his soon-to-be ex-wife had to take her to the emergency room. I asked him what time all of this happened. He said they took her to the emergency room around 4:45 p.m. and they were there until eleven p.m. I asked why he hadn't called me or responded to my pages. He said he'd left it in his hotel room. I asked him why he hadn't taken at least two minutes to call me. He said his daughter was afraid and didn't want him to leave her side. He claimed that he stayed with her the entire time. He told me that if I had been sick, he would've done the same for me. I was getting more and more livid with every word he spoke.

"I asked him what he had eaten for dinner on Valentine's Day. He acted confused. I asked if he'd had a snack from the hospital's vending machine, the cafeteria, or if he'd eaten something else. He claimed he only ate a mint that was already in his pocket. I couldn't take his lies anymore, so I confessed that I'd called the restaurant he'd reserved for the two of us on Valentine's Day, and the hostess informed me that he was there having dinner with his wife." I started laughing until I coughed as I recalled Eric's response. "It wasn't funny, then.

"Let me tell you, Officer Reese. If you thought I was livid when the hostess told me that he was there, heck that was nothing compared to how angry Eric became when

I told him the hostess informed me that he was there at the restaurant with his wife.

"He claimed that the hostess was lying, and he would personally sue her and the restaurant. He was going to have her fired for lying about him. He swore he had been tending to his sick daughter at the hospital. Blah, blah, blah. I informed him that the hostess had checked his ID and verified that it was him and his wife. I thought about threatening to call the hospitals to find out if a patient under his daughter's name had been seen in the past forty-eight hours, but I didn't know if privacy laws would make that impossible. But he was caught. Yet, he wouldn't admit to the truth. He said he was not going to rest until that hostess had been fired.

"It was at that moment that my feelings for him changed permanently. I understood that if he had lied to me about that, then who knows what else he'd lied to me about. I asked him to leave, explained that I no longer wanted to see him. He begged and pleaded, but I was done. He handed me a box of chocolates, a card, and a smaller box, but I told him to take it with him, to give it all to his wife. He left it at the foot of my bed, and left my apartment quietly, but I wasn't having it. He closed the door to my apartment and started down the stairs, but I hopped up, grabbed the gifts, opened the door, and threw it all at him. Then I went back to bed."

I swatted at an annoying fruit fly as it buzzed near my ear.

"By the time Monday rolled around, I was still a bit bummed emotionally, but I went to all my classes and took care of my responsibilities. Eric called every day, several times a day, for a week straight, but I never answered. Then

I got sick at work one day. It just so happened to be the day that he decided to show up at my job. I was vomiting all over the place, feeling dizzy . . . just not feeling well at all. He offered to take me home, and I agreed.

"He stayed with me for a little while, tucked me into bed, and told me he was sorry about everything. He finally admitted that he had lied. He said he didn't want to hurt me and he was ashamed that he had fallen for his 'soon-to-be-ex-' wife's tears and pleas to try one last time before they made it final. He claimed that he didn't love her, and it was her last-ditch effort to save their marriage.

"He asked me to open the smaller box that he'd gotten me for Valentine's Day—I guess he'd brought it with him when he came to my job, hoping to convince me to open it. I agreed and inside was a heart-shaped diamond necklace. It still had the price tag on it. He'd paid over a thousand dollars for it. I felt like he must've really loved me to go through the trouble to spend that much money on me. That since he'd finally admitted he was at the restaurant, maybe I could somewhat trust him again."

The sound of unravelling empty nicotine wrapper filled the room. I spit my gum into it, and balled it back up.

"I listened to him go on and on about how his marriage was over, and his divorce was almost finalized, and how I was the love of his life. And oh how sorry he was for what he had done to me on Valentine's Day. He told me he had only spent fifty dollars on her meal, but he had spent more than a thousand dollars on this diamond necklace for me as proof that he loved me and not her. He was convincing and, again, I forgave him. We kissed and hugged, and he left. I went to sleep, still feeling tired and sick."

I got up to get myself something to drink.

"The next morning, vomiting is what woke me up. Roxie helped me to the campus clinic. I thought I had the flu or mono. There were a lot of sick pick on campus with one or the other. Roxie left me there and went about her business. After the doctor checked me out, he told me he wanted to have me take a pregnancy test. Looking back, I don't know why, but I was shocked. When he explained that he was concerned that since I was sexually active, and my last menstrual period had been six weeks earlier, it could be the reason for my vomiting.

"Before I left the clinic, they confirmed that I was pregnant. I had mixed emotions. My parents raised me in the church. I knew they would be disappointed. Embarrassed. But I was comforted by thinking about how happy Eric would be, because, after all, he loved me. The moment I got home, I paged Eric. He called right back. I told him I needed to see him when he got off work. He was more than happy to hear that.

"That evening, I made him take me to the nicest place on campus to eat when he got off work. He was acting a little strange, and claimed he had a bit of an upset stomach. I didn't think much about it. I didn't know how to tell him that I was pregnant, so we ate first and made small talk. While we were having desert, he expressed how much he loved me, and how he was going to make everything right for us real soon. I thought that was the perfect opportunity to give him the good news. I explained how happy I was to hear that he wanted to make things right between us. Then, came right out and told him that I was five weeks pregnant. I'd never seen Eric turn so pale, or sweat so profusely. His mouth was open and moving, but no words came out. When he did manage to speak, he asked for the check."

Officer Reese stopped writing and just listened now.

"It was in the car that I wished he'd never opened his mouth to speak at all. He pulled an about-face on me. Went from in the restaurant, talking about making things right between us, to talking about how having this child with me would be his ruin. It turned into a horrible evening.

"I made it very clear to him that I certainly hadn't gotten pregnant on purpose. I had him drop me off at my apartment, and vowed to him that I would just figure it all out on my own.

"It must have bothered him all night because he showed up at my apartment at six thirty the next morning. My first class wasn't until nine, so he waited in my living room while I showered and dressed. He wanted to take me to get some breakfast, but I was still having morning sickness and didn't have an appetite.

"When I sat next to Eric on the sofa, he handed me an envelope that contained four one-hundred-dollar bills in it. He said, and I will never forget his words, 'This should be more than enough to take care of our little problem.' I was furious. I handed it back to him, told him I was going to keep the baby. He told me that was not a part of the plan he had for us. I told him I was so sorry to ruin his plans, and that I was even sorrier that he felt like our baby was going to be the ruin of him. Then, he pulled the ole 'how do I know it's really mine' on me. Before I knew what was happening, my hand was slapping his face."

Realizing I'd just confessed to assault, I asked Officer Reese, "Surely I can't get into trouble with the law today for slapping him way back in 1987, can I?"

Officer Reese smiled. "No ma'am. I am certain that the statute of limitations has already run out on any assault charges."

"Good. Well, yeah, I slapped him! He knew that I was at his beck and call. He had never questioned if I had messed around on him before. In his heart, he knew better. He let it go and apologized. He started playing a lot of mind games with me though. And they worked. He went into his lawyer, negotiation mode.

"Till this day, I still don't know how he got me to agree to something that I was completely against."

I dug through my purse again, needing another stick of nicotine gum. "He told me he loved me. Said his feelings toward me and plans for us had not changed. He asked if I would be willing to work with him, meet him halfway—for . . . how did he put it? . . . 'for us.' He went into this spiel about how the best relationships could not be one-sided, and that's why his marriage was coming to an end in the first place. He loved me, and had plans to marry me because I was a great team player, and he could always count on me to do what was right for us as a couple. He told me what was right for us as a couple was for me to finish college when I was supposed to finish. Said having the baby would interfere with me being able to finish college on schedule, and how he knew countless people who had every intention of having a baby and finishing college, but none of them ever did both. He said I had worked too hard to not finish. I must say. He laid it on thick. Said I owed it to my whole family to finish since I was the first person in my family on both sides to go to college. He made some really good points that got me thinking."

My hand started to shake, so I popped a fresh piece of gum into my mouth.

"When he stopped to take a sip of coffee, that's when I took the opportunity to explain that I had overcome a lot in life already. I knew it would be hard, but I would do everything in my power to finish school and raise our child. I asked him if he would help me. That's when the bottom fell out. He hovered over me, pointing his finger in my face, yelling. I had never seen him so . . . so angry and scared. He was yelling about how he didn't understand why I was trying to ruin us. He claimed he was trying so hard to build a future for me and him, but I was doing everything in my power to break down what he was trying to build. He calmed himself and sat back down, then went back into lawyer mode. But it was time for me to go to class.

"I couldn't concentrate in any of my classes. Roxie was very supportive when I told her I was pregnant. She confided in me that she'd had an abortion her freshman year, and she wasn't sure she had made the right choice. She offered to be there for me any way I needed.

"Eric kept calling. He told me he'd found the perfect clinic, and they were discrete. It was located two towns over in Tolono. I told him I just wasn't ready to make that decision yet.

"That next weekend, I decided to go home to visit my folks. I needed to be around them. While there, I couldn't keep my eyes open or my food down. Sunday afternoon, right after church service, my mother pulled me into her room. She came straight out and asked me, 'Nancy, when were you planning on telling me that you're pregnant?' I was speechless. I confessed that it was the whole reason for my visit. She cried and held me; we cried together. She wiped my tears. I wiped her tears. She asked about Eric. She had a fit when I told her that he was still married.

"After the initial shock wore off, my mother expressed how disappointed she was in me. How she and my father had sacrificed a lot to send me off to college. What my mother advised me to do on that day affected our relationship for many years. She, just like Eric, told me that I had to have an abortion. Her logic was that she had not raised me to have sex outside of marriage. We were good Christians. 'For heaven's sake, what will all the church folks say when they find out? Oh, Lord! What will they say when they find out you're pregnant by a married man? They'll put us out of the church!' According to her, I absolutely could not have some married man's baby. She made it clear that I was the worst person in the world for having sex in the first place."

I wanted to smoke a whole pack of cigarettes. Right now.

"That was really the first time that it hit me. Up to that point, I had not really seen Eric as a married man. I looked at him as a man who was separated and almost divorced, who was choosing to move forward with his life. By the time my mother finished with me, I felt like a fool. She told me that God would understand. I asked her how she could say that God would understand if I took my baby's life, but not forgive me for adultery. She had no answer for me. I never looked at my mother the same after that. I could hardly wait to get back to my own apartment."

After a jangling of keys at the front door, my husband walked in wearing a bright orange-yellow construction vest and matching pants that were covered in dust. I sprang over to him.

"Oh no you don't. Give me that lunch pail! You know the drill, Burt. You're not tracking all that dust and dirt through my clean house. You know you're to leave all that construction gear in the garage. I already have a clean pair of shoes waiting for you out there."

"I know. I know. I just saw the police car in front of the house and wanted to make sure that everything was okay. Looks like it is, so I'll change in the garage "Hello, officer. I'm Burt, the husband."

Officer Reese stood and made haste to shake my husband's hand. "Nice to meet you, Burt. I'm Officer Paul Reese."

"Is my wife in some kind of trouble, officer?" The residue of a smirk remained on his face.

We all shared a laugh as I leaned in and pushed my husband, twice my size, out the door. "Burt, out. You know good and well I told you weeks ago that a couple of officers wanted to interview me about something."

After Burt went into the garage, we sat back down. "Now, what was I saying?"

"You had just told your mother you were pregnant and could hardly wait to get back to your own apartment."

"Oh, yes. When I got to my apartment, there were a dozen red roses sitting on my little kitchen table with a card attached that read, 'I love you! Please call me. E.' I paged him once I got settled in. It was late. Around ten on Sunday night. He called me back and said he was coming over. I was mentally drained after dealing with my mother. I never told my father. My mom said that it would be our little secret as long as I agreed to the abortion.

"Eric came over. He hugged me with one of those lingering, 'can't get him off me' kind of hugs. He said he'd missed me and knew I'd left to visit my folks. He was anxious to hear what they'd had to say. He was beyond happy to hear that my mother, like him, wanted me to abort the baby. He really picked up the pace once he found out my mother's wishes. He started saying that everyone who loved me just wanted the best for me. I was really drained after about an hour of him and I asked him to leave. I needed to rest something awful.

"After that, I stopped taking Eric's and my mother's phone calls. I started doing poorly in my classes because all I wanted to do was sleep day and night. I was miserable because I felt outnumbered two to one. I overslept on three occasions and was late to work by like two hours. Eventually, they just told me to take the month off. I really needed that money, and life started taking its toll on me."

Burt came into the house wearing clean jeans, a plaid shirt, and brown shoes.

"Nancy, I need to run over to the grocery store to pick up a few items for our cookout this weekend. Did you need anything?"

"Yes, I do. Wait a minute."

Burt stood by me, waiting as I dug through my purse before I pulled out a purple notepad. Fumbling through it again, I found a pen and wrote down several items before handing him the list. He gave me a quick kiss to the cheek and said, "I'll be right back."

"Thanks, Burt!"

"Yup."

"Nancy, it sounds like you were set against having this abortion. How did you end up at the abortion clinic?"

"I avoided my mother and Eric for two months. But my grades continued to slip and I was put on academic probation. Then, I was let go at my job. I couldn't pay my portion of the rent or bills.

"I had to call both my mother and Eric for help. I was one day from being put out of my apartment, because I had fallen two months behind on my rent. That was the perfect opportunity for both of them to start in on me again. I had no recourse. I was unaware of the fact that Eric had contacted my mother. He gave her the same story that he gave me. How he didn't love his wife. They were planning on getting a divorce. He wanted to marry me. But, he couldn't do it yet. She didn't buy it the same way I did. But, they agreed that I should finish college and a baby would stand in the way of accomplishing that.

"He told her that he was willing to pay for the abortion and to stay with me during the entire process. So, they plotted behind my back when I wasn't talking to either of them, and put a plan in motion. I called home to ask my dad for money, but I knew better. My mother handled the finances. She wanted to know what I needed money for. I was desperate, so I told her.

"She agreed to pay my rent, but she said I had to agree to have the abortion. I hung up on her. I paged Eric. He called right back. Do you know he gave me the exact same ultimatum? I had to agree to have the abortion if I wanted my rent paid. I hung up on him too. I felt all alone in the world at that moment. I was so angry with them both. I felt like they were taking advantage of my bad situation.

"I started packing my things. I was crying. I made up my mind that I would move into a shelter for abused and battered women that I had volunteered at during my freshmen year of college. I did not want to go there, but I felt like it was my best option. While I was packing, Eric stopped by. Like he knew I was up to something.

"He made me sit down on my bed, and he began to rub my feet. He asked me to just listen to him. He started in on how much he loved me. He promised that he would marry me, but first he had to get his divorced finalized. He said that his wife knew that he was in love with me, but she could never find out that I was pregnant with his child. He said if she ever found out that he got someone pregnant while they were still married, she could take everything he had. He explained that my being pregnant was the only thing that could jeopardize our future together. He promised me if I got the abortion, he would be able to finalize the divorce within a month. He assured me that he would marry me the day after I graduated. He told me to start planning our wedding.

"He told me he had already explained all of this to my mother. I felt betrayed, but at the same time, I needed some good news in my life. And everything Eric was saying to me was what I wanted to hear. He told me that all I needed to do was agree to have the abortion, follow through with it, and he'd even give me the money for my wedding dress the day after the abortion. He promised that we would have more children once we were married. I was tired, emotionally. I understood that I was running out of options. Eric told me to consider the fact that I could not take care of myself, so how was I going to care for a baby too? He was right. I felt defeated, and he was promising me the world.

"He called my mother and told her that I agreed to have the abortion. She told me that I had made the right choice, and nobody ever needed to know about it besides the three of us. I felt so much anger toward her for encouraging me to go through with it. At the same time, I was tired of fighting the two people I needed the most.

"Eric had already called the abortion clinic. They told him that because I was nearly four months pregnant, it would be a two-day procedure. I would have to go back on a third day to make sure they got all the tissue out. Eric made it clear to me that if I wanted half of my rent paid that day, I had to agree to go to the clinic and begin day one that very day. I would get the second half after the procedure on day two. I was defeated, so I agreed.

"He took me that same day. When we got there, Eric dropped me off, then parked his car about five blocks away at a little shopping center. The clinic made him pay with cash up front. They took us to a back room where a lady explained the procedure. She told me I had nothing to worry about because all they were planning to do was remove a blob of tissue out of me. A blob of tissue.

"They ran tests to confirm how far along I was. Took some blood. Did an ultrasound. I was sixteen weeks pregnant. On the first day of the procedure, with Eric in the waiting room, they placed what they called a cervical dilator into my cervix. This, they said, was to help me to dilate for the procedure. The next day they performed the abortion, or so I thought. They sedated me and numbed my lower half, so I didn't really feel much, other than pulling and tugging. Then came that loud vacuum sound. I think that's what bothered me more than anything. The very thought that they were vacuuming out my child made me feel sick. I wanted to get up, but I was heavily sedated. It was over before I knew it. Next thing I remember, Eric was helping me into the car. He took me to my apartment, and called my mother. They talked, but I was still a little out of it, so I can't tell you what they talked about. The next day when I woke up, my mother was in my apartment. By afternoon, she was taking me back to the clinic to make sure they had gotten all of the "tissue" out of me. They basically just wanted to make sure the procedure had been successful."

"So, you went back to the clinic a third day?" Officer Reese started writing in his notepad.

"Yes."

"Who checked you out on day three?"

"It was the doctor."

"Was it the same doctor who performed the procedure?"

"As far as I could tell it was. He looked the same. I had no reason to think otherwise."

"Now, this is important." Officer Reese leaned closer to me. "Did he say anything to you about the procedure?"

"Yes. I would have thought it odd if he had not said anything."

"What exactly did he say?"

"Oh, I could never forget. He said, 'Everything looks good.' Then, he winked at me before he left the examination room. I got dressed and met my mother out in the waiting room. The receptionist handed me the paper work. My mother gave me a hug. Then, we left. I was angry with her, Eric, the doctor, the nurses, the receptionist. I was angry with the world. My mother tried to tell me that this was best for me, now I could graduate, and all that mess. She drove me back to my apartment, but I did not want to hear any of it."

Another fruit fly hovered around the center of the table. No longer able to conceal my disdain for it, I slammed my hand down. But missed.

"When we got to my place, before we got out the car, I asked her for the rest of my past-due rent money. She handed it to me. I told her not to bother coming inside because I was tired. I saw her wipe tears as I closed the car door.

"Once I made it inside my place, Roxie met me at the door. She had a sad—no, more of a sympathetic—look on her face. She handed me a white envelope and said Eric dropped it off earlier and if I needed anything, she would be in her room. I opened the envelope. There were two one-hundred-dollar bills inside. There was a sticky note attached to one of the bills that simply read, 'Hope this helps' in Eric's handwriting. I called Eric's beeper right away, but it didn't go through. I thought I had dialed wrong, so I called it a second time, but it had been shut off. I couldn't believe it. I waited all day for him to call. I didn't leave the house, even though I felt fine health-wise. But, he never called. I got angrier by the minute. I made up my mind that if I didn't hear from him by the next day, I was going to his job. So, that's exactly what I did."

My nails made a tapping sound on the table.

"I caught the bus to his law office. That was the first time in the year that we had been together that I had ever been to his job. The receptionist asked how she could help me. I told her that I was there to see Eric Dade. She wanted to know if he was expecting me. I told her that he would definitely be interested in hearing what I had to say. She said he was in his office having lunch with his family at the moment, but she would inform him that I was in the waiting room. She asked my name, and I gave her a fictitious name. She picked up the phone, but before she could push a button, I asked her where the restroom was located. She pointed down a hallway and told me to turn left and it would be the third door on the right. I remember this because once I turned down that hallway, Eric's office was the first door on the right. He had an office that had one of those glass windows with the white venetian blinds. Except, he had the blinds slightly opened. I could see right into his office. I'll never forget what I saw.

"He had boxes of Chinese food on his desk. He was sitting in his big brown swivel chair. His wife was standing behind him giving him a neck and shoulder massage. He looked relaxed, his eyes closed, as he held and fed a sleepy baby in his arms. If I had to guess, the baby was maybe five or six months old. His daughter was standing in front of his desk coloring something. She had all her crayons lined neatly across the front of his desk. She would color a bit, then jump up and down, then color a bit more. His son was sitting on the floor stacking some wooden blocks.

"I didn't want to believe my eyes. I started telling myself that what I was seeing was not really what I was seeing. Next thing I know, I was turning the handle on Eric's door, and walking into his office.

"When I walked in, you would've thought he was a jack-in-the-box, the way he popped out that chair. The chair must've injured his wife because she immediately started whining and grabbed her foot. He was still holding the baby in his arms, but the bottle hit the floor. The baby started screaming. When I came in, I hurled questions at him like I was the attorney. Questions like: 'Who is this woman, Eric? Is this the wife you told me you were divorcing? I know you have a daughter and son, but whose baby is this? Why haven't you returned any of my phone calls since the day you took me to abort our baby?' His wife asked who I was. Officer Reese, the way he passed that baby to his wife, you would've thought he was in a football game passing off a ball that his life depended on.

"He came charging at me, shoved me into the hallway, and yelled to his wife that he'd take care of it. Then, he closed the door to his office and pushed me down the hallway. Oh. He was furious with me. That's what he said. But I know he was really angry for getting caught up in all his lies, mad that I'd exposed him in front of his wife and children.

"In the hallway, he kept saying I had no right to just show up like I did. I was hot! I told him he had no right to disappear out of my life after he made me have an abortion. When his colleagues started stepping out of their offices because of all the commotion we were making, he grabbed me by my arm and forced me outside. It got really intense out there. Now, I'm a lot better at keeping my hands to myself, but I wasn't so good at it back then.

"When I confronted him about how he still had pictures of his wife throughout his office, and how they were not interacting like a couple who was about to get a divorce, that's when he came clean. 'I'm sorry, Nancy, but it's over between you and me,' was his response to me. Can you believe that?"

Officer Reese nodded.

"I was in shock. I had about a hundred different emotions followed by a hundred different thoughts go through me in about five seconds. I thought maybe I wasn't hearing him correctly, so I asked him to repeat what he'd just said. He told me that I just needed to get back on a bus and leave because . . . he and I never happened.

"I'm sure my face turned beet red because I could feel the heat coming off my skin. I told him that I would leave, but I just needed him to tell me whose baby he was holding back in his office. He said that was his son. I wanted to make sure that I was understanding him correctly so I said to him, 'Let me get this clear. You have an infant son with your wife, yet you made me get an abortion?' He told me that he didn't make me get an abortion, that I was a grown woman who made a choice on my own to get an abortion. That's when I lost it and just started hitting him with all I had in me. Eric kept grabbing me, then trying to walk away, then I'd start grabbing him, but my anger kept getting the best of me. People starting going in and out of the building, but I only saw him. I heard one of his fellow attorney co-workers yell that he was going into the building to call the police. They came out and arrested me.

"I spent the night in jail. I chose not to call anyone to come get me out until the next day. I called my father and he came. Eric filed an order of protection against me. I was not allowed to go to his place of employment, call him, contact his wife, or be anywhere near him or his family. That's how our relationship ended.

"I told my dad everything because I felt like my mother was as guilty as Eric. My dad was disappointed in me, but he surprisingly became the person who helped me get through the devastation. He loved me through my ordeal.

"Once out of jail, I wavered between being angry and sad. Instead of staying depressed, I became proactive. I took on two part-time jobs. When I wasn't working, I lived at the library. It was just something about the way that Eric handled me . . . like I was nothing to him . . . that made me want to be successful. So, I channeled all my anger, frustration, and depression into working on becoming a better me. But whenever I slowed down long enough to think, I cried. So, I stayed busy as much as possible.

"For about a month after the abortion, I had these awful bouts with nausea. One of my part-time jobs was in a grocery store. From time to time I had to work in the deli whenever someone called off work. The smell of certain meats had me feeling like I wanted to vomit. That was very unusual for me. When I could no longer fasten my jeans, I knew something wasn't right. At the abortion clinic, they told me that my period would be irregular for a while due to the abortion, but that it would eventually regulate itself. But I felt like I was still pregnant. I swore that I could feel a baby moving inside of me. I thought about buying a pregnancy test, but that would have done me no good. At the abortion clinic, and on the follow-up instructions they gave me about the termination of pregnancy, it said that pregnancy tests could still show a positive for some time even after an abortion. It said something about pregnancy hormones still being in my system. So, I thought maybe my mind was just playing tricks on me.

"I tried not to think about it. I just stayed busy with school and work. But my belly kept getting bigger to the point I could only fit into my sweats. The nausea eventually went away. Then, one day while I was at the grocery store working as a cashier, an older African-American lady asked me when my due date was. I told her I wasn't pregnant. She looked at me and smiled. In the sweetest voice, she said, 'Darling, I was a midwife for forty years. You're probably somewhere between twenty-two and twenty-four weeks pregnant. Go visit a doctor, sweetheart. I'm rarely wrong about these things.' She smiled at me, took her groceries, and walked out the store.

"I couldn't shake what she said, so I left work early and went straight to the campus clinic. I told the nurse I had an abortion, but I wasn't sure if it had been successful. They had me take a pregnancy test. It came back positive. The doctor referred me to a clinic off campus. They did an ultrasound. All the medical staff was stunned. Just like that former midwife had said, I was twenty-three weeks pregnant. They scheduled prenatal visits for me, and the doctor wrote me a prescription for some prenatal vitamins.

"I must've imagined every possibility as I tried to figure out how the abortion had failed. I pulled out the documents they gave me at the abortion clinic. I studied them. The papers indicated that the abortion had been successful. The doctor and nurse signed off on a paper stating that the termination of pregnancy was a success. To this day, I still have all the papers as a reminder of the miracle my child is.

"I was happy. My anger turned to happiness." I couldn't hold back the laughter that rose up and came out as I relived the moment as if it was today.

"I had been given a second chance, and I promised myself that I would do everything within my power to protect my unborn child. I chose not to tell my mother or Eric this newfound information. Well, I couldn't contact Eric even if I wanted to because of the order of protection. But since they pressured me to get the abortion in the first place, I was determined not to go through that again. So, I kept my mouth shut and chose not to go home.

"Roxie was the only person I told, and she was very supportive. She was as shocked as I was to discover I was still pregnant.

"By the time I was seven months along, anyone who saw me could tell that I was pregnant. The day I went into labor, Roxie drove me to the hospital. I was okay with just her there with me, but she encouraged me to at least call my parents and let them know that I was in labor. I did, but I took my sweet time. They lived three hours away. By the time they arrived at the hospital, I'd already given birth.

"Neither my mother nor my father knew what to think. My mother was afraid to ask me any questions because our relationship was strained. My father just came straight out and asked how I could have a baby when I had gotten an abortion. I'm convinced that they both thought, and most likely discussed on their drive, that I had gotten pregnant again. When I got home, Roxie informed me that she overheard my mother asking a nurse if my baby was premature. The nurse told her that my baby was a full-term, healthy, eight-pound baby girl.

"Do you believe in God, Officer Reese?"

"I can't say that I do."

"At any rate, my dad was genuinely confused when he questioned me. I told him that apparently the abortion had failed. My father was a man of few words, but he was a good man. I will never forget what he said to me next. He sat on my bed, touched my cheek, and said, 'Sweetheart, God allowed that baby to live because He has a plan for that child's life. Now that the child is here, you have a responsibility to protect and nurture her. Do you hear me?' I told him I did.

"I allowed my dad to hold Natasha. I wouldn't let my mother touch her. She stood there. Watched the three of us interact. She left the room in tears. My dad hugged me before leaving. Mom was too emotional and simply waved on her way out.

"Some hours later, my parents called. I thought it was to say they'd made it home safely. Instead, it was to inform me they checked into a nearby hotel. They planned to stay until I was released from the hospital. The next day, they came back.

"My mother, still in tears, apologized. She was inconsolable, saying how sorry she was for pressuring me to abort Natasha. She confessed that as a mother and a Christian, she had failed and sinned. We cried together. Hugged. I forgave her. She held Natasha that day for the first time.

"I tell you, Officer Reese, I never saw my mother cry so much in my combined life the way she cried in that one day while holding her granddaughter. She was truly broken. I thank God that He gave us both a second chance with Natasha. With all this talk about Natasha, let me show you some pictures of her."

In the living room, the ottoman squeaked as I opened it and pulled out a box and photo album.

"This is my miracle baby right here." I pointed to a large hospital picture of an infant wearing a pink hat and wrapped snuggly in a pastel multicolored hospital blanket. Written on the picture was the date August 3, 1987, 8 lbs 1oz, and 21 inches.

Staring at the photograph, Officer Reese looked lost in his thoughts. He handed the large photo album back to me. I flipped through the many pages and showed Officer Reese pictures of Natasha through the years. I kept every single school year picture of her. From kindergarten to college graduation.

I handed Officer Reese a picture. "This here is my favorite picture. Same one is over there on the wall. This is Natasha and my mother. Natasha is about fifteen years old in this picture. My mother liked the *Chicago Tribune*, but her eyesight started failing her, and she had Natasha to prop her up on those pillows you see and read to her.

"My baby ended up being an incredible blessing to my mother while she battled breast cancer. My father had his own health problems, so he was limited in what he could do for my mother.

"My mother was dying in this picture. She had to be turned several times a day in bed, so she wouldn't get bed sores. She had to be fed, bathed, and changed. I worked a full-time job, so I couldn't do it. My father was almost to the point where he needed someone to look after him. I convinced him, though he was completely against the idea at first, to place my mother in a nursing home for proper care and medical attention.

"It was Natasha who volunteered to care for my mother during her summer vacation. We thought it would be too much for her, but my child is very convincing, like her biological father. We gave her a one-week trial period.

"A home healthcare nurse came out and showed her what to do. That child of mine blew all our minds. She was great at it! My mother's health even improved during the time Natasha cared for her. We believe it extended my mother's life. Even for a short time, Natasha brought a reason to live back into Mom's life.

"Every day, she told Natasha that she was her angel, sent to her from God. My mother eventually passed away in 2002. Just before New Year's Day. My father passed away almost one year to the day in 2003. They had been married for thirty-nine years. Because of her experience in taking care of my mother, Natasha went on to become a registered nurse. Today, she's the head nurse in oncology over at Providence Hospital. With both of our schedules, I don't get to see her as much as I would like. Well, anyway, that's the story of my miracle child, Officer Reese. Now that I've talked your ears off, what did you want to know?"

"Were you ever contacted by anyone asking you about Natasha or your abortion experience?"

"Do you mean other than police officers and FBI agents?"

"Well, yeah."

"Eric had one of his lawyer buddies contact me once in an attempt to scare me when I sued him for child support. Natasha was a year old.

"How did that turn out?"

"Eric and I hadn't seen each other or talked after I got arrested. As far as he knew, I'd had an abortion. I can't blame him for thinking I was crazy. But the courts made him take a paternity test.

"He was beyond surprised when it came back that he was indeed the father. He was ordered to pay me almost two thousand dollars per month in child support. But he had friends and colleagues in high places. They created a lot of legal red tape for me. I was back and forth in court. He was able to get his child support reduced to three hundred dollars per month. I had an opportunity to see him only once after Natasha was born. Outside the courthouse, he approached me. He wanted to know how I had pulled off such a feat as to fake an abortion. I told him that I had gone through with the abortion, and since he was there he should have known that. I attempted to explain that the child we had together was a miracle child. I offered him a picture of Natasha. He refused it and then proceeded to tell me how I almost ruined his life, marriage, and career. He walked away. I never saw him again."

Burt came through the door with several bags of grocery. I jumped at the opportunity to help take some of the bags from my hard-working husband.

"I've got them, Nancy. Let me handle this. Go ahead and tend to our guest."

I was fighting a losing battle.

"You know, Officer Reese, three weeks after I had Natasha, I was back in school finishing up my senior year. It was hard. I had to juggle school, motherhood, and work all at the same time. But she was worth it. Then, I met this man over here when Natasha was fourteen. We married a few months before her sixteenth birthday. Burt has been a wonderful father to Natasha. I'm so sorry. Did I even answer your question?"

"Yes, you did. But, I have one more question before I leave. If we capture the Chameleon, would you be willing to testify against him?"

"And what would I say, Officer Reese?"

"You could tell how he violated your life and body."

"Officer Reese, I get what you're trying to do. I do. But the only thing I could say about the Chameleon is that he gave me my miracle baby. I don't know what he looks like. He never hurt me as far as I know. And Natasha is here because of him. So, that's what I would say if I testified against this Chameleon. I mean, how do you know that it wasn't the doctor who chose not to terminate the pregnancy? I don't believe there is a "Chameleon." It just seems odd that there's someone doing all of this who looks *exactly* like the doctor."

"Well, all I'm at liberty to say is that we know for certain that it was not the doctor. We have overwhelming evidence that proves that the doctor was not the one in the room with you on the day that your supposed abortion was performed."

Officer Reese stood up, closed his notepad and placed it into his shirt pocket, and extended his hand. "Mrs. Smith, thank you very much for agreeing to this interview, and for sharing your story. Here's my card. If you think of anything out of the ordinary that happened when you visited the clinic, before or after, please don't hesitate to contact me. Have a good day, ma'am."

"Well, I hope something that I said helps you in some way, Officer Reese."

He walked into the kitchen area, extended his hand to Bert. "Thank you, sir. Good day."

"Good day to you too, officer." Burt shook Officer Reese's hand.

As he left, I heard him mumble something like, "Well, that's zero for three." Whatever that meant.

6

ILLNESSES

JENESIS

"Hey, Jen! I didn't expect you to be here this time of day." Knowing today was his day off, I'd left Paul sleeping when I slipped out to work this morning.

"Yeah, I know. I had a doctor's appointment during my lunch hour, but decided against going back to work." I leaned in to give him a hug.

"Careful. I'm returning from the gym and have a bad combination of sweaty and smelly." He stiff-armed me, but made up for it by planting a smooch on my forehead. "What's all this?"

"I figured I'd prepare a few days of meals for your mother since you're always asking me to package up our leftover dinners for her."

"When were you planning to take it to her?"

"Soon as I'm done here."

"Mind if I go with you? I just need to take a quick shower if you have about fifteen minutes to spare."

"Like I would deny you the opportunity to go with me to visit your mother."

By twos, up the stairs he glided.

Twenty minutes later, he opened the car door for me before removing the half dozen containers from my grip and stacking them in two rows on the floor behind his seat. The additional bag of goodies, he allowed to remain in my possession.

"So . . . what? How did this doctor's appointment go?" He pressed the button to lower the garage as we backed out of the driveway.

"Not so well."

"What do you mean?"

"Today wasn't a good day." I turned to look out the window so he wouldn't see the tear escape my eye. I wasn't as interested in the March snow flurries that melted upon hitting the window as I pretended.

"Tell me about it."

"My test results came back. They confirmed that I have PCOS." I felt the words getting stuck in my throat.

"Okay. And what exactly is that?"

"It stands for Polycystic Ovary Syndrome." I'd much rather not have this conversation, but he had a right to know.

"I have no idea what any of that means."

"Basically, my androgen levels are too high, and my progesterone levels are too low."

"Jen, you might as well be speaking Greek to me."

"In laymen's terms, my body is not functioning properly for me to get pregnant."

"Oh. Okay." His strong hand caressed mine. With a gentle squeeze, he held it. We drove in silence.

"I'm hopeful though. My doctor put me on a low-calorie diet. She wants me to lose ten pounds. She also prescribed a medication to help me ovulate. Prayerfully, this will remedy the problem and get my body back on track to conceive."

"Prayerfully?" He let go of my hand.

"Yes, prayerfully! My ultimate trust is in God. You made it clear to me that you don't believe in a God who's never been there for you, Paul. And I respect you. And your beliefs. But God has been there for me, and I need Him if I'm to get through all of this. I hope you can reciprocate the respect."

"I don't want this to turn into something ugly. Just know that I love you." He interlocked his fingers with mine. We stayed that way until we pulled into his mother's driveway.

Paul knocked on the front door, and we stood waiting in the icy cold, teeth chattering, huddling together.

"I'm coming. You have to wait a minute now," his mother yelled from a distance.

Huffing and puffing, she opened the door. The big green metal oxygen tank hissed as it dangled from her shoulder like a purse. Bent over, she rested her forehead on her walker.

"Oh, son!" She looked up in between breaths. "It's so good to see you!"

Paul guided me in first. We wiped our feet on the entry mat. Leaning down, he gave his mother a hug.

"How are you feeling, Momma?"

"I'm feeling a lot better today, son. My fever finally broke, so I've been sitting here in the living room reading and doing some crossword puzzles."

She stood up straight and then waved for me to come near.

"Have you been keeping my son in line?"

Careful not to crimp the long plastic tubing supplying her oxygen, I leaned in to hug her. "I've been trying, Momma. But you know he's a handful."

"I know. But don't give up on my son. He's got a lot of good in him."

We laughed and made our way into her living room.

"When was the last time you heard from Mark?" Paul hadn't talked to his older brother in over a year.

"Oh, well, it's been a couple of months now." Her voice quivered.

"Do you ever see any of your Bingo buddies?" His face was covered with a look of concern.

"Every now and then one of them drops by, but it's becoming less and less."

Paul didn't have far to walk before he was in the open kitchen.

"What about food, Momma? Do you have enough?" He was operating in full detective mode now. Before she could answer, Paul had swung open the refrigerator.

"An empty water jug. One egg in the egg carton. Mustard, ketchup, mayo, jelly. Some dried up hotdogs! Molded cheese! And a rotten assortment of vegetables!" He slammed the door so hard, several magnets fell to the floor.

"Momma, why don't you have any edible food the fridge?" Paul, veins looking like tree branches growing in his face, charged back into the room where his mother now sat in a recliner.

"Well, son, that young lady you hired to run my errands took my money to go grocery shopping a couple days ago, but never came back."

"Why didn't you call me and tell me about this?"

"You do so much for me already. I didn't want to bother you."

"Momma, what bothers me is finding my mother's refrigerator looking like that."

"Good thing we brought you some prepared meals to last you for a couple days. Breakfast. Lunch. And dinner. Got you some beef stew. Let's see." Plastic bags fell to the floor as I unstacked large and small containers. "Chicken, broccoli, and potatoes. Hotcakes, eggs, and turkey sausage. Times two. Oatmeal. Just add sugar and milk, which we have a small container of here. And all your other favorite toppings too. What else . . . Oh! Homemade chicken and dumplings. Two servings. Broccoli cheese soup. Two more servings. Got you a variety of breads here. Some salad. And some sweet tea. We know how much you like your sweet tea."

She smacked her lips. "Mind if I start with those hotcakes?"

"Don't mind at all. Coming right up."

While reaching in the cabinet to get a plate for the microwave, Paul had made his way back to the kitchen and whispered into my ear, "Thank you!"

Paul did a load of laundry and emptied all her trash bins. I washed some dishes and put them away.

"Momma, how much grocery money did you give to that woman?"

"All eighty-five dollars."

"Okay. I'll handle it the moment I get home. Did you need us to do anything else around here? And please don't feel like you're bothering me. That's why we're over here today . . . to help you."

"Well, that television you bought me for my birthday is still in the box. If you can set it and the television stand up for me in my bedroom, that would be nice."

"Momma, your birthday was two months ago. But it's cool. It's cool! I'll do it now." Within twenty minutes Paul was finished setting up his mother's television and its stand.

Though new, the wheels screeched as he rolled both into the room where his mother and I sat finishing up a crossword puzzle together. We stayed to watch the movie *Mully* he'd bought her. My hand snapped up to my mouth to capture the contagious yawn before it escaped. Paul stood and signaled for my hand. He helped me stand.

"Momma, I'm gonna do my best to get over here twice a week instead of once every two weeks. I'm sorry. I didn't know your hip had you in such bad shape. I thought you were healing faster than you are." He kissed her on the top of her head.

"Oh, Paul, don't you go feeling bad now. You're a wonderful son. I would be in a home somewhere right now if you weren't paying my copays for my home healthcare nurse. They're doing a really good job with me, but they're only here three days a week." She tugged on his arm until he leaned down where she could hug him. "Thank you, son! I love you and appreciate everything you do for me."

"You're welcome, Momma. But I'm still gonna come over here twice a week now to check on you. I'll have Jenesis see if we can get your home healthcare nurses out more frequently. I'll locate that crook of an errand lady, and I'll have your eighty-five dollars for you by the beginning of next week."

He held my coat until I disappeared inside of it. I put on my hat, gloves, and scarf, and braced myself for the fierce Midwest cold that chose to stick around into the month of March.

"Don't even think about it, Momma. Stay seated, and I'll lock the bottom lock on my way out."

7

OR ELSE

PAUL

Following our day off, we were back at it, *Operation Almost* in full effect. I was already situated, studying older reports, with several files spread across the table. The whiteboard, filled with facts, scenarios, diagrams, timelines, and victims, looked like it lost a challenge in a paintball fight.

"Good morning, partner." Jeff, juggling two large cups of coffee from his favorite coffee shop, made it to the table. He drank coffee throughout the day. I drank it when he chose to bring me a cup.

I rubbed my eye and yawned a "Good morning."

"I got something for you. Hopefully it'll make your morning a little better. I know how much you liked that caramel cappuccino last time. But I don't know if there's enough caffeine in there to wake you up. You look like you got zero rest on your day off."

"Thanks for the cappuccino. I didn't sleep well last night."

"Is everything okay on the home front?"

"Yeah, everything's a'ight. I just need to slow my mind down when it comes to this case. Too many things not adding up for me. Couldn't sleep, so I've been here since five a.m."

"Find anything?"

"Oh yeah!"

"Care to share?"

"First, there are about twenty-five missing files. I also found eight files that had names and addresses completely blacked out. Second, there's approximately $750,000 in abortion money missing from local clinics over the course of the last forty-four years. It's still unaccounted for. There's a lot of sketchy reports concerning the missing money. But I have yet to find one charge of robbery brought against him.

"The more I look at these files, the evidence, the reports, the more I'm convinced that someone here—right here at this police station—knows a lot more than they're letting on. Fourth, every report I've read through on a victim, which is over a hundred now, ends with these same exact words, 'I almost had him, but he escaped.' How? I keep coming back to this question. Why hasn't this raised red flags? Why would they name this case *Operation Almost* and highlight their own incompetence? I need some answers. Which leads me to number five. I think I'm going to ask the chief if I can interview some of the officers who've worked this case in the past."

"Paul." Jeff raised his eyebrows. "Are you sure that's a good idea? They seem to be a bit unsettled that you volunteered for this case in the first place."

"That's exactly why I think it's a good idea to interview them. Why are they so agitated over a case dealing with abortion fraud and stolen abortion money unless they're somehow involved? I'm looking over everything, and starting to believe we're questioning the wrong people. I believe those who really know what's going on are right in front of us. They were too determined to keep us off this assignment. I need to find out why."

"That's some theory. Not saying you're right. Not saying you're wrong. Just. Are you sure you want to go around accusing people you work so closely with? That could get a little messy, you know?"

"I know. But they've already come at me reckless regarding this case. I need to find out why they don't want me on this case. I understand if you don't want to pursue this with me."

"No, I'll stay on the case. But I'm going to let you lead the charge."

I slurped the cappuccino. "This is really good. Thanks."

"Not to change the subject, but how'd your interview go with the last victim?"

"Like all the other ones. She couldn't identify the Chameleon. He looked just like the doctor. She can't remember anything out of the ordinary. If we ever capture him, and she testifies at a trial, she'll basically testify in his favor. She had quite a story, though. How'd your presentation at the school go?"

"Really well. The kids were receptive. A handful came up to me afterward and thanked me. One little boy had tears in his eyes, said he hoped my presentation would make some of the boys in his class and on the bus stop bullying him. I asked him to point them out to me. So,

I had a real police-friendly conversation with them—if you know what I mean. I asked the kids who came up to me to give me their names." He tapped the notepad that rested inside of his uniform pocket. "I'll stop by the schools every couple of weeks to check on their situations. See if things are improving."

"That's great, Jeff! You really do have a way with kids."

"That's because I care. Children can tell if you care or if you're faking it."

"True." My attention was divided between talking with Jeff and trying to recall and decipher my coworkers' behavior.

"Who are we interviewing next? Today right?"

I scrolled through my phone. "Let's see. Tom's got us meeting with . . . No wait. Looks like he had to reschedule. It was Abbarane Chaikin for today. It's been rescheduled for Friday. I'm going to head over to the chief's office and see won't he let me interview a few of our folks."

"Go ahead. I'll try to make sense of this board I'm looking at."

Sargent Stevens was leaving as I arrived.

He nodded. "Officer Reese."

"Sargent Stevens."

Off he went.

"Chief. Got a moment?"

"Sure do. Come on in, Reese. I needed to talk to you anyway."

"What about?"

"You're off the *Operation Almost* case."

"What! Why?"

"Numerous complaints. And a couple requests that you be pulled from the case. This is a big case, Reese.

Besides, these types of cases really should be handled by our detectives."

"I know, but they don't want anything to do with it. No one does. Isn't that how it landed in our meeting as a volunteer assignment? Plus, what I'm investigating is old news anyway. Cold cases. Why does it matter to anyone?"

"Give me one good reason why I should keep you on this."

"I'm all in. If you want someone who cares about this case, I'm the person. Plus, Jeff and I are making progress."

"How?"

"That twenty-foot whiteboard in the conference room is loaded with reasons why. If you'd like, let's go, and I can break it all down for you. Right now."

"Not necessary." Chief Lewis steepled his hands and looked off into the distance.

"C'mon, Chief. Don't pull me. Us. I eat, sleep, and drink this assignment. I know we can crack this. Besides, it'll just be sitting in the basement with Cheddar and Buddy collecting dust if we're not on it."

"You've mentioned you want to train to become a detective. This is a good start. You seem to have an aptitude for investigative work. Maybe you can learn some valuable lessons."

"It'll be great for helping to lay a foundation for when you're ready to promote me to detective. Also . . . no one else wanted this case. Just thought I'd remind you."

"Listen. If I'm going to allow you to stay on this case, you need to capture the Chameleon once and for all. Bring him in, Paul. All this 'dog chasing its tail' stuff ain't good for nobody. Becomes a waste of time and resources."

"Thanks, Chief. Yes, sir."

"Not so fast! What did you come here to see me for?"

"I want your permission to interview Officers Prince, Rodriguez, Johnson, and Sergeant Stevens."

"What for?"

"More than $750,000 in abortion money . . . gone with the Chameleon. According to some of these reports, the Chameleon is arrested and brought in for questioning, but then escapes. He has been brought in to our precinct for questioning more than thirty times. Chief, who escapes thirty times from a police station full of armed officers, detectives, and lieutenants on duty? It makes no sense. None! More specifically, I need to know how the Chameleon escaped their custody."

"Now you're thinking like a detective. It's what I would do." He bit his fingernail and spit it out. "Permission granted."

"Thank you."

"Not so fast. You're skating on thin ice with me. I'm not going to allow you or anyone else to tear the department down with a bunch of conflict and strife. I've worked too hard to build a solid bunch. Now, you find a way to get along with you coworkers, or you're off the case. Got it?"

"But, Chief, they're the ones—"

"They're not on the case. You are. Don't allow them to get you taken off the case too."

"Got it." Knowing some of my colleagues had just attempted to persuade Chief to take me off the case had me a bit wary of the stipulations I'd just agreed to. I knew it was going to be a challenge getting an honest interview from any of them, but I had to try.

I had Tom schedule interviews with two of my colleagues for the next day.

In a small interrogation room with the station's video surveillance set up, I waited. This room, containing only two chairs and one small table, was normally used for difficult criminals. I tapped my watch to make sure it was still working, then stood. I walked into the hallway and asked one of the officers who was passing by for the time. Sergeant Stevens was more than fifteen minutes late. I used that time to review my notes and the questions I'd prepared. I fiddled with the camera in the room. Several minutes later, Sergeant Stevens knocked hard on the already propped open door before entering. I never looked up. Knocking hard on the door to startle was a tactic we all had learned in this department.

"Let's get this over with. I have some real work to do." Sergeant Stevens stood two inches taller than my six-foot frame. He was in his late fifties, in good shape, and had a head full of silver hair.

"Thank you for meeting with me today." I didn't mean a word I said. But even though Sergeant Stevens was not my supervisor, he was a man who deserved respect, and I had to be careful how I handled this questioning, even if I did suspect foul play.

"Please, have a seat, Sergeant Stevens. I've hit a roadblock in my investigation of the *Operation Almost* case, and the purpose of this interview is to tie in your knowledge of this case with my knowledge so we have the best possible chance of bringing the Chameleon to justice."

"Officer Reese, I'm here to assist you the best way I can. What I don't understand is why you have me in this interrogation room. I typed up everything I investigated and put it in a report."

"Yes, sir. I see that. I have your report here. And it reads, 'I had the Chameleon in the interrogation room for questioning. I stepped out and left him alone for a few minutes. When I returned, he was gone. I almost put the Chameleon away for life, but he escaped.'"

"Let me see that." Sergeant Stevens studied the report.

"Did you write that, sir?"

"I sure did." He handed the report back to me.

"How did the Chameleon escape from *this* interrogation room, Sergeant?"

"We still don't know, Officer Reese."

"Were the investigation cameras rolling?"

"Yes, they were, Reese." He exhaled a long breath through his lips.

"Why can't we locate the video of the interrogation you led, Sergeant Stevens?"

"Reese, if you're insinuating that I have done something wrong regarding my investigation of the Chameleon, why don't you just come out and say it, young man? I would respect you more."

"No problem." *Ahem.* "Are you conspiring with the Chameleon in some way?"

"No."

"Have you taken any money from the Chameleon for any reason?"

"No."

"Did you assist the Chameleon with his escape, directly or indirectly?"

"No."

I walked to the camera on the tripod, and took a look again at its buttons.

"Thank you, Officer Stevens, your testimony is recorded, and you're free to go."

"Be careful, Reese. Don't go around here accusing innocent coworkers. You never know if one day you might need their help." The firm pat Sergeant Stevens gave me on the shoulder before leaving the room stung. "You don't have a clue what you've gotten yourself involved with," he said as he walked out the door.

Ten minutes later, Officer Rodriguez was already seated in the interrogation room when I arrived. The video camera had been removed.

"Officer Rodriguez." I extended my hand and offered a firm handshake. "Man, thank you for being on time. I moved us over to interrogation room five."

As I lead the way, Officer Rodriguez jingled some coins in his pocket. "Why are we going over to the state-of-the art interrogation room? What is this really about, Reese?"

I stopped and turned around to look Rodriguez in the eye. "This is about me getting to the truth, Rodriguez."

I held the door for him to enter. The door automatically locked behind us and would require being buzzed out by someone externally. All cameras were set to record, including the four that hung from the ceiling. Still, on the tripod I set up the same camera I'd just used to record Sergeant Stevens.

This larger room came with a bigger table and four chairs. The two-way mirror built into the wall allowed other law enforcement personnel to observe interrogations while in progress. Only Jeff stood on the other side of the wall to watch.

"So, what's this all about? What you got a camera running for, ese?" Rodriguez sat on the edge of his chair.

"I'm not your ese. The camera is running in the hopes that you'll be honest—in case there's a follow-up internal investigation. Or if the FBI ever needs to review this interview or your investigative techniques."

Rodriguez bolted from his seat. "Are you trying to say I'm not an honest cop?"

"Are you?" Our eyes remained locked for a full five seconds before he looked down. I flipped a page of my legal pad and curled it under.

"I'm an honest man." Rodriguez straighten his shoulders and lifted his head.

"Please," I whispered, "have a seat."

"I don't have anything to lie about."

"Great! Then this should go real quick. Do you know the Chameleon's real name?"

His nostrils flared as his lip curled up. "No, I don't. Do you?"

"Are you assisting the Chameleon in any way?"

"No, I am not. Are you?"

"Have you ever assisted the Chameleon in any way, big or small?"

"No . . . wait . . . yes, I have."

Caught by surprise, I looked up and swallowed hard. "How exactly have you assisted the Chameleon?"

"It was small. I'm not sure you'd even care to know."

"Great or small, I need you to tell me." I offered him a nod with a little smile.

"Okay, if you insist. After I handcuffed the Chameleon, I assisted him in making sure he didn't hit his head when I placed him in the back of my car."

I understood that the rest of this investigation was going to be full of mind games, so I decided to just ask the questions I'd written down and let him go.

"Has the Chameleon ever offered you any money?"

"No."

"Did you have the Chameleon in this interrogation room when you brought him to the station?"

"Yes."

"So, how did the Chameleon escape this— how did you put it?—'state-of-the-art interrogation room' while you were interrogating him?"

"Well, Reese, he just walked right out the door."

"You mean that metal door, with the secure locks, that requires someone externally to buzz a person out?" I stretched out my long, pointer finger.

"Yep, that's the one."

"And who buzzed him out?"

"I don't know."

"And where were you when he escaped?"

"I was talking to the chief."

"I looked at the interrogation tapes of your interview with the Chameleon. Why are they so fuzzy? You can hardly see or hear anything."

"I don't know, Officer Reese. Perhaps you should investigate the people who installed this state-of-the-art video equipment too."

"Thank you for your time, Officer Rodriguez. You are free to go."

Rodriguez got up and walked over to the door. There he waited for someone on the outside to buzz him out.

"Real funny. Ha, ha. But somebody better open this door."

"Oh, you're talking about the same door that the Chameleon was standing at when he escaped?"

"Reese, you think you're so smart, but everything you think you know is about to change."

"What is that supposed to mean?"

"Oh, you're about to find out."

Jeff buzzed the door. Officer Rodriguez walked out, but not before he looked me up and down with a face that looked like he had been sucking on lemons.

I would have to be creative in gathering information from Officers Johnson and Prince. But first, I had more victim's interviews to contend with.

"The Chameleon just walked right out the door." I wonder what kind of fool Rodriguez takes me for.

INTERVIEW #4

ABBARANE CHAIKIN

The receptionist at the library's front desk called to inform me that the officers were running behind schedule, but shouldn't be more than ten minutes late. When they arrived, she called me down.

"Hello. I'm Officer Paul Reese. And this is my partner, Officer Jeff Hughes." They took turns shaking my hand.

"It's a pleasure to meet you, Officer Reese, Officer Hughes. You probably know by now, but for the record, I'm Abbarane Chaikin-Bachman. Chaikin is my maiden name. I got married several years ago."

"Thank you for agreeing to this interview," Officer Reese said.

"If you two had arrived about eight minutes earlier, you would've run into two of your fellow officers hauling away two longtime thieves who've been stealing our DVDs and Blu-rays. Two teenagers who should've been in school anyway."

"Maybe this will be exactly what they need to get back on the right track," Officer Hughes said.

"Well, let's hope so. We all could use a second chance. After all, that's what I'm about to talk to you two gentlemen about now. This way, please." I had to be mindful not to walk too fast. I've often been told that I walk like I'm on my way to fulfill some top-secret mission. Then again, I'm sure these two officers, standing a minimum of six feet each, could keep up with my five-foot-four self plus three artificial inches in the form of my shoes. I led them to a private elevator for employees only. "Here we are, officers." They followed me into my office and I shut the door.

I enjoyed my spacious office. Officer Hughes stopped in front of an oversized, gilded-framed oil painting of an old wooden cross illuminated by the sun. The words *God Is Merciful* was written underneath the cross. The officers scanned the office, taking it all in.

"I only have an hour to spare before I'm off to a meeting." I sat in a chair that nearly swallowed up my small frame and repositioned it so I was no longer hidden behind my computer.

"So, how can I be of assistance this time around in dealing with this mysterious, yet fascinating individual whom you have so appropriately named the Chameleon?" I folded my hands on the desk as I leaned forward.

"We have a number of questions to ask you, but, first, how should we address you?" asked Officer Hughes.

"Abby is fine."

"Abby, what do you know about the Chameleon?"

"According to the officers who interviewed me in the past, the Chameleon is responsible for impersonating abortion doctors across the state. I've been told that he assumed the identity of the abortion doctor who performed the intended abortion I was forced into. Apparently, he's very good at what he does since he's been doing this for forty some odd years, and he's still a free man. That about sums up my knowledge of him."

"Have you ever met the Chameleon?" Officer Hughes asked.

"I've been told by some of your colleagues that I have met him, but I just didn't know it at the time."

"From your personal experience, can you tell us anything about the Chameleon?"

"Unfortunately, Officer Hughes, I cannot. If you were to place the Chameleon in a lineup, obviously, by the sheer nature of this case, I would not be able to pick him out. If he truly stole the identity of the abortion doctor, then he deserves some type of award because I certainly could tell no difference. I would have never allowed some fraud to touch me if I had known. He could have really botched up the abortion. But I feel fortunate—no, blessed, actually, by the outcome."

"Did you desire to have an abortion?" Officer Reese interjected.

"No, sir. I did not want an abortion, and I did not keep that a secret."

"Who did you tell that you were against having an abortion?"

"I only told those who already knew I was pregnant."

"Try to think back for me. Prior to the abortion, or attempted abortion, do you recall having any encounters with strangers you may have told of your desire not to have an abortion?" Officer Reese scooted to the edge of his chair and rested his clasped hands on my desk.

Thinking back to that painful time in my life, I searched my memory to recall if perhaps I had a forgotten conversation with a stranger. "No, Officer Reese, I only shared my disapproval with everyone who already knew of my pregnancy. Unless you consider the medical staff at the abortion clinic strangers."

"What do you recall about the actual day of the abortion procedure?" Officer Reese sat back in his chair.

"I was sixteen years old. My mother took me to the abortion clinic against my wishes. I cried the entire ride there. According to the staff at the clinic, I was eleven weeks pregnant. That meant I would have to undergo a two-day procedure. The first day, they started the abortion process by prepping my cervix for the removal what they referred to as a blob of tissue. They told me that a baby had not formed yet, so I had no reason to be upset. That only made me more upset. The second day, they had to sedate me to perform the abortion because I was too hysterical about going through with it. My mother allowed them to give me a general anesthesia although they could have performed the abortion using only a local. They prepped me and placcd a port in my arm for the IV.

"The entire time, I begged and begged them not to do it. I made it clear to the nurse, doctor, receptionist, and my mother. This was not something I wanted. My mother came over to me while I was laying on the table in a hospital gown and whispered into my ear that she knew it wasn't what I wanted, but it was the best thing for me. The next thing I recall was being transported to the recovery room. When I was fully awake, able to comprehend, the nurse told me everything had gone as planned, and that my life would return to normal."

"Do you recall the doctor's reaction before or after the abortion itself?" Officer Hughes asked.

"He just waited for everyone to finish with the prepping. He looked like he was getting his tools in order. While everyone else was trying to calm me down with their great insights into my life, he just watched. Never said a word. His eyes were the only part of his face that I could see because he was wearing a surgical mask. From across the room, he looked as if he were seeing right through me. I never saw him again after that. Only the nurses came to the recovery room. When I was lucid, a nurse helped me get dressed, and then walked me out to the waiting room area. My mother was there, and she helped me to the cab."

I had already decided that I would comply with the officers interviewing me. I had also determined I would answer any questions asked, but would not willingly volunteer information about how I became pregnant.

"Abby, please explain the story behind your pregnancy which led to your mother . . . I guess, *forcing* you to have an abortion, which of course didn't happen because of the Chameleon." Officer Hughes had a gentle, sympathetic way about him.

"Please, if you don't mind my asking, why is it necessary for me to give you the details related to how I got pregnant?"

"That's a legitimate question. We are not trying to be nosy. It's part of being thorough in our investigation. We don't know why the Chameleon chose you. We don't know if it was random or if there is a connection between you and the other victims. Any time we can get the full details of the circumstances surrounding the pregnancy and attempted abortion, it allows us to see the big picture and connect the dots.

"I see." I closed my eyes and inhaled as much air as could fill my lungs and tried to brace myself for this bitter-sweet trip down memory lane.

"Please, take your time. We are not here to judge you."

I exhaled. "I had just turned sixteen. It was the middle of my sophomore year in high school, the first year that I thought of myself as attractive." I smiled recalling the moment. "I had finally grown out of that awkward phase. You know, where your looks are trapped between a child and an adult. I had gotten to the point that year where I thought I was pretty. You have to understand why that was so important to me. My mother and I were very poor. Dirt poor to be exact. I never knew my father. Mom and I lived in a trailer park a couple miles from school. I lived far enough away to catch the school bus, but not far enough because my schoolmates knew where I lived and made fun of me. I was an average student. I was more concerned with trying to stay warm at home and overlook the fact that we ate hotdogs or peanut butter and jelly on stale bread almost daily. I escaped by watching an enormous amount of television, when I should have been doing homework. I wasn't dumb, I just didn't put any effort into my schoolwork."

While speaking, my telephone rang.

"One moment, please." I turned my chair to face the window. Officers Hughes and Reese sat quietly. It was the circulation desk asking me about a book I had on hold for someone. I answered their questions quickly, then hung up and turned my chair back around.

"I'm sorry about that. What was I saying?"

"You were telling us that you were not a dumb student," Officer Hughes said.

"Oh, yes. So, I wasn't a scholar. I didn't have money, which meant I didn't wear the best clothes, let alone drive a car like the popular kids. I didn't play any sports. But that year, I started getting a lot of attention from boys, and I always had a bubbly personality.

"Yeah. I was having a pretty good school year for the first time in a long time. Then, to top it all off, the very handsome, popular, basketball captain, and school president who was a senior, Chad Evans, took an interest in me. Me! A friend told me that Chad had been asking around about me. I thought she was playing a sick joke on me, and I told her that I was not silly enough to fall for that. It seemed absurd that this handsome senior who seemed to have it all would be interested in me. But he was.

"He approached me the day before Thanksgiving break. I will never forget it. He handed me a Thanksgiving Day card that he'd made himself. He placed it in an envelope that he had drawn a turkey on and colored burnt orange. After he handed me the card, he just said, 'This is for you,' and walked away. Let me tell you"—my cheeks began to hurt from the big smile I had no control over—"I was standing there in the hallway at my locker, speechless, mouth wide open. I wanted to respond, but I was in absolute shock. I could not even open the envelope at school. I went through the next three hours of my day like a zombie. Friends harassed me, trying to get me to open the envelope because they were just as curious as me to know what was inside. I can be pretty stubborn. I refused. I held on to that envelope like there was a million dollars in it. I rode the bus home, then I sat on the couch for ten minutes just staring at his drawing and the way he'd written *Happy Thanksgiving* on the envelope. I was afraid of what was inside. I wasn't sure if this was a joke that I would be the butt of. I wasn't sure if he was really interested in me, or if he saw me as a charity case. I knew that the answer was inside, so careful not to rip it, I slowly opened it. Let me tell you, I was unprepared for what was inside."

I paused and could feel tears forming, but I blinked them back.

"He'd made me a card out of orange construction paper. He cut some brown construction paper in the shape of a turkey and glued it to the front of the card. Inside, it read something like, 'I know you don't know me, *yet*, but I hope you will allow me to prove that I am worthy of your time. I have watched you for two months now. You are a kind person. That is hard to find around here. On this Thanksgiving, I am thankful for your kindness. I am thankful for your smile. I am thankful for your beauty. But, I will be most thankful if you would call me at the number listed here, so I can get to know you better. I hope you have a Happy Thanksgiving. Don't eat too much turkey. (Well, eat as much as you like, I guess.) Sincerely, Chad Evans.'

"Those were the nicest words anyone had ever said to me. I just sat there on that couch in shock. My mother couldn't always pay the phone bill so I wasn't sure if there'd be a dial tone. Sweet relief, there was. I called a friend and read the card to her. She screamed so loudly in my ear . . ." The memory made me smile.

"I talked to her for a while longer, but then realized I should call him before my mother got home. I dialed the number and waited, stomach doing somersaults. Chad answered. We talked for two hours. He was friendly and easy to talk to. Chad had a way about him that made me want to open up. He cared. I told him how I'd feared he was playing some bad joke on me or that he saw me as a charity case. I said I feared his friends wouldn't approve and he'd care more about what they thought. There was also the issue of him being a senior and me a sophomore. I just didn't want to start something that was going to be over in a month. He heard my fears, but, most importantly, he heard my heart. He promised me that I would be safe with him. He asked me to trust him. And, well, I did."

I had to stop talking because I could feel a lump in my throat and my breathing was shallow. I closed my eyes, and the tears began to roll down my cheeks. Officer Hughes spotted a box of tissues tucked behind a photograph on my bookshelf and handed it to me.

"Thank you." I pressed the tissues against the tears, careful not to smear my make-up. "Chad was good to me. He was everything he said he would be. He didn't allow anyone to speak badly of me. Gradually, he bought me some really nice clothes. He was gentle toward me. He had a really good heart."

I got choked up all over again, and could hardly get my words out. "I really . . . really loved Chad. And I believe he loved me too."

I cleared my throat. "My mother worked a lot. She also went to bars and drank when she wasn't working. That allowed me and Chad to spend way too much time together. We were pretty much inseparable after school, which was not good for two teenagers. We started having sex. A lot. I was so focused on my relationship with Chad,

I wasn't paying attention to my own body. I didn't realize I'd missed my period that first month. It wasn't until we were at a drive-in, watching a movie that it became apparent that something wasn't right. We ordered our food, and they brought it out to us. The moment I smelled Chad's burger, I threw up all over him and his nice Mustang. Then, he threw up all over me, and his nice Mustang. We got cleaned up, and left. Right away, I figured I was probably pregnant and I told Chad so. The next day, we both skipped school and he drove me to a doctor. They confirmed that I was indeed pregnant. I cried and he hugged me and told me that everything would be okay. He asked me what I wanted to do. I told him I wanted to keep our child, but I didn't know how to raise a baby. He said that by the time the baby was born, he would have graduated from high school, and he would get a job, and get us a place. He wanted us to raise our child together as a family. He said if my mother would agree to it, he would marry me after he graduated. Suddenly, the situation didn't seem as scary anymore."

Someone knocked on my office door. I got up and whispered to one of my coworkers at the door that I would be finished in about twenty minutes. The officers exchanged a look that seemed to have a hidden meaning.

"Gentlemen, I apologize for the interruptions." I sat back down.

Looking at his watch, Officer Hughes asked, "You two were planning on getting married. So, what happened?"

"We didn't tell anyone while we tried to figure everything out. Chad's behavior with me didn't change. He remained a good man . . . a man of his word. I knew other girls who had gotten pregnant before me, and their boyfriends dumped them and then acted like they never even knew them. I expressed to Chad that I feared he would do the same. He assured me that he would not, and he didn't. I loved him all the more for how he treated me during that difficult, scary period of our lives. Close to two months passed and I knew I had to tell my mother about it sooner or later. I wasn't scared to tell her since she had me when she was sixteen. But Chad wanted to wait to tell his parents until after graduation. He didn't think they would be as understanding. When I told my mother, she yelled at me a little. Then, she just told me the baby would totally be my responsibility the same way I was hers as a teenager. She was over it in a day or two. It wasn't a big deal to her."

The officers were sitting up and leaning forward. I couldn't tell if they were just uncomfortable in their seats or personally curious as to what would happen next.

"All was well until Chad's mother found a note that Chad had written me detailing his plans for us upon his graduation." I felt that knot lodging its way into my throat again, but this time I fought through it. "She found the note on Friday morning while Chad was at school. She met him that afternoon at school. She parked behind his car in the student parking lot. It was my first time meeting her. She refused to shake my hand when I extended it to her. She just wanted to know if my name was Abby. When I told her yes, she looked at me with such hatred. Almost like she wanted to hit me. But she restrained herself. She told Chad that he had better get into his car and follow her straight home. It was the first time in several months that I was back on the bus. I didn't hear from Chad for the entire weekend. I was afraid to call him, but I did. When his mother answered, I hung up."

"It was the longest weekend of my life. On Sunday evening, the phone rang. It was Chad's mother. She asked to speak to my mother. I handed my mother the phone. She took it into another room. When my mother came out of her bedroom, she started cleaning up the living room area in our trailer. When I asked her what was going on, she said we were having company. We never had company over, so it made me really nervous. Thirty minutes later, someone knocked on our front door. Guess who? Chad's mother. She'd come alone. She had on a winter white pants suit, with a matching coat, hat, gloves, and boots. She had diamonds everywhere—in her ears, on her neck, on her wrists, and on her fingers. I'll never forget—with her white pants, she was hesitant to sit on our sofa, because it wasn't in the best shape. I asked what was going on, and she said she wanted to conduct a business deal with us. My mother just sat back, lit a cigarette, and allowed Mrs. Evans to talk. She made a proposal. She offered me five thousand dollars to have an abortion and leave her son alone. Forever."

My stomach began to churn so I rested my arm on my abdomen.

"I immediately told her no. I told her that Chad and I were going to get married, and that I did not need or want her money. Then she laid a guilt trip on me. She asked me if I loved Chad. I told her of course I did. She asked if I loved him, then why was I trying to ruin his life. I told her that I would never attempt to ruin Chad's life. She told me that Chad had been accepted at Harvard, and they were offering him a scholarship. She asked if I knew that

Chad was an A plus student, who had scored in the top 5 percent of all the standardized tests. She reminded me how good Chad was at basketball. I told her that I knew all that about Chad, but she continued to interrogate me. She wanted to know how I could love him, and take all of those opportunities away from him by letting him stay in our town, get married, get a dead-end job, and raise a baby? I told her that had been Chad's idea, and I'd had nothing to do with it. She told me Chad was throwing away his promising future because of me, and she wasn't going to allow that to happen. I told her she couldn't stop it, and that we loved one another. She went on a rant about how young love was fleeting, and everyone made mistakes. She said she didn't blame me, but she was willing to help me fix the mistake I'd made. Then, she offered me and my mother ten thousand dollars if I would have an abortion right away. I told her that I didn't want her stinkin' money and she could shove it."

I rested my face in the palms of my hands remembering this terrible encounter.

"The woman slapped my face, and my mother had to restrain me. I was yelling at her and crying. I was so angry with that lady. My mother made me go wait in my room. I took the phone and tried to call Chad, but their house phone only rang. My mother talked to his mother for a few more minutes before she left. The next day, my mother took the day off work. She woke me up, and told me I needed to get dressed to go with her. I reminded her that I had school. Then she informed me that she was pulling me out of that school. I asked her why. She told me she would tell me later, and insisted that I get dressed. She called a cab, and it was on our way that she told me I was going to have the abortion. I cried and tried to reason with her all the way there. I told her I didn't want an abortion. She said Chad's mother promised her that I would never see Chad again. His mother told her that if I attended that school the next day, they were going to pull Chad out and send him to live in another state with relatives. She offered my mother the ten thousand dollars if she'd agree to make me have the abortion within a twenty-four-hour period, and then send me to an alternative high school or night school."

I could only shake my head at the memories.

"My mother made a deal with the devil. She agreed to everything that lady told her she needed to do in order to keep me and Chad apart. Starting with the abortion. She gave my mother a thousand dollars cash as a down payment for their agreement, plus the cost of the abortion. She promised that she would give her the rest over the next several months until Chad graduated just to ensure that my mother made me comply with all of her demands. My mother cried in the cab. But her tears were over how badly we needed the money."

I had to stand. As I paced the length of the room, I massaged the knots that were starting to form in my shoulders.

"We were bad off financially. We had no heat the day Chad's mother gave my mother that money. But no amount of money made me want to have an abortion. I tried to bargain with my mother. I begged her to let me get a job. I told her I would get two jobs if she let me keep my baby. She started crying and telling me it was hard out there, and how hard she had it in life since she gave birth to me, and that I could do this one thing. Just this one thing. To pay her back. I told her that I could work, and pay her back that way. She said by having the abortion and going to another school that would be the best way for me to pay her back."

I stood behind my chair and rested my forearm on it.

"I was torn between my mother's cries and the cries of my heart for my unborn child. I told my mother I did not want to end my child's life. She told me that I could always have other children, but an opportunity like this one only came around once in a lifetime. We went back and forth like that until we reached the clinic. I cried all the way into the building. It was a two-day procedure. I told you the rest."

I sat back in my seat, wishing it were my bed.

"Oh, on the second day, Chad's mother was waiting in her car outside the abortion clinic. She made my mother show her the papers showing that the abortion had occurred."

The bottom half of my face felt heavy with sorrow of the memory.

"My mother enrolled me in an alternative school. She moved us out of the trailer park and into a nice little two-bedroom house with the money she received. I hated that house. Chad's mother sent her a thousand dollars every month until Chad graduated."

"I fell into a state of depression. I dropped out of school completely and stopped leaving the house. By the time my mother received her final payment, I think she realized that the money had been a down payment on my soul. I lost weight. I stopped eating. I had no will to live after that. I think she understood that she'd made a huge mistake. But it was too late. Or so I thought.

"I discovered I was still pregnant when I felt my child move inside of me. Trust me when I say there is nothing in the world quite like a baby moving inside you. That is not something you can mistake. It seemed so impossible to me at the time. I was highly conflicted. I started telling myself that I was in denial because I didn't want it to be true. But my body wasn't lying to me. So, I started monitoring myself. I still didn't have the best appetite, but I could no longer button my pants. I started to rapidly gain weight. I wore lots of layers and big clothes, so no one could see my belly becoming rounder and bigger.

"What do you know? I quickly came out of my depression. I told my mother that I wanted to enroll in night school. She was happy. I really wanted to find some answers to questions. So, I enrolled. There were so many young teenage mothers there. I started asking them questions about where they went to find out if they were pregnant. They knew about all the free clinics and free programs. I became good friends with one girl who had her own car. I asked Michelle if she would take me to a doctor to find out if I was still pregnant. The next morning, she took me. At the free clinic, they confirmed it. I decided that it would not be smart of me to tell my mother that the abortion had failed, so I kept that to myself. She had already proven to me that money was more important to her than the life growing inside me. I felt like I needed to get a place on my own, but I was clueless as to how to go about it. I continued going to night school. Outside of class time, I asked the other young women in night school with me a lot of questions. Most of them were eighteen or nineteen and already living on their own. They gave me contact names and phone numbers of agencies that could assist unwed teenage mothers who were attempting to make it on their own. I contacted one. They assigned me a social worker, Ava, who started by making sure I received the proper medical care and vitamins. Then, she started the process of helping me become emancipated from my mother. She called the house several times to talk to Mom, but each time when I answered the phone, I had to tell her that my mother wasn't there. But a few times, that wasn't true. I knew it was wrong to lie, but I also knew that if they would have talked to her, it would have ruined my plans to keep my child and to become emancipated from her. Ava wanted to know when the best time was to stop by to talk to my mother. I told her between ten a.m. and four p.m. Again, I knew those were the hours she worked. Even if they tried to show up between four and eight on most nights, she wasn't there. She went straight from work to the bars. They sent her mail about me asking her to contact the agency, and to appear in court if she wanted to object to me becoming emancipated. I tore it all up and threw it away at school.

"I continued to hide my pregnancy from my mother. Ava took me to another agency that helped teenage mothers. I filled out all the necessary paper work, and was placed on a waiting list to live in a home for teenaged mothers. I had to agree to rent a room for me and my baby. There was on-site day care in the home, which allowed young mothers the opportunity to go to school and work. All residents were assigned a schedule to cook, clean, or do yard work. I signed more papers agreeing to the terms and conditions of the house. While I was on the waiting list, I still had not been emancipated from my mother by a court. My ability to stay in that particular home rested on if I could get through the court process of being emancipated without my mother showing up at court.

"Well, the court date came, and I could hardly contain myself. Ava and I waited in the hallway of the courthouse for about an hour before they called my case. I felt like time was standing still. Finally, we made it inside of the courtroom for my case. I kept looking at the door wondering if my mother would put an end to everything. She never did. So, I became emancipated in late June. I was sixteen years old. I allowed Ava to drive me home to get my things during a time when I knew my mother wouldn't be there. Ava made me leave my mother a note. I basically told her that I was leaving her house. I explained that I was receiving a lot of professional help, and for her not to worry about me. I let her know that I was going to continue school and get my diploma, and, that I was going to get a job. I told her that I loved her, and that when I was ready, I would contact her. Ava left her card and court documents showing that I had been emancipated. But as we were pulling out of the driveway, I pretended like I'd left something I needed in the house. I ran back in and removed all the papers off the kitchen table. I folded them up and placed them in the elastic waistband of my pants. I didn't want my mother to have the court order overturned. My hope was that by the time she found out the truth about everything, I would be at least eighteen.

"Ava took me to the home for teenage mothers, and because my status on the waiting list was dependent upon my ability to become emancipated, they got me into a room that day. I continued to go to school, got a job, and did everything required of me to stay there. Ava and some of the other ladies who worked at the home took me to my doctor's visits. I had my baby in September of that year. I named him Chad, like his dad. I wanted to contact Chad when I had the baby, but I was afraid of what would happen to my baby if Chad's mother or my mother found out. So, as much as I missed Chad and wanted to share the moment of us having a child together, I chose self-preservation. I valued protection for me and my son above all else.

"I have no words to convey how happy I was that the abortion failed, and I just wasn't willing to risk Chad's mother trying to harm my baby. I loved big Chad with a love I didn't even know existed. But there's just something about the love of a mother for her child. It superseded any love I had ever had for another adult. So . . ." I clasped my hands. "I chose my baby.

"I chose to forget about Chad. I felt like he allowed his mother to dictate his life. Don't get me wrong, I didn't blame him. I had personally experienced his mother, and she was scary. I knew he didn't stand a chance against her. None of us did. I accepted that . . . and chose to move forward in life. Once I turned eighteen, Ava helped me to get my own apartment. I graduated that year. I still had a job. I enrolled in the community college. I had my own little car. I met a lot of great people and friends by living at that house for unwed teen mothers. I had a wonderful support system for my baby boy. I moved forty minutes away, to Danville, because it was just far enough that I knew my mother would not go to the places I needed to go to, like grocery stores and gas stations. But it was still close enough that I could get to work, school, and day care for Chad. Places she would never go. I was in a really good state of mind that year.

"It was toward the end of that year, on Christmas day, that I finally chose to stop by to see my mother. When I knocked on the door of the house, some man I'd never seen opened it. I apologized and turned around to leave. He came running after me and told me that I must be Abby. He said he was my mother's boyfriend. And that my mother would be very happy to see me. As he led the way, I followed him inside. He told me to make myself and the baby comfortable while he went to get my mother. I was sitting on the couch taking Chad's snowsuit off him when my mother came into the living room and saw me.

"She ran up to me with the biggest smile, knelt on the floor in front of me and started hugging and kissing me all over my face. She cupped my cheeks in her hands and studied my face, then hugged me and proclaimed how happy she was to see me. She kept hugging me up until Little Chad started crying. I picked him up. My mother, frowning and scratching her head, watched me and Chad. Finally, she asked who this baby was. I told her that he was my son, Chad. She asked me how that could be. I came right out and told her that the abortion had failed. She picked Chad up in her arms and examined him like he was an alien. Now, I don't believe I ever saw my mother so spooked in all her life. She apologized profusely. She asked me to forgive her. She tried to explain why she'd 'had to do it.' I had already made peace with the whole situation. In spite of everything that had occurred, I had my baby. That was more than enough reason for me to forgive her.

"My mother's boyfriend helped her cook a small Christmas dinner. They asked me to stay, and I did. After dinner we sat and talked for a while. Then I was ready to go. Before I could make it to my coat, my mother asked how I felt about what had happened to big Chad. I told her that I didn't understand what she was asking me. She went into her room and brought out a box of newspaper clippings. One year earlier, around Thanksgiving, Chad was returning home from college. He hit a patch of ice, lost control of the car, and died in a car accident. I sat there on that couch, looking through newspaper articles. And for the first time, I began to grieve the loss of the only man I had ever loved, and my child's father. I was overwhelmed with emotions: shock, grief, regret, unbelief, you name it, and I'm sure I felt it."

I could feel the tears welling in my eyes, but this time, none fell.

"I suddenly understood why he'd never tried to find me. I left my mother's house very broken that night. I cried all the way home. I had a newfound anger against my mother and Chad's mother. I felt like they'd taken him from me. I could not believe it. I did not want to accept that he was dead.

"But I had to accept it. Eventually. I continued on with my life. I became an Illini and got my bachelor's degree. Chad grew up, and he was just like his dad in so many ways. He was a very smart child. He actually started reading at age two! He made straight *A*s in school.

"Now here's what's interesting. When Chad was about seven years old, we were in the shopping mall at one of the department stores. I was shopping in the women's clothing section, and Chad was bored beyond measure." I laughed at the memory.

"He was running, hiding in between clothes, knocking clothes off the racks, and begging to leave. You know how kids do." I looked the officers in their eyes.

"I couldn't find him at one point, so, I started calling his name. I saw him dash from a rack of dresses and run smack-dab into a lady. He almost made her fall, and left her doubled over. I grabbed him by his little arm, knelt so that I was eye level with him, and reprimanded him on the spot. When I stood to apologize to the woman, I was shocked to see who it was! Big Chad's mother, Mrs. Evans. She looked flushed in the face, like she'd seen a ghost. She recognized me right away, and called me by name."

I walked over to my window and peered out at the people in the parking lot. "She asked me why my son's name was Chad. Before I could stop it, she grabbed my baby's face. Looking down into his big brown eyes, she started shaking and hyperventilating. I thought she was having a seizure. With her other hand, she gripped him by one arm, and I tried to pull him away from her by his free arm. There we were in the store performing a tug-of-war on my baby. She finally caught her breath, and repeated like five times, 'This is my grandchild.' I finally pried her fingers off his arm, and positioned him behind me. She started telling me she was sorry for what had happened, and that my son was a splitting image of her son. And even though she didn't know how it was possible, she knew without a doubt that my baby was Chad's son. She hurled all kinds of questions at me, then begged me to answer her. I never answered her a word. I positioned Chad in front of me, put those clothes back on a rack, and left in a hurry. She followed behind me the whole time. Apologizing. Asking questions. Making demands. She followed me out of the store and into the parking lot still asking questions and screaming how if he was her grandson, she had rights to him. My baby asked me who that strange woman was. I told him that she was nobody."

I sat back down.

"I still don't know how I made it home. Everything around me was a fuzzy haze. I don't know if I ran red lights. My son was talking to me, and I didn't hear a word he said. All I could think about was how interesting life can be. Mrs. Evans did everything in her power to take my son from me. She bribed my mother. Tried to intimidate me. Probably did intimidate Chad. She manipulated circumstances to the point of me laying on a table to have an abortion. Then, there's this man you all have named the Chameleon who interferes with the abortion. I secretly go off and have my son. But, her son, who she tried to save from me, leaves me alone, goes off to an Ivy League school like she planned, and on his way home from school, he dies in a car accident. She did everything in her power to take my son.

"What's most interesting, officers, is that my son remained a straight *A* student throughout school. He was the valedictorian of his class. He got a perfect score on the standardized tests for college. He was smarter than his dad, but not nearly as good in sports as him. He was accepted to three Ivy League schools. When he turned eighteen, I told him the truth about everything. I do mean everything, from the abortion, to his dad, to his dad's mother, to my mother, everything. I explained to him that if he wanted to develop a relationship with his dad's side of the family that would be up to him, and I would not be angry or hurt. He did visit Chad's mother. She still lived in the same house. Chad's father had passed away by then. Chad had been her only child, and my child, the one she almost had aborted, became her only living offspring. My son still talks to his grandmother. I don't get involved in their relationship."

I picked up a picture that was sitting on my desk, and turned it around to face the officers. "This here is a picture of my son Chad, his wife, and their three children. He got several degrees all in the science field. Today, he is a medical scientist who studies diseases. He got his degrees from Yale. He's a really bright young man."

"Abby, how do you feel about the Chameleon?" Officer Hughes asked.

Their hour was up five minutes ago. I looked at my cell phone.

"Oh, that's easy. He's my hero. Whoever this criminal is, he interfered with my baby almost being aborted. He changed my life. I don't know who he is or what this man's motives were, but he changed my life for the better."

"So, I guess that means you wouldn't be willing to testify against him in a court of law if he were brought to justice?"

"What would I say, Officer Reese? That he stopped an abortion that I was forced into? I mean, I could say that, but I don't know how that would help with what you are trying to accomplish. The Chameleon saved my son's life. Yes, I eventually married and had two other children." I removed a picture of my two other children and husband from one of the bookcases and handed it to Officer Reese. "But Chad is my special child."

Officer Reese passed it to his partner.

"He's the child that forced me to grow up and strive to be better. I learned perseverance as a result of having Chad. Because of what I went through at such a young age with my son, there is not too much in life that has been able to shake me up. That whole ordeal made me stronger. I don't know what my life would be like if the Chameleon had not committed that crime. I don't know if I want to know."

"Abby . . ." Officer Hughes stood. "Thank you very much for taking the time to answer our questions."

He handed me back the photograph, and shook my hand.

Officer Reese did the same. "Have a nice day, ma'am."

I led them out of my office and pointed them to the elevator.

8

TWICE A PREGNANT TEEN

PAUL

Jeff and I spent the next several days going over the reports we'd typed up for the four victims we had interviewed. We ran out of space on the whiteboard, and had to bring in a flip chart to write on. The one trend we noticed so far: every victim was grateful for what the Chameleon had done. No one had any memory of him doing anything physically inappropriate. But most of the women had been sedated in some way. Our final victim interview was looming days away. I called Tom into the room and asked him to set up a few more interviews with a doctor and a nurse. Maybe they could shed some light on the Chameleon from a medical perspective that the victims would never be able to offer.

The next victim on the list to interview was Tamika Jackson. We were meeting her at a gym located in a rougher part of the city, but tucked away on a couple acres of private land. I had heard plenty about it from some locals at another gym where I lifted weights. According to those who were so impressed, the gym we were heading to was not a typical workout facility. This was a one-of-a-kind, custom-made gym and everything was top-of-the-line: a boxing ring, swimming pool, indoor and outdoor track, football field, indoor and outdoor basketball courts, tennis courts, a baseball diamond, and all types of workout equipment inside.

Once we arrived, we observed the outdoor equipment, courts, and fields.

"This place stands out like a sore thumb in this neighborhood. Check out the turf on that football field."

Jeff said what I was thinking. "Better yet, look at those courts. Those basketball courts look brand spanking new."

"I wonder who owns this place. I would love to know the story behind why they put it here," Jeff said.

I parked the patrol car in the large parking lot across the street from the gym, and we walked into the building through the front entrance. The inside of the facility was just as nice as the outside. We approached the counter and were greeted by two African-American teenage receptionists.

"Good afternoon, officers. How may we assist you?" one of the young ladies asked.

"A lady by the name of Ms. Tamika Jackson is expecting us. Do you know her?" I asked.

"Ms. Jackson. Oh, yes sir. Her office is right there." She pointed her finger toward a door down the hall. "I'll call her now, and let her know you're here." She picked up the phone and pressed a single button. "There's no answer. Ms. Jackson must have stepped out of her office for a moment. I'll go look for her inside the gym."

"We want to take a look at the gym while you get Ms. Jackson," I said, unable to contain my curiosity.

"Okay, follow me," she said.

Inside the gym, she walked off as we stood near the front watching everyone. The gym was full of African-American men of all ages. The sound of activity filled the room. Some young men boxed in the ring. Older men coached and yelled at them. Others practiced kickboxing on punching bags. There was a pick-up game of basketball going on. When we looked up at the upper level, there were about twenty-five African-American teenagers running on the track. There was a weight room off to the right of the gym that was enclosed in glass. It was full.

"I didn't know this place existed. Did you?" Jeff asked.

"Yeah. It's all I hear about at the gym over off Mattis Avenue."

"You know what? Now that I think about it, a couple of the kids at one of the high schools I presented at mentioned that they spent a lot of time here."

While we talked and took everything in, a man about forty years of age approached us. He wore a gray and black sweat suit that had "Better You Gym" neatly stitched on it in lime green, and the name "Ty" stitched on the other side.

"Good afternoon, officers." He extended his hand. "Can I assist you all in some way today?"

"No, sir," Jeff quickly but politely replied. "We're just waiting to speak with someone. And one of the nice receptionists is looking for her now."

As Jeff was speaking, a woman in a pink and gray sweat suit, in her mid- to late fifties, with short black hair and of a medium build, approached.

INTERVIEW #5

TAMIKA JACKSON

As the officers talked with Ty, I walked up and touched him on the back. "I see you gentlemen have met my son Tyrone. I'm Tamika Jackson. And I bet you're Officer Reese." I made my way around Tyrone and stood in front of Officer Reese.

"Yes, ma'am, I am." He extended his hand to me.

"So, that means you're Of-fi-cer . . ."

"Hughes. Officer Jeff Hughes."

We shook hands.

"It's nice to meet you both. I guess we should get started then."

"Ty, son, they're here to see me about something. I'm going to be in my office with them for . . . How long do you think the interview will last?" I looked to Officer Reese for a response.

"About one hour," he answered.

"Should I be concerned?" Ty looked me in the eyes and awaited my reply."

"Oh no."

"It's nothing like that."

"Not at all."

We all answered simultaneously.

"Well, okay then. I'll let you all be." Ty nodded at the policemen and then walked away.

As I stuck the key into my office door, I directed the officers to each grab a chair from the lobby. In my small office, they placed their chairs in front of my desk. A few gray file cabinets with locks, a wooden desk, and an office chair was all the furniture that could fit comfortably without feeling cramped.

"So, is the Chameleon still on the loose or what?" No sense in beating around the bush.

"Yes, ma'am, he is. That's why we're here. We hope to bring him to justice once and for all, and something you say today could help us make that a reality," Officer Hughes said.

"Ms. Jackson, what year did you have your attempted abortion?" Officer Reese asked.

"That was April, 1974."

"Were you forced into having an abortion?" asked Officer Reese.

"No. Wanting an abortion was 100 percent my choice."

"I hope you don't mind our asking, but we need to know why. Can you explain the circumstances that led you to seek an abortion?"

"I had my first child when I was fourteen. At fifteen, I was pregnant with my second child. I knew that wasn't something I could handle."

"What made matters worse was who I was pregnant by. Both my first and second child were conceived with a big shot drug dealer back then. I was drawn to him because he was a leader in the hood I grew up in. That sounds silly to me now, but that was alluring then. Whatever he told people to do, they did. He was charming. Had a lot of money, along with a whole lot of nice things. You have to understand, my family didn't have much of anything. But it wasn't so bad because all our extended family and neighbors had about as much as we did. So, to see a black man around our neighborhood driving a shiny clean Mercedes was very attractive to me.

"One day I was walking home from school, and he pulled up next to me. He told me I was the most beautiful woman he had ever seen. I was already star struck with the man, so he didn't have to say much to win me over. We exchanged phone numbers, and within a week he was picking me up at my house. I lived with my mother and three siblings. My father left when I was six. I'm the oldest. My mother heard from the neighbors that King Mike, that's what everybody called him, was picking me up. But he was giving me money, and I helped her pay the bills, so she never said anything, except to be careful. Two months after meeting him, I became pregnant with our first child.

"When I started looking big and pregnant, he stopped picking me up or coming around. One day, I saw him driving another girl around in his car. When I was about eight months pregnant, I confronted him about it at the gas station. Super emotional. Big and broke. I saw him when he pulled up to the gas station and went inside, but he didn't see me. I stopped at his car first and talked to the girl in the passenger seat. I just asked her what her name was, and how old she was. I told her that he would do to her just like he was doing to me if she became pregnant with his child.

"When he saw me talking to her, he ran out of the gas station and started yelling at me. We argued. I said something he didn't like, so he slapped me and then pushed me to the ground. Then, he sped off like a madman. Two weeks later I had our first child, Gregory. He stopped by the hospital to see the baby. I lost all my pregnancy weight, and he started coming around me again—picking me up, buying clothes and things for the baby. Things were good between us again, so I eventually moved in with him.

"He had a nice, big house. Still in the hood, but nice. There was a lot of traffic in and out of his house all the time. Day and night. Every night was a party. People were smoking, drinking, and getting high. When I complained to him that the excessive, constant noise was too much for our newborn son, he'd hit me and tell me I was ungrateful. The abuse lasted for about four months when I finally decided that I'd had enough. So, I moved back home. I was only fourteen at the time. Sometimes I can't believe how much life I lived in such a short amount of time." It was like having an out-of-body experience remembering the hard times I had been through.

"So, that was your first pregnancy? Did you attempt an abortion then?" Officer Reese asked.

"Yes and no. Yes, it was my first pregnancy. No, I did not attempt an abortion then. King Mike was not the type of person you walked away from. Oh no. He could walk away from you anytime he pleased, but you had better not walk away from him. I was back in school by then, my freshman year of high school. A neighbor who used to watch me and my siblings when we were little, watched my baby while I attended school during the day. One day, King Mike decided to go pick our son up from the neighbor without telling me anything about it. So, when I went to pick Gregory up after school, and she told me his father had him, I was a combination of furious and scared.

"He wasn't that interested in our son. In fact, by then, I learned that he had children all over the place. I called him and asked him what he was doing. He said if I wanted to see our son again I had to come back and live with him. So, I moved back in with him. I wasn't happy about how he forced me back into an environment I didn't want any part of. Living with him the second time was a nightmare. It seemed like every night he was bringing home a different woman. It got to the point that I didn't want him to touch any part of my body. Anytime I rejected him, he physically and emotionally abused me. I had black eyes, swollen lips, bruised ribs, and welts all over my body pretty much every day. When Gregory was seven months old, I discovered that I was pregnant with our second child.

"I had no pleasant feelings toward King Mike, and the only thing I wanted was out of that relationship. I had no intention of bringing another one of his children into the world. My feelings of hatred toward him intensified with all those pregnancy hormones. I started challenging him in ways that he had never been challenged before. I became reckless, and just as crazy as him. One time, I initiated a fight between us and hit him with a high heel shoe. He retaliated and hit me so hard he thought he killed me. He had one of his girlfriends and another close guy friend of his to drop me off at the emergency room. He dropped Gregory off at my mother's and told her that I was no longer welcome at his house. I had a concussion and had to stay in the hospital for a week. They confirmed that I was pregnant with my second child. I was fifteen. A child having her second child. Lord have mercy!"

I had to shake my own head at the absurdity of what I had just confessed. The expressions on the officers' faces remained neutral the whole time I was talking.

"They made me stay at the hospital to monitor the health of the baby. King Mike's friends had told the hospital staff that I fell down a flight of stairs and hit my head on the floor. I didn't tell them any different.

"When I got out of the hospital, I knew I was going to do whatever was necessary to abort the baby. I located an abortion clinic, found out how much it would cost, then I dropped out of school and started babysitting the neighborhood kids myself. But the abortion was five hundred dollars. I knew that at the rate I was saving money, it would be more than three years before I would have enough money. Gregory needed diapers. Formula. We had bills. Had to eat. In four months, I was able to save forty-five dollars. Then something would come up and I'd have to spend everything I'd saved. I didn't want to, but I started calling King Mike telling him I need things for Gregory. He wouldn't take my calls, so I started tracking down his girlfriends. I started giving them notes that were open for them to read. The notes were asking him for money for diapers and formula.

"Any girl I had ever seen him with, I would give her a note to give to King Mike. They were prewritten. I kept several in my purse."

I had to laugh out loud at my own crazy self.

"He got so frustrated with me that he gave me a stack of hundred-dollar bills that totaled fifteen hundred dollars, and told me to never contact him again. So, when I was twenty-three weeks pregnant, I went into the Woman Health Needs Clinic with five hundred dollars cash and asked for an abortion. I was already starting to show, and they thought I was too far along to have an abortion. But the doctor agreed that I could have it after I told them that if they wouldn't do it, I would just go somewhere else. The doctor explained the procedure to me. He had to place something called laminaria sticks into my cervix the day before the actual abortion. That was to dilate my cervix. The next day, he was going to inject a saline solution into my uterus with a large needle to make me have contractions. The doctor explained that the saline solution would kill the baby while it was still inside of me. Then, my body would have contractions, and that would cause me to pass the dead fetus.

"I didn't care how it was done, I just wanted it to be over with. So, I laid on the table and let the doctor place the laminaria sticks in me. At the end of that first day, the nurse told me that I had to bring someone with me the next day to help me get home so, the next day, I brought my thirteen-year-old little brother with me and made him stay in the waiting room the whole time. He had no idea what I was there for. I told him it was because I was still having headaches from the concussion, and they were going to give me some medicine that would make me drowsy.

"On the surgical table, the doctor told me that it would be best if he used anesthesia on me during the procedure because it could be painful. When I saw how long the needle was that he was planning to use on me, I agreed. They placed a mask over my nose and mouth, I started counting, and then I woke up in a completely different room. While a nurse was helping me get dressed, the doctor came into the recovery room and told me that the procedure had been successful. I thanked him, and he left."

"Ms. Jackson, was the doctor you saw on the first day the same doctor you saw on the second day?" Officer Reese asked.

"Yes, he was. I would not have allowed a new doctor that I didn't trust to touch me. You have to understand. I was young, yes, but I was nobody's fool. I knew of too many girls who had died because of faulty abortions done by people who were not actual doctors at all. I did not want to die, so I did my research. I went to the same doctor that most white girls went to when they had their abortions.

"In my neighborhood back then, most black girls my age were still going into the back of somebody's uncle's store. Or, some man or woman claiming to be a medical professional would show up at your house or in your friend's kitchen and do the abortion there. Many times, you didn't even know their names. I heard too many horror stories. Too many girls. I knew a couple of girls who died from those back-alley-type abortions because they were cheaper. And this was in 1974, so abortions were legal. But most black people couldn't come up with five hundred dollars to have an abortion at a clinic. I know I paid more than the average cost at the time—way more. I expected everything to go just like they said it would. The nurse gave me the recovery papers. It said to expect some bleeding, cramping, and soreness. The nurse suggested that I should stay in bed for a day or two and to see how I felt after that. If I felt okay, then I could get up and move around. I felt great the moment I got home.

I was still a little drowsy from the anesthesia, and ended up sleeping it off."

"When did you discover you were still pregnant?" Officer Reese asked.

"When I was about seven months along. My stomach got bigger and I was waddling all over the place just like I did when I was pregnant with Gregory.

"The month before I knew I was still pregnant, my mother made me angry when she told me that she was disappointed that I was only fifteen and was going to be a single mother of two children. We got into a heated argument over that. I tried to convince her that I was not pregnant. She told me that as a mother of four, she knew when someone was pregnant, and that I was pregnant. Big and pregnant. So, when I was seven months, I went back to the abortion clinic, and clowned. I was livid, and they were 'bout to learn why. When I first walked in, the nurse greeted me. But I had no time for small talk. I told her to give me back my five hundred dollars. She looked at my belly in disbelief. There were other people in the waiting area, so she quickly escorted me to an empty room, said to wait there while she got the doctor. She came back with the doctor and he was more confused than me. He asked the nurse who I was. She started reminding him about me, and the procedure. He claimed that he had never seen me before. Had never laid eyes on me. He denied that he'd ever performed an abortion on me.

"His nurse pulled my chart and handed it to him. The chart was missing the medical details of the abortion, but it had information regarding the first day I was there. There were notes written in the doctor's handwriting. The doctor swore that he had never done the abortion.

Me and the nurse started talking and blasting him at the same time, telling him he had. He got mad. Red-hot mad. And stopped us both. He said he was certain he had not performed the abortion because no black teenager had ever been able to afford his services. The nurse and I looked at one another and started again, trying to convince him. He just got angrier. He told me to leave before he called the police on me. The nurse pulled him out into the hallway and talked to him for about a minute. She came back in very apologetic.

"The nurse even got a little teary eyed, and said that if he called the police, they would believe a medical doctor over me. She took ten dollars out of her own pocket and handed it to me. She said she knew it was not much, but maybe I could use it to get back and forth to a doctor for some prenatal care. The last thing she said to me was that I shouldn't attempt to have another abortion this late in my pregnancy because it could kill me.

"I walked out of there so angry. I had been robbed and cheated by a lying doctor. I wanted to harm somebody, but the kindness of the nurse helped to calm me down a little. She wished me all the best and escorted me out of the clinic through the back door. The clinic had my money, and I was still pregnant. I left and went straight to the police station. I filed a report that day. Nothing ever came of it. No one ever followed up with me until almost five years after my initial report. That was the first time I ever heard about the Chameleon. When they called, I thought they were just trying to make a mockery of me, so I told the cop not to ever contact me again unless someone had my five hundred dollars waiting for me. I hung up on him."

"Did anyone ever follow-up with you after that?"

"Oh, yes. The FBI, the CIA, and local cops were all at my house almost every day for a week after that call. That's how I knew the Chameleon was real. Or, I figured there must be something to him. I must have told this same story more than twenty times since that initial callback."

"What can you personally tell us about the Chameleon?"

"Well, if the first doctor I met at the clinic was the Chameleon, then he is a genius in what he does. Physically, he looked exactly like the doctor I confronted when I discovered I was still pregnant. Their voices were exactly the same. The only difference is when I first encountered the doctor, or the person y'all call the Chameleon, for my procedures, he was nice. He made me feel comfortable. When I confronted who I thought was the same doctor when I wanted my money back, he was rude and obnoxious about the fact that he had never seen me before. I just thought he was a crook. But five years after I filed my report against that clinic, I was told by a local officer that he was one of many abortion doctors across the state that this had happened to. That's when I believed it was possible. Since then, it seems like every several years, a new batch of officers needs to interview me about this Chameleon."

"So, what are your views about the Chameleon now?" Officer Reese asked.

"I don't really know what to think of him now. But, once I learned that the Chameleon was a real person, I hated him."

"Why is that?" Officer Reese sat a little straighter.

"Because I still had to deal with the reality of being a young mother struggling with two children. It was very hard raising two baby boys when I was still a minor myself. King Mike eventually was shot and killed by a fourteen-year-old girl's father. He beat that poor girl something awful, just like he did me. And, well, her father put an end to it. By the time I gave birth to my second son, Tyrone, King Mike was already dead. As Tyrone grew up, I couldn't understand for the longest time how a child who'd never met his biological father could turn out just like him.

"Tyrone was a bad child. Yes, he was my son, but he was bad. He got into fights from the time he could grab. He was fighting his big brother before he could walk, and was getting the best of him too. He got put out of kindergarten more than any other child in the history of the school. He was a really smart kid, but he was just so misbehaved. He fought girls, he fought boys; he sometimes fought them at the same time."

I rested my chin in my hand and my elbow on the desk.

"The boy fought the teachers, cafeteria workers, janitors, substitute teachers, principals, school nurses, and social workers. He even fought the police who came to the school to scare him. My son was a terror.

"When he was about thirteen years old, he really got out of hand. One day he got mad at me for turning off the TV and telling him to wash the dishes instead. We got into a shouting match, then he hit me. The next thing I knew, Gregory was pulling me off him, telling me I was killing him. I said some really hateful things to my son that day."

I stammered. I wasn't fond of this part of my story. "I told him that I never wanted him in the first place. I confessed to my son that I tried to abort him. Said the devil made it fail. I could see the hurt in his eyes. In his soul. I pretty much lost all control of him after that. He spent nights at friends' houses without telling me. He was absent from school a lot. Even had to fill out a missing person report on him so I wouldn't go to jail because he wasn't in school on a regular basis. He got hooked up with some of King Mike's old running buddies. They gave Tyrone a job selling drugs! Next thing I knew, it was like looking at King Mike all over again. Tyrone, at the age of fourteen, was driving nice cars, wearing gold chains, and had gotten an apartment with two older drug dealers. People were telling me that he was going to be bigger than King Mike, because he was smarter. Then, I heard that he had gone to a juvenile detention center for beating up one of his girlfriends.

"He was my son, but I didn't want nothin' to do with him. I had no respect for any boy or man that put his hands on women. Even if he was my son. It wasn't long before he got out of the juvenile detention center for that incident, but he went back something like twenty more times. It all caught up with him when he was seventeen. He got caught with drugs, a pistol, and no license. They tried him as an adult. He was found guilty, but the judge had mercy on him and sentenced him to only one year in jail.

"Then. There were some folks who had a prison ministry. They drove two hours once a week to minister to the inmates. There was this one older gentleman, a black man, who was a former kingpin. He'd given his life over to God. My son tells me that man is the biggest reason he turned his life around."

"How so?"

"You know what, Officer Reese . . . I'm going to go get my son and let him tell you how so. I'll be right back."

I had to squeeze past the officers before I could get out the door. Leaving it open, I went looking in the gym for Tyrone.

After a whole lot of walking and asking, I found him. We headed back.

"Is everything okay, Officer Reese?" I wasn't sure why he was standing in the hallway and why his partner was missing.

"Oh, yes, ma'am. I'm just waiting on Officer Hughes, who's down there buying us something to drink."

I nodded. "On our walk back over here, I filled Tyrone in on the reason for y'all's visit today. This isn't the first time Tyrone's heard about the Chameleon either. The first time was a couple years ago when two other officers investigated.

"I've shared everything I know about the Chameleon and my attempted abortion with my son. We have no secrets when it comes to that. So, go ahead and ask him what you were about to ask me." I sat back in my chair and relaxed while observing the officers interact with my son.

"Tyrone, I understand from your mother here that you were a bit of a terror in your earlier years. And you spent some time in jail. But your mother tells us that an older gentleman who used to visit you in jail helped you turn your life around. Can you tell us about your experience?" Officer Reese asked.

"I will be happy to. I was really an out-of-control kid. Bad . . . if you let my mother tell it." He winked at me.

"I was angry that my father was killed before I was born. Children said a lot of mean things about me, my brother, my dead father, and my mother. I didn't go back and forth with them with words. I had too much anger for that. I chose to hit them in their mouths or wherever.

"I'm certain my mother told you that I got into selling drugs as a teenager. By the time I was seventeen, I sold all kinds of street drugs, carried pistols, juggled women, and made a ton of money. I had seen too much life and done too many things that I am not proud of today to have been so young. To make a long story short, as you two are all too aware, that lifestyle landed me in jail. The judge was merciful. He only gave me a one-year sentence followed by a year of probation.

"On lockdown, an older black man named Bernie, along with seven other men, came to the jail to teach Bible studies. The first week I was there, I just wanted to get out of my cell for an extra hour, so I went to hear what they had to say. Of all the men who spoke, I most related to what Bernie had to say. He was this old cat who had a past that represented what I was trying to become before I ended up in jail. He talked about all the money he made slinging dope. How all the money in the world meant nothing without Christ. Stuff he said didn't make sense in my head, but it resonated in my heart. He taught on the love of Christ. How this Man loved His enemies enough to die for them. How Christ died for people who hated Him. How he took a beating for the same people who mocked Him something awful. I'd never heard of that kind of love, let alone experienced it. After that, for the next week, I couldn't get the things I'd heard him speak about outta my mind. I didn't show it, but I was excited to hear what Bernie and this ministry had to say the next week.

"The second week, after they finished speaking, Bernie came up to me and said, 'Young man, I know you cannot see it now, but God has a plan for your life that only you can fulfill,' then he turned and walked away.

"So, for the next week, that's all I thought about. I started living for those once-a-week, one-hour sessions. When the sessions ended, I stayed a few minutes over and talked to Bernie. He gave me scriptures to read and study. I asked questions about why he changed, how he changed, and the Bible. He got approval and started visiting me one-on-one twice a month to mentor me. That man poured so much into me. He was the first and only example of a man that I admired to the degree that I wanted to be like him. He led me to a relationship with Jesus Christ. Right there. In that jail.

"I had plenty of time to read the Bible. He helped me to grow spiritually. He challenged me mentally. He taught me how to use the good in me to bring out the good in others. He showed me how I had leadership abilities that came naturally, but out in those streets, I used them for evil. He explained to me that God had given me my leadership abilities, but God wanted me to use them for good. For God's glory, and not for my own selfish gain. That sure was an eye-opener for me. Bernie encouraged me to get my education. Everything he told me to do, I did. I got my GED in jail. He encouraged me to take some junior college courses in jail. I started, but then it was time for me to be released.

"He told me that he knew with absolute certainty that if I went back to hanging around the same people I was with before I went to jail, I would be back in jail within the year. I trusted him, because he understood human behavior like no one I'd ever met. He invited me to stay on a farm! Can you believe that?"

Tyrone flashed his million-dollar smile.

"He and some men at his church put together their money and purchased a farm not too far from here in Mattoon. Are y'all familiar with Mattoon?"

"Yeah. 'Bout an hour south."

"Yes. Bernie had helped me get registered and attend Lakeland Community College there in Mattoon. He helped pay for half of my education, but it was on the condition that I work and pay for the other half. I took him up on his offer. I got my associate's degree. After that, I was accepted into to Eastern Illinois University, in Charleston, about twenty minutes from Mattoon. With financial aid, scholarships, a part-time job, and small loans, I graduated with a bachelor's degree in Business Administration. I was on a roll, so why stop, right? I pressed on and got a master's degree in Divinity from Moody Bible Institute.

"I stayed with Bernie the first two years after I got out of jail, and he poured the Word of God into me. He, and the other men who formed that prison ministry, became like fathers to me. I went from having no father in my life for the first seventeen years to having eight fathers from age eighteen onward. The way they kept God before me, the ways they challenged me and held me account-able when I messed up . . . completely changed my life. Bernie saw me graduate with my Masters of Divinity at the age of twenty-four. He pushed me every step of the way, encouraged me when things got difficult. Working two jobs while in graduate school full time taught me perseverance.

"That Bernie wrote me a long letter for my graduation. I still have it. Pull it out from time to time and read it. In it, he basically told me that I had a duty to give back to the community I came from. Told me the same way he had been changed, and gave back to me, that I had a responsibility to do the same thing for other young black boys and men needing direction. Two weeks after my graduation, Bernie died. He was seventy years old. He was not my biological father, but he was the father God gave to me to fill in that gap. I only had Bernie for seven years, but the wisdom and insight he poured into me, I will never forget."

I heard Tyrone sniffle prior to quickly changing the subject.

"I worked as an accountant and a bookkeeper at some local businesses. I also prepared taxes during tax season and made some good money. I lived way beneath my means and saved my money because I had a vision. I wanted to create a community center that could help young and old black boys and men to become better. I wanted to have a place where they could discover their God-given gifts and abilities. But I couldn't leave out the spiritual aspect. I needed them to have access to the One who changed my life, and that was God through Christ Jesus. I wanted to offer what helped me.

"So, I opened this gym. There are classrooms both upstairs and on this main level. We have Bible studies. We have tutoring sessions. We have GED and college preparatory classes here. There are coaches who come from all around the state, and even some from out of the state, who offer free clinics for all our sports.

"When I see young men on the streets who look like they're on the verge of getting into trouble, I invite them over here. We don't tolerate disrespect of any kind—no profanity, drug usage, drug selling, alcohol use, or negativity. We tell people to come here if they want to become a "Better You"; hence, the name of the gym. We've had a few young men who have come up through some of the training camps and clinics here who have since become professionals in their sports. We have three who are now professional baseball players, four play football professionally, two who are professional basketball players, and one who is about to have his first professional boxing match in two weeks.

"We have hundreds of young black men who have come through here who have gone off to college, and that's since I opened the doors of this gym in January 2003. My only request of everyone who passes through here is that they commit to becoming a "Better You" in every area of life, and that they give back to other black men, young and old. So, a lot of our funding comes from young men who have come through here, but now have careers of their own.

"While we have great supporters, we also have some who don't like how I do what I do. I've had some people to come through here really offended by all my "Jesus talk." They tell me that 'it don't take all that.' I always tell them maybe it don't take all that for them, but I was a mess before 'all of that.'"

I couldn't hold my outburst of laughter.

"Yeah, officers. Some people look at my son today and think because he's so polished and professional, that he's never been in a fight in his life. Folks have no idea what they're sayin' when they try to tell someone what it does or does not take."

"She's right. I would probably be dead, just like my biological father, if I had not surrendered my life to Christ Jesus back in that jail cell when I was seventeen years old.

"Officers, I can't speak on behalf of anybody else. I don't know their story. But I know mine. I can say that change did not occur in my life until I surrendered completely to Christ, and learned of His ways and expectations of me through His word. The Bible. Now, I live to do His work right here in my community at this here gym. Now my children have a father, and my wife has a husband that she can be proud of. That's my life in a nutshell."

Tyrone stood up. Before he left, he asked the officers, "If you ever catch the Chameleon, do you think I could meet him?"

"Now, why would you want to do that?" Officer Reese bit his bottom lip.

"I kinda want to meet the man who saved my life. That's all."

Also standing, Officer Reese said, "I'm sure you could visit him in prison if you desire."

Tyrone extended his hand to the officers, one at a time. "It has been a pleasure meeting you both, but I've got to get back to the duties of the gym."

Officer Hughes joined them and the three of them stepped into the hallway. Tyrone removed his chair to make more space, then the two officers came back into my office and sat down.

"Ms. Jackson, is there anything else about the Chameleon you want to add?" Officer Reese asked.

"If you ever catch him, I guess I'd want you to ask him, why me? Why did he do that to me personally?"

"Jeff, did you have anything you wanted to add?" Officer Reese asked.

"No."

Both officers stood, and I followed their cue.

"Ms. Jackson, thank you for your time today." Officer Reese extended his hand. "If you think of anything else, here is my business card."

Officer Hughes shook my hand. "Have a great day, ma'am."

"Same to you."

9

SUSPICIONS CONTINUE

PAUL

I returned from lunch and made my way to Interrogation Room 5. Officer Johnson, the only other black officer on the force, was pacing with his arms crossed. "Don't even think about locking me in this room like you did Rodriguez, brotha."

"Or else what, brotha?"

"Or else you will see *what.*"

"Are you threatening me?"

"Are you paranoid?"

I left the door open. Not because I was afraid of Officer Johnson, but because the chief's words rang loud in my ear. He'd worked too hard to build this force, and he wasn't tolerating any conflict or strife. So, I humbled myself—this time—and walked over to the camera on the tripod and pressed the record button.

I adjusted the camera. "State your name for the record."

"Officer Ronald Johnson."

I pulled a chair up close to him and sat. Our knees almost touched.

"Why are you partnering with the Chameleon?" I asked.

"Why are you on this case? You're going about it all wrong because you're blind. And to top matters off, you're completely wasting your time. But, most importantly, you are completely wasting *my* time."

"Why are you evading the question, Officer Johnson?"

"Officer Reese, I am *not* evading the question. It's just a really *dumb* question. I tell you what. If you answer my next question, I will then answer the next question you ask me after that. Deal?"

"Okay. I'll play your childish little game. Shoot."

"What will it take for you to get off this case?"

"That's a great question, Officer Johnson. I vow that I will *not* get off this case until the Chameleon has been captured once and for all, tried, convicted, and is behind bars. And once every crooked cop who has assisted him shares the same fate. That's when I will get off this case, and not a moment before."

"Careful now, Reese. Your mouth shouldn't go around here making vows that all the fellow officers who have ever worked this case know that you can't deliver on. You won't capture the Chameleon once and for all. I guarantee it!"

"I've answered your question, now you need to answer mine."

"What's the question?"

"Have you ever assisted the Chameleon in any way for any reason?"

"No, I have not."

"Has the Chameleon ever given you any money?"

"No, he has not."

"How did the Chameleon escape from you?"

"I honestly have no idea."

Lies! I hit the table with my fists. "What do you mean you have no idea? You had the man in this holding room. The door was locked from the inside. You captured him. Then, he escaped. How? How did it happen?"

"When you capture him, I guess *you* can ask him how he did it. But one thing I do know for sure, you have forgotten who it is that you're talking to. So, I will remind you only one time. I am an officer of the law." Officer Johnson stood up and leaned over me. I could feel the heat from his breath on my forehead. "And you better not insult me like I'm some common criminal ever again."

The chair he'd been in flew under the table. "And I don't lie." He walked out the door.

I spread my hands on the table and took a deep breath. A moment later, Jeff entered the room. He'd been observing from behind the two-way mirror.

"I understand where you're coming from. I do. Bizarre that no one will fess up to the truth about how he escaped from here. Just a word of caution. You're a grown man, and you can do what you like, but you're making enemies for yourself."

"I'm not trying to make enemies, I'm just doing my job. Trying to get to the truth. What's wrong with that? Why won't anyone tell me how the Chameleon escaped from this interrogation room while in custody? They're all hiding something. I have studied every other possibility. I have the architectural designs of this room. It locks down like Fort Knox. The only way for him to get out of here. Is. With. Help. From the inside." My heart raced.

"I have thirty minutes before I meet with Officer Prince. I'm wondering if I should delay it."

"Might as well get yourself calmed down, and handle it."

I rubbed my temples with my thumb and index finger. "You're right."

I did the only thing I could think of to get control of myself; I dropped to the floor. *One, two, three . . .* My arms burned. *Breathe. Forty-eight. Breathe. Forty-nine.* "Ahhhhhh!" *Breathe.* "Fifty!" I collapsed onto the carpet and caught my breath.

Minutes later, I sat with a bottle of water, ready to conclude my internal investigation by interviewing one of my biggest nemeses. Again, I looked over the report that Officer Prince had written up five years earlier.

Memories returned like a flood breaking over a river-bank. The evasion, mind games, and aggression displayed by all the other officers had me ready to do battle with Officer Prince. The last time we'd met face-to-face was when we'd had an argument in the breakroom. Jeff asked me to pull back a little. It wouldn't be easy, but it was wise advice.

I closed my eyes and visualized my approach. It was like watching a movie. One moment, I smiled and spoke gently. The next moment, I was firm. Direct. No nonsense.

Eyes still closed, I suddenly heard, "Reese! Still causing trouble. Can't leave well enough alone." My heart leapt in my chest, but I was glad I hadn't visibly startled.

"Prince of corruption. Welcome to the beginning of the end for you. Please, have a seat." I smiled and walked over to the camera, pressing the record button before sitting.

"Listen, let's get something straight here, Reesie. If you didn't go around accusing people of things that you have no knowledge of, we would all make life much easier for you. But since you insist on making the rest of us who've already worked this case look bad, then you're only making things harder on yourself."

"What's with all the threats?"

"No one's threatening you. I'm only stating the facts."

"How did the Chameleon escape after you arrested him?"

"It's truly a mystery."

"Where were you when the Chameleon escaped?"

"Here at the station."

"Was the Chameleon in this room here?"

"Yes."

"Was he handcuffed?"

"No."

"Why not? Especially if you knew he had a history of escaping."

"Because this room has no windows. And, well, you already know about the door."

"Where's the tape of your interrogation of the Chameleon?"

"You're the current officer on the case. You should know."

"The tape was not in evidence."

"Well, I don't know what to tell you."

"How much did he give you to assist him?"

"Who? What?"

"How much money did the Chameleon pay you to help him escape your custody?"

"Man, you're crazy. And for the record, I have *never* taken any money as a bribe from anyone, and never will. I'm done with your charades." Officer Prince stood up.

I stood nose-to-nose with Officer Prince. "I'm going to find the most pleasure in seeing you get locked up for being corrupt, because you're just so cocky about it."

Officer Prince pushed me in the chest and I hit the wall hard. Like a raging bull, I charged at him. Officer Prince's legs went up and over the chair as it somersaulted through the air, cascading into pieces upon touching the floor. He bounced up like a ball, and looked like a hurricane coming at me. We cleaned the already spotless floor with our uniforms as we squirmed about. I could only see darkness as my head was tucked under his arm. Our combined grunts weren't enough to cause either of us to stop landing single-handed punches to the other's side. Jeff buzzed his way into the room and performed his best imitation of a crowbar, to no avail. Yelling for help, he and three other officers succeeded in doing what Jeff could not do solo. Within minutes, the chief was in the room. Everyone except Officer Prince and I were dismissed.

The three of us were sitting at the table, Prince with his arms crossed looking at the floor through a swelling eye and me breathing heavy, heart racing, with a throbbing lip. We each told our accounts of what had just happened. Looking at the glass, the chief asked Jeff if our encounter had been recorded. Jeff affirmed that it had. Chief informed us that based on what we both had shared with him, he was placing us both on a two-day suspension without pay. Minimum. He dismissed Officer Prince for the day, telling him to expect a phone call in a couple of hours, once he had reviewed the tape and determined if our suspension would be extended. He instructed me to stay put.

"Paul, apparently I need to pull you off this *Operation Almost* case? Is that what you want?"

Arms folded, standing against the wall, I was back in third grade, being scolded for a scuffle with Darrin . . . Darrin somebody.

"No, sir. I just lost my cool. It won't happen again."

"Every time someone takes on this case, it nearly tears this department apart."

I noticed a line of blood smeared across the back of my hand after running it across my bottom lip.

"Your suspension is effective immediately. If I get a single report from anyone that you blinked wrong, I'm taking you off it. Do you understand?"

"Yes, Chief. I understand."

"Follow me!" he barked.

In his office, Chief pushed a suspension form into my chest. "Sign this!"

I could hear myself swallow as I, with the stroke of the pen, flitted out two wavy lines.

"Now, get outta here, and get your head together!"

Jeff caught up with me on my way to the lockers.

"I heard what Chief said to you. Would you like for me to do anything while you're out?"

"Naw, man. If you think of anything, or run across any new leads, just follow up on them." Hands shaking, mind racing, heart thumping, I attempted to open my lock three times before it clicked.

"I'll keep things moving forward."

A two-day suspension turned into four total days off. Two without pay. Two prior arranged days off with pay.

10

SICKNESS

JENESIS

I gathered all the wadded-up tissue off the coach and table and stuffed them in my robe's pockets. I hadn't seen him pull into the driveway before I heard the garage door opening. *What time is it?* It would look too suspicious for all that tissue to be in the kitchen's trash bin. Since he was taking his time coming in the house, I had enough time to fix my smeared make-up and put on a brave face. When he still didn't surface, I opened the door and peeked in a dark garage. I flipped on the light switch and waved. His shoulder curved inward as he walked looking down. With a swollen lip, he looked worse than me.

"Why are you home so early? And what happened to your lip?"

"I got suspended. And Officer Prince."

He brushed past me.

"Suspended!" I followed him into the living room.

"Yeah. Just for two days. It's no big deal."

"No big deal! What happened? And please don't tell me it's that *Operation Almost* case again." I grabbed his face to examine his lip.

"Yep. That's exactly it." He pulled away, and flipped through some channels on TV, before setting the remote on the couch.

"I want you off the case, Paul!" I followed behind him and pressed the mute button. My heart racing.

"Not gonna happen. I'm vested now, and this just strengthens my resolve."

"But I told you if something like this happened I wanted you off the case. It's enough to have to worry about you out in those streets. Now—"

"Let's not talk about this. Let's—"

"Now I have to worry about you at work too." I felt overwhelmed.

"Let's talk about something else, Jenesis!"

"I told you I didn't need anything stressing me out. And you're . . . you're stressing me." I couldn't control the tears flowing. "On top of everything else . . . it's too much!"

I was scrambling for some tissues when he pulled me close, burying my face into his chest. He held me tight, his chin resting on my head.

"It's not like you to cry like this. What's really troubling my beautiful wife?"

I pulled from the embrace and sat on the coach. "Paul, the medicine to help me ovulate isn't working. The doctor thinks my condition is worse than they initially thought. Now they want to try some additional treatments."

My tears flowed like a steady stream, and he wiped them with his thumbs.

"I'm so sorry, Jen." Tears welled in his eyes too.

The next morning, I woke with my heart and my eye sockets aching. I peeled his arm from around me as I eased my feet onto the plush carpet. The bed squeaked as I stood. I ran cold water on my eyes to relieve the swelling and sinus pain that had begun to increase.

"Girl, you look a hot mess," I whispered to myself, not realizing Paul was hovering near our bathroom door.

Yawning, he staggered in. Eyes half open, Paul rubbed his fingers through my hair, then pulled me close for a hug.

"You coming back to bed, beautiful?"

"Yeah."

He flicked off the bathroom light and ushered me out. 5:53 a.m. illuminated my bedside table in green.

"Give me a moment. I need to text my secretary to let her know I won't be in to work today and tomorrow. I'm in no shape to think."

"Well, you're the manager and you haven't taken a whole sick day off at the university since you started working there. I'm sure your staff will survive Human Resource duties. Besides, we rarely get to spend a full twenty-four hours together. The last time was during our honeymoon. It'll be good for us. It'll be good for you. Rest your mind."

We slept awhile longer, then lounged around the house until noon. When Paul realized I wasn't moving from the couch as I watched one courtroom show after another, he made a breakfast consisting of most of the foods I was advised to avoid because of my condition. I couldn't even eat without being reminded that I couldn't have a baby. Now, a commercial for diapers. I ate the last bite of my pancake dripping in syrup, and washed it down with a glass of milk. I still had an omelet to conquer, but that would have to wait till later.

"I'm going to take a shower now."

"I'll clean up. Hey. Think you can hang out with me as I run a few errands today?"

"Sure. It'll do me some good to get out the house."

The April showers and gloomy skies didn't help my mood as we went to the bank, a couple hardware stores, and finally the grocery store before heading to his mother's.

As we pulled into the grocery store parking lot, Paul said, "Are you coming in or do you want to wait here?"

"I'll stay."

"Can you help me put together a list of food items you think will be easy for my momma to cook for herself?"

I dug and retrieved a pen. He handed me a mini black notepad. It hurt to think but I managed a few items that should last her three or four days. I looked up and spotted a woman struggling with a set of twin toddlers, shopping cart, and umbrella, in the rain. Warm tears filled my eyes again.

Paul handed me a mini package of tissue from the middle console. "Are you going to be okay?"

"I sure hope so." I handed him the notepad.

While Paul shopped, I connected my cell phone to the radio and allowed the worship music of William McDowell to minister to me. I mouthed the words of the song as I leaned my head back and closed my eyes. I must have drifted off because I awakened to Paul loading groceries into the trunk. I unplugged my worship music to ensure it wouldn't lead to an argument I had no energy for.

Ten minutes later we stood outside his mother's door, Paul's arms filled with grocery bags. Holding a single brown paper grocery bag with one arm, I held an oversized umbrella in the other hand.

We knocked. And knocked. The bags were getting wet and I struggled to keep the wind from turning me into a wet Mary Poppins.

A home health nurse jerked the door open, visibly sweating.

"Couldn't hear you over all the commotion. Come on in." She left us in the foyer as we created a puddle.

Suddenly we heard Paul's mom's voice from the living room. "I don't want it! I keep telling you! Why won't you listen?"

Like he'd been dispatched to a burglary, Paul darted to his mother. "What's going on here?"

The way the peas, mashed potatoes, and meat loaf covered the furniture, floor, and walls, you'd have thought a bunch of kids were having a food fight.

"She's doesn't like her microwave dinners, but she hasn't eaten all day."

"Momma. You've got to eat something."

"Ahhhh!" She covered her face with her arm and sunk into her recliner. "Please! Please, don't hit me! I'll be a better wife. I promise!"

No movement. No blinking. Just standing. Staring.

"Mr. Reese. Can I have a word with you in private? Ma'am, will you please stay with her, and holler if you need me."

Paul finally blinked and walked into the kitchen. I got as close as I could to them so I could overhear the conversation.

"Your mother is not well."

"I know that. It's why we hired you all."

"No, you don't understand. We were hired to help Deborah with her physical therapy related to her hip replacement, but her Alzheimer's is progressing rapidly."

I heard Paul sigh. "What does all of this mean?"

"It means that us home healthcare folks visiting her once a day for two hours is not enough. She needs someone with her around the clock. The way I see it, you have three options: a nursing home facility, pay for an around the clock home health provider, or move her into your home and hire a part-time home health provider to help you care for her. Depending on her insurance and Medicare status, you may still have to pay out-of-pocket."

There was a pause before Paul responded. "How much time do I have to decide?"

"Today. I have a responsibility to report that she isn't safe being left alone. Now, understand me. Deborah's mind comes and goes. She was speaking very sensibly a few minutes before you arrived. But the next moment, she had no clue who I was. Mr. Reese, your mother is a danger to herself. You need to make arrangements today. I'll give you the card of a social worker before I leave, and she can help you with the paper work and next steps. I'll see if she can come out to meet with you today. If not, you'll have to schedule it yourself. But your mother cannot be left alone, beginning right now. I have to report this while you're here. I'm going to run out to my car and get some forms for you to sign. I'll be right back."

Paul joined me in the living room where his mother was drinking a bottle of sweet tea and nibbling on a slice of lemon cake.

"Did you hear any of what she said?" he asked

"I heard everything. I'm so sorry, baby."

Paul sighed. "Is it okay with you if we move her in with us? I don't know what it's going to cost to have a home health nurse with her most of the time, but with our combined salaries, we should be able to pull this off. What do you think?"

"Well. Let's go ahead and get her moved in today. Then we can see what the social worker has to say and crunch some numbers."

"Let me be straightforward now. I do not, under any circumstances, want to put my mother in a nursing home. I'll get a second and third job to provide around the clock care for her, from our home, if I need to."

"Okay, Paul. I'm with you. With four bedrooms, our home is big enough. We can turn the office into a room for her so she doesn't have to fool with those stairs. I'm sure it'll all work out."

The next day, Friday, Paul got her bedroom furniture moved in and our office furniture move into one of the empty bedrooms upstairs. It's not like we were using it for the children I couldn't have. Helping Paul get his mother situated helped me to get my mind off my problems. At least for the day.

The next two days were Saturday and Sunday and, working at a university, I always had weekends off.

Paul spent his entire Saturday transitioning Deborah into our home, talking to her and caring for her needs. The only break he took was to meet with a social worker to become acquainted with the duties of the home health-care team.

Meanwhile, the new medicine they'd put me on had me feeling sick. I couldn't keep any food down, and the only comfort I could find was in bed. And boy, I needed comfort since the nurse I'd called less than an hour prior told me to discontinue the medication. They would have to consider another method to help me with my infertility issues. By dusk, I felt a little better and joined Paul and Deborah downstairs. They sat at the dining table eating and laughing.

"Jenesis!" Paul shot up. "We didn't leave you out. You were sleeping so peacefully, I didn't want to bother you. But I made you a plate, it's on the stove covered in aluminum foil. Have a seat and I can heat it for you."

He'd cooked meat loaf and mashed potatoes and gravy by way of his mother's instructions.

"Paul filled me in on some things," his mother said, seeming lucid. "And I'm real grateful that you would allow me to stay in your home, Jenesis. I wish there was some way I could repay you."

"You're welcome, Momma Reese! You just feel better and be comfortable. That'll be repayment enough."

We sat and visited while I ate my dinner. Awhile later, Paul asked me to keep an eye on his mother so he could install a video camera in her room, the kind new parents use for infants in a nursery. It was yet another reminder that hit me hard. This time, I choked back the tears.

The next morning, I felt better but was awakened by arguing and objects hitting the hardwood floors downstairs. The smell of biscuits and coffee filled the air.

Still in my robe, I ran downstairs to check out the commotion. Paul was standing in the kitchen and I could see someone in green scrubs in Deborah's bedroom.

"Headed to church?" Paul asked as I opened the fridge and pulled out a container of mixed fruit and cottage cheese.

"Naw. What's going on in there with your mother?"

"She's not allowing the nurse to help her get dressed this morning. She's a little out of it. Breaks me to see her going in and out like that. Why aren't you going to church? I don't recall you missing a Sunday since we've been married."

"I don't see the point in going. But I am about to head to the gym. Need to do my part and get these last five pounds off, especially with the pancakes and meat loaf we had yesterday."

I poured a cup of joe and headed up the stairs with my mug in one hand and fruit in the other.

11

DOCTORS AND NURSES INTERVIEWS

PAUL

Fresh off my suspension, I stopped by the chief's office.

"Chief, mind if I have a quick word with you?"

"Not at all, come on in, Officer Reese." It was one of the only times the chief actually stopped what he was doing to look me in the eyes.

"I just wanted to apologize for my behavior. I know I disappointed you. I'm sorry."

"Thanks for that, Paul. I'm glad you stopped by. I'm going to allow you to remain on the *Operation Almost* case under one condition. You and Jeff will investigate it on a reduced schedule. You two are back on field duty for half days. You may pick which half you'll investigate and submit it to me in writing."

"Yes, sir. May I ask how you came to your decision?"

"I saw that whiteboard. If it reflects your thoughts, it looks like a dog on steroids chasing its tail in a cluttered maze. Still, I can see that you genuinely care about this case, but you've become too attached. You need periodic breaks from it. Allow your mind to process some of what you've discovered. Get some fresh air. Besides, you're not a detective yet. We need you two back on the streets. At least part time, anyway. The other option was to pull you from it all together."

"Part time works."

"Paul, the day will come when you will understand your fellow officers are not your enemies. I had something to do with everyone here who was hired on as a police officer. And for you to go around here making accusations that several officers are crooked is an accusation that you better be ready to prove with hard evidence, and plenty of it. Otherwise, you make me look bad for selecting them."

Chief walked around and planted himself on top of the old, solid wooden desk. "Now, if you have hard evidence, I have no choice but to put my ego aside, listen to you, and take action. Until then, you need to get along with everyone on this force."

Arms folded, his blue eyes pierced through to my soul. As he approached me and gave a firm squeeze to my shoulder, I braced myself. "I reviewed the video of you and Officer Prince. You owe each other an apology. I'll tell you like I already told him, no one here is going to make either of you do it, but the first to apologize is the better officer. Good day, Officer Reese. I have a lot to accomplish today." He slid open a file cabinet that was in the corner, and thumbed through files.

At least one weight in my life had been lifted. I still had my job. I was still on this case. I took the stairs down to the conference room. On my way, I ran into Officer Mint, whom I also suspected of corruption.

"If it isn't the vigilante cop himself. Back from suspension already?" Officer Mint said.

"Have a great day, Mint." Still walking down the stairs, I never broke my stride.

Mint remained in the staircase, scratching his ten-strand comb-over. His jaw hanging open. I flung open the door and found Jeff seated, a sea of files before him.

"Hey there, partner." I plopped in a chair near him. "What are you looking at?"

"Welcome back, Paul!" He extended his fist for a pound. "This is testimony from some former local clinic employees. While you were out, the chief had me to interview some former abortion clinic employees who encountered the Chameleon. So far, all three of them have similar stories. They thought the Chameleon was the doctor until they found the doctor unconscious somewhere in a remote place in the building. Some doctors claimed that they had not come into work at all on the day the Chameleon saw the patient. Most of the local clinic workers on the list are no longer in the area, or don't have a working phone number. The ones I could reach still work at some of these clinics. There is one doctor who is retired, but lives here in town. If you're up for it, we have a nine a.m. interview with him."

"I'm definitely up for it." I was pleased to see Jeff had taken the lead and kept the momentum going on the case while I was gone.

"Here's a list of former and current clinic workers who may be able to give us interviews in the next few days to a week, if they're reachable. We should be able to get through this list before we leave for our interview with Dr. Peterson."

Only two people agreed to an interview under such short notice, a former nurse of Lafayette's Women's Clinic, and a former doctor of Begin Again Health Center. Jeff and I had learned the importance of clearing our schedules to interview the witnesses as quickly as possible before they changed their minds.

We secured an interview at noon with the former nurse, but couldn't schedule an interview with the former doctor for another two weeks. Even then, the doctor wouldn't commit to a date or time. We straightened the messy conference room and then left to meet Dr. Peterson.

We arrived at his very nice house and before we could reach the door bell, the doctor had opened the door.

"Come on in, gentlemen. We're going to have to make this quick. I don't like the idea of two uniformed police officers showing up at my house. My neighbors will start speculating. By the way, I'm Dr. Peterson, and you are?" A tall, thin man, he looked as if he could be a distant relative of Abraham Lincoln. His salt-and-pepper hair hung over his thin-framed glasses.

"I'm Officer Paul Reese." I extended my hand.

Jeff did same. "Officer Jeff Hughes."

"We can step right here into my office." His office was just to the right of the front door. It was a nice large room with bay windows that allowed a view of the front area of the house.

"Have a seat right there." He pointed to an old-fashioned burgundy leather sofa to the right of his desk. He pulled the big and tall executive chair from behind his desk and joined us in sitting.

"I'm not really big on small talk, so the sooner we can get this interview started, the sooner we can get it finished." As long as he didn't break the law, I didn't mind him being alpha male.

"Great." Jeff took the lead. "What can you tell us about your encounter with the Chameleon?"

"The first time I encountered the Chameleon was an ordinary day."

"You encountered the Chameleon more than once?" I made a note of this.

"Yes. I know for certain two times I encountered him face-to-face. I believe I also saw him several additional times because of the mere circumstances."

"Please describe to us your face-to-face encounters," Jeff asked.

"It was strange. The first time, I had just arrived at the clinic around seven thirty in the morning. I pulled into my reserved parking spot. I reached over to grab my belongings off the passenger seat, and suddenly, sitting in the passenger seat, out of nowhere, was . . . me. Or, I guess I should say, someone who looked exactly like me. My very next memory after that encounter was waking up in the car. I remember looking at the car clock. It was 2:18 p.m."

"How long ago did that happen," Jeff asked.

"It was April 4, 1999."

"Tell us about the second time you encountered the Chameleon," Jeff continued.

"It happened on November 18, 2003. I was at home preparing to go in to the clinic."

"When you say at home, do you mean this house here?" I asked.

"Yes, this house. I had just finished getting dressed for work. My wife was out of town on a business trip. I made a pot of coffee, and placed a couple pieces of bread in the toaster. I took a sip of my coffee, placed the cup on the counter, and went over to the coat closet and put on my coat. I was heading back to the kitchen, and there he was, standing in the middle of my living room. For a split second, I thought I was looking at myself in the mirror. A man my height, with my eyes, my nose, my mouth . . . my everything, was just standing there looking back at me. He had on the exact same clothes I was wearing, including the coat I had just put on. I remember opening my mouth to ask him a question. The next thing I remember was waking up on the couch. When I got up, it was 5:45 p.m. The clinic had been closed for more than an hour by then.

"I called my mother and asked her to confess. I interrogated her. Way worse than what you fellas are doing to me now. I asked her if I had a twin. Then, I asked her if I had been adopted and she just hadn't told me. When she said I was acting strange, I had her put my father on the phone. He came right out and told me I needed to see a shrink, because none of what I explained happened to me that day made any sense. He was convinced that I was hallucinating. After their responses, I didn't tell anyone about my encounter. That was, until several years ago when a couple of FBI agents stopped by my office and told me about the Chameleon. It was the first time that everything made sense, and I knew that I wasn't crazy."

"So, you said there were several other times that you believe you encountered the Chameleon, but you didn't see him? Can you tell us about that?" Jeff asked.

"The third time I believe I encountered the Chameleon was inside the clinic. I was preparing to do a procedure. I had just finished putting on my scrubs and scrubbing in when I heard the door to the scrub room open. The scrub nurse was responsible for putting on my mask, gloves, and the light we surgeons sometimes wear around our foreheads. I figured she was coming in to do what she did. Next thing I recall was waking up in the coat closet in my private office. The clinic was closed, and the lights were off. Everyone was gone. The place was clean. It looked like business had gone on as normal. Similar events happened many more times while I was there. There were a few occasions when the nurses and receptionists found me unconscious in closets, under my desk in my office, in the mop room, and in corners of rooms that were not in use. I thought I was blacking out, even went to see a neurosurgeon. They ran a series of tests and did an MRI on me, but found nothing wrong. Like I said, it wasn't until I got the visit from the FBI, and subsequent visits from police officers throughout the county about the Chameleon, that it all made sense to me. I was just happy to know that I wasn't crazy. But I was angry that someone had access to me like that. He could have done anything to me, and I couldn't stop him. The very thought of that nearly drove me crazy."

"So, tell us about his disguise. What did it look like?" I asked.

"Disguise, huh? That man looked exactly like me. I honestly thought I had a twin. There was nothing about him that looked suspicious. I literally, for a split second, thought I was looking in the mirror when I encountered the Chameleon standing in my living room. That's how much he looked identical to me. In fact, when the FBI visited me and started telling me about the Chameleon, I made them give me an official document stating that any crimes seemingly committed by me in the past, present, or future could very well be committed by the Chameleon before I would give them a statement. I understood that this man could ruin my life if he wanted to. But over the years, it seems to me that his only interest was in my profession. I know that for sure now."

"And how do you know that?" Jeff asked.

"I've been retired since 2007. Since I've retired, I've had no more incidents of waking up in remote places, confused about how I got there."

We asked a few more questions, then wrapped up the interview.

"Dr. Peterson, we know how valuable your time is. Thank you for granting some of it to us." Jeff and I shook his hand.

"You're welcome. Good day, gentleman."

We headed to the patrol car. While we walked, Jeff said, "That. That there was something." His eyes were wide.

"That Chameleon is something. I wonder if there's a group of people going around committing these crimes. Did you see how tall he was? It never occurred to me that it could be multiple people until I saw him. I'm glad we interviewed him. I'll have a height check done through the DMV. There can only be so many people who are six five. We'll catch 'em. One way. Or another.

It was time to interview the former nurse from a clinic on the other side of town. After handing out a few warning tickets, we headed over to the address on file for Mildred Owens. She lived in a gated apartment complex. We drove up to the bricked-in area where the gate attendant stuck his head out the window and asked, "Who are you here to see?"

"Mildred Owens in 1810 C," I replied.

"One moment, please." The attendant closed the window and picked up a phone. After a brief conversation, he reopened the sliding window. "Go straight until you reach the end of the street, then make a right, then make another right. Her building will be the second on the left."

"Thank you, sir." I waited for him to open the gate.

When we arrived, Mildred was standing in the door waiting for us. A heavy-set woman in her early forties with dark hair cut evenly at her shoulders, you could tell she took pride in her appearance. When she wasn't tugging at her jeans, pulling them up as if they were too big, she made her hands disappear inside her cashmere sweater like a turtle in a shell.

We stepped out of the car, introduced ourselves, and she invited us in. Her light-yellow living room and white furniture matched her cheerful disposition. Her home smelled of fresh baked cookies. We sat on her sofa.

May I offer either of you something to drink?" Mildred asked.

Jeff spoke up first. "No, thank you."

"Nothing for me either. But thanks for offering."

Mildred sat in a living room chair across from us.

"So, how may I assist you officers today?"

I flipped open my mini notebook. "We understand you used to work at Vine Health Center for Women. Is that correct?"

"Yes, it is." Mildred sat at an angle facing us. Sitting forward with good posture, her back never met the chair's.

"Why did you end your employment there?" I asked.

"It got to be too much for me."

"What do you mean?"

"In your profession, I'm sure you see a lot of things that ordinary people will never see. I think for someone in your profession, you either become desensitized to something like death, or it's just something you can never come to terms with no matter how often you see it. Abortion is death. And some of the things I saw as a nurse in that abortion clinic started affecting me both in my dreams, and in my waking hours. I was haunted by images of baby parts. I started having nightmares about the little dismembered arms and feet and fingers I had witnessed from procedures. It overwhelmed me. Other nurses I knew who worked for abortion clinics told me to hang in there, and it would pass, but it never did. It got worse for me. Then, when the stuff with the Chameleon started happening, I knew it was time for me to leave."

"What happened with the Chameleon?"

"I assumed that I was working with Dr. Andrews at the clinic, but some weird stuff started occurring. Dr. Andrews had a certain way about himself. He liked things a particular way, and rarely did he deviate from his preferences. You ever meet anyone who eats the same breakfast, the same way, on the same plate, with the same fork, everyday? Well, that's the type of person Dr. Andrews was. He liked the surgical room where he performed the abortions to be set up just so. If one surgical tool was out of place, he was not happy. And he would let you know on the spot. He wanted a nurse near him at all times during the abortion. And when I say near him, I mean like a front-row view. There were seven separate occasion when Dr. Andrews, or someone who looked exactly like Dr. Andrews, was behaving out of character." She paused as she seemed to recall in her mind specific events.

"How so?"

"He moved the surgical tool table way over to the side of the room where I could not visually see him perform the abortion. I had to walk the tools to him one by one; whereas, normally, I was so close to him, I simply handed the tool to him without ever taking a step."

"So, let me make sure I am understanding you correctly. The majority of the time, Dr. Andrews had you right next to him during the abortion procedure. The surgical tool table was near the patient, and you just handed the doctor whatever tool he needed from where you stood. But, on seven separate occasions, he moved the tool table a nice distance from the patient and you had to walk the tools to him from across the room. Is that correct?"

"That is correct. Something else that was out of the ordinary, with each of those seven occasions, was he had me leave the room to get an extra towel or something that in my mind was not necessary. What was even stranger was that when the procedure was finished, he said he would handle the disposal process of the fetus. Now, you must understand, Dr. Andrews never cleaned up. Not one time outside of those seven times."

"During a typical procedure was there ever any blood on the table, sheets, or other places?"

"Absolutely!"

"During the seven times you mentioned, was there any blood anywhere?"

"I could see a little blood, but I don't know how much because of where he had me standing, and since he was the one who cleaned up."

"Did he touch the patients inappropriately while you were in the room?"

"Officer Reese, I cannot answer that question because I don't know if he did or didn't. From where I stood, it didn't seem like it. But I couldn't see what he was doing."

"When did you resign? Or were you fired?"

"I resigned two years ago."

"Other than a change in behavior, did you notice anything else different about Dr. Andrews?"

She shook her head, and then paused for a moment. "I take that back. Once. I had just finished assisting Dr. Andrews with a procedure when I helped a patient get settled in the recovery room. I saw, with my own two eyes, Dr. Andrews, when he came out of the washroom where he showers. He was wearing a suit. It's not unusual for him to put on a suit, especially that late in the day. It was around four p.m. I went to my desk to enter in some notes regarding the patient's vital signs, and Dr. Andrews went into his office. For my rounds, I had to check on the patient every five minutes. During my rounds, I saw Dr. Andrews was wearing scrubs. When I asked him how he had changed so fast, he looked confused. But it was his response that threw me for a loop. He said, 'I've been wearing these scrubs since this morning. Do you have the patient prepped for surgery yet?' Officers, it was the end of the day, and he had already performed all the abortions for that day. I told him that he had already finished the procedures. He stood there in the hallway, hair going in every direction, looking disoriented. Then, he just turned and walked away. He went into his office and shut the door. I remember trying to figure out how in the world he had changed his clothes that fast. I could never figure it out. I guess I forgot about it until now."

"Do you know who the Chameleon is?" I asked.

"I do now. But I didn't know back then."

"How did you learn about the Chameleon?"

"I'm still a registered nurse. I just don't work at the abortion clinic anymore. I work in a hospital now. As you can imagine there are a lot of women working in hospitals, and sometimes we like to talk. Well, a nurse on the same floor I work on was the one to tell me about a lengthy investigation going on at abortion clinics about some former CIA agent going around faking the identity of abortion doctors, and fondling women. She and another nurse knew that I used to work at an abortion clinic, so they asked me if I had ever seen the Chameleon. I told them I didn't know. So, when you called me for this interview, I knew I had to share my experiences. Is what they told me right about the Chameleon?"

"Unfortunately, it is," I answered.

"That's sad. If I had known he was fondling women, I would not have allowed it. But if it was the Chameleon that I encountered, he looked just like the doctor. I mean, he looked *identical* to the doctor."

"Can you remember any other incidents that seemed out of the ordinary to you at the clinic or with the doctor or a patient?" I asked, not wanting to leave if Mildred had not shared everything she knew.

"No." She paused for a moment. "I've told you everything I can remember."

I reached over to retrieve one of Jeff's business cards. "Here's my card, and my partner's card. If you think of anything, please contact either one of us."

Working part time on the case, we spent the next couple weeks studying the information we'd gathered from interviews. We did some fact-checking. I contacted the CIA about the possibility of an operative adjusting their height. They agreed that it was possible to do so with special shoes, but only up to a point. An inch was doable. Two inches was stretching it. Three to five inches was most likely someone else. Six inches or more was definitely somebody else. Body suits to adjust size were not unusual either.

But it was rare, if not impossible, to go from being a naturally big person down to a thin one as a master-of-disguise operative in a short span of time. Prosthetics and heavy make-up were their way of changing facial features. Jeff and I studied some video to understand how it was done. We felt confident that we had more answers to our many questions.

But that still didn't fully answer my questions as to if there was more than one individual committing these crimes. I got special permission from the chief to patrol the streets near abortion clinics. I stopped inside every couple days just to ensure that all was well. I wanted to be nearby these clinics in case the Chameleon decided to strike again. Jeff had his school presentations, so occasionally I rode solo.

12

LOSING HOPE

JENESIS

When Paul came home, I was on the phone with a friend I'd known since seventh grade. Evenly spaced snoring sounds emerged from his mother's room. She'd worn herself out fighting the nurse and knocking medications across the room. I could assist neither. I'd used all my energy just getting out of bed and going to work every day. This wasn't my battle.

"You're not helping me by saying that, Teresa." I had the phone on speaker as I sat curled on the couch, dipping sliced celery into almond butter.

"All I said was it'll happen when you least expect it and to enjoy this time with your husband while you're child-free."

"You still don't get it! So far, none of the treatments have worked, and I am classified as infertile. As things currently stand, they're saying I cannot have children. So, how is it going to happen when I least expect it? Please help me to understand what the doctors don't know."

"I'm sorry. Maybe I shouldn't have said that. If it makes you feel better, you can have one of my four children. I'm overwhelmed over here."

She couldn't see the tears now gushing from my eyes, the lump the size of a cherry forming in my throat, or my own personal dark cloud looming over me courtesy of her insensitive comfort. *Rub it in my face, why don't you? You have four children and I have none.* I couldn't speak.

"Jen,"—Paul had been listening while rustling through the refrigerator for something to eat—"should I go pick up some dinner?"

My voice quivered. "If you'd like to eat, you should."

"Would you like me to pick up something for you too?"

"I'm not hungry." Though I had been before answering this phone call.

"Jen. Jen, are you there?" Not to be rude, I was covering the speaker with my thumb.

"Yeah, I'm here, but I need to go now."

"Okay. You know that I'm here for you, anytime, day or night, right?"

"Yup."

"Okay. I'll check on you soon. Bye!"

"Good-bye."

I let myself fall onto my side and pulled up my knees so I was in a fetal position, then buried my face in the couch cushion and started sobbing.

"Jen, what's wrong?"

I could hear Paul's heavy breathing outside of the fortress I'd created around myself. He sat near me in silence for a minute before he rubbed my arm.

"Can I see your eyes, please?"

I raised my head, looking him in his big brown eyes that were trying their best to peer into my soul. I went back into my fortress.

He rubbed my arm again. "I need you to talk to me, Jen. What about that conversation just set you off?"

Maybe he'll understand. So far, no one else seems to.

"I'm starting to hate people. I hate talking to them. I hate that I ever told anyone that I'm battling infertility. I hate the stupid things they say to me. They think they're being helpful, but they're hurting me more than I'm already hurting. I can't talk to anyone!"

"You can talk to me. Tell me what people are saying to you that's hurtful, so I'll never hurt you."

"Well, it's stuff like 'Stop stressin' and it'll happen.' Or 'You can always adopt.' Or 'You should try this herbal concoction.' And 'Stop trying so hard.' Oh, here's the best one of all, 'Just pray about it!' I'm really starting to hate people, Paul."

"I'm not trying to upset you with my next question, I'm just trying to understand you. What about each of those things upsets you?"

"I've stopped stressing many times. Made love to you after the most relaxing massages. For years now. Well, you know that. And nothing's happened. Don't they know that I know that I can adopt? But I want to carry my child in my own body. I want to know what it feels like to have a baby kick and move inside of me. I want a child to have my eyes or my quirky ways. I want to be able to breastfeed a baby that came out of my body. I want to see a little person who's a mixture of you and me. Adoption doesn't give me that. There's nothing wrong with adoption, it's just not what I've dreamed of my whole life like I have of carrying a baby in my own body, experiencing pregnancy and labor. I feel like a piece of me is missing. And that herbal concoction sh—"

"Jen, you don't talk like that!"

"What? I was about to say 'shenanigans.'"

"Oh. Well, what's wrong with prayer? You try to get me to pray about everything."

"Paul." I grabbed his hand. "I should've listen to you when you first told me to stop talking to you about prayer. I'm sorry I didn't, but I understand now! I won't be praying any more. Why? Nothing happens. I've prayed. I've fasted. I've cried. I don't even know that God is real anymore. I mean, what kind of God would do such a cruel thing to me?"

He stared at me like he was trying to look into my soul again.

"If there is a God, He sure isn't listening to me!"

Back and forth across the crown molding his eyes shifted. Only he appeared to be trying to see through the ceiling, as if he could peek into heaven, if there even was a heaven.

"I'm grabbing some Chinese food. Sure you don't want any?"

"I'm sure."

"I'll grab a large of everything I order, just in case you change your mind."

"Suit yourself."

"What did Momma eat?"

"Paul, I don't know. I wasn't here during her breakfast and lunch. When I got home at five thirty, she was battling with the nurse over some pills. She just fell asleep about an hour ago. Don't they have a chart or something with all her meals on it?"

"Yeah, I just thought I'd ask. No worries. I'll get enough food for her, too, in case she's hungry when she wakes up."

Days later, Paul asked to join me at my next doctor's appointment. I agreed and he met me there.

"Mr. Reese, it's a pleasure to meet you. I've heard a lot of nice things about you from your wife. I must say, you've picked the perfect appointment to join your wife," Dr. Creek said.

"Why is that?" Paul asked.

"Mrs. Reese, I'll be frank with you. We haven't had success with what we've tried up to this point. The next phase for treatment would be in vitro fertilization or IVF."

"What's that?"

"This is where you come in. We would need a semen sample from you to ensure that you're not experiencing infertility also. If we detect challenges, then we'll see if it's treatable and move from there. If the semen analysis is all clear, we move to the next phase of the IVF process. Mrs. Reese, you would have to inject yourself with hormones. These hormones would cause you to ovulate. We would retrieve a number of healthy eggs from you through a minor outpatient surgical procedure. Those eggs would be fertilized in our laboratory here with your husband's sperm. After a few days we would surgically place either one or two of those fertilized eggs, which would now be embryos, into your uterus. We then wait and hope that implantation occurs and becomes a viable pregnancy. I have some literature for you here that will explain the entire process in greater detail. Do either of you have any questions?"

"Yes. What does this cost?" I asked.

"Between twelve and seventeen thousand dollars."

"Wow! Does insurance cover it?"

"With all that has taken place recently with health care reform, unfortunately no it doesn't."

"I have a few questions," Paul asked as he embraced my hand. "What is the success rate? And what are the drawbacks of this procedure?"

"Let's see." Dr. Creek clicked the mouse, scrolling through pages on the computer screen. "Your wife is twenty-eight years old, and uh-huh, success rate, I would say is about 40 percent. And that's for just one round of IVF."

"What do you mean by one round?" I asked.

"That's the cost and success rate to go through the entire process including returning the embryo(s) to the uterus. A second round, if needed, may be slightly less expensive. It all depends on egg quality, sperm, and ultimately, your health Mrs. Reese."

"Well, we certainly don't have that kind of money just lying around. We just bought a four-bedroom home that came with a big mortgage attached. And my mother-in-law just moved in. We're paying a small portion of her medical expenses. If I'd known this a year ago, we could've stayed in our apartment and saved. Uhh! The timing is bad. We would have to save for it, and that could take us years."

"You don't want to wait too long. Research finds that your chances at success are greater if you have IVF before age thirty-five."

I chewed on my nails. *Yikes! Twelve to seventeen thousand? The cost for me to attempt to have a baby, with a 40 percent success rate. One round.*

"Do either of you have any more questions for me?"

"No."

"No."

"Okay. Then, Mr. Reese, should I have the receptionist set up an appointment with you to do a semen analysis? Just so that it's already done if you two should decide to proceed with IVF in the future."

I nodded at him.

"Ye-ah. Yes."

We headed to the receptionist desk.

"I need a really strong drink to help numb all this pain I'm feeling right now."

"Baby girl, you don't drink. And that's not a habit you want to pick up. Besides, it wouldn't help anything should we attempt IVF at a later date."

The darkest, loneliest, most depressed place would have been a welcomed vacation to where I was now. Though his mouth moved, I could hear nothing Paul said. The drive home and the remainder of the day were no different.

I couldn't sleep. Rolling out of the squeaky bed, I slapped on my house shoes and clunked my way down stairs.

I grabbed a half gallon of black walnut ice cream, a large spoon, and a stack of mail before heading to the couch and clicking on the television. I turned the volume down too low to hear what they said, but loud enough to know they were talking.

Fumbling through the mail, I came across it. A trigger. In the form of a cute, blue, five-by-seven envelope, with itty bitty feet making a path. My heart froze in time only to feel like it was bursting into flames when the contents of the envelope confirmed what I knew before I opened it. *She's not even married. All she ever talked about was partying. And her smartphone's call log would show a dozen calls made to 911 for domestic issues.* As far as I knew, she didn't even want kids, and now I'm being invited to her baby shower. My cousin was only twenty-two years old, and I envied—hated even—her big, round belly silhouette of an invitation. I couldn't escape my present darkness. No matter where I turned, everything was a reminder. I ached down through my soul to my toes and back up again.

I had to get the pain out somehow. "Whyyyyyyyyy! Ahhhhh! God? What have I ever done to You to deserve this?"

Balled up in a knot on the floor, I entered my fortress and attempted to hush myself. I could feel him touching. Attempting to pull me out of my knot. He lifted me onto the couch. I heard only mumbles. I refused to leave my fortress. The darkness I could expect here. Here was safer than the real world. The real world was torture. I wanted no part of it anymore.

"Jen! Jenesis! Jen, look at me!" He sounded like he was yelling down a tunnel.

Sleep. I'm just going to sleep.

The next morning I woke up on the couch. I overheard Paul talking to his mother, who was coherent.

"I don't know what to do, Momma. When I go in to work today, I'll ask Dr. Langley if she could recommend a therapist for her."

"Hear me, Paul. Your wife is suffering. The Bible speaks about barren women and the anguish they endured as a result of their condition. It's all-consuming when a woman's body betrays her. Pick up your Bible, son. Read about Hannah and Rachel, and you'll understand your wife a little better."

"But, Momma, she's talking about how she hates people and doesn't believe in God or prayer anymore. I've always struggled with whether God was real because of what He allowed our family to go through when I was growing up. But Jenesis was always well-grounded. Now, she's worse than me. It's scary."

"Pray for your wife, pray for her! You hear me?"

"How can I pray to a God I don't really know exists?"

"You say you don't know whether God exists based on how you saw me struggle? How we struggled? Yes, we struggled, but where's your memory of the rest of the story, Paul?"

"The rest of the story?"

"Yes. Or don't you remember me praying and crying out to God? When our food supply was low, and payday wasn't for another week, and all that money was already spent on rent and still not enough for utilities, all I had was prayer and God. I would pray and remind God of His own words in the Bible about how He cares for the little birds of the air, and if He cared for them, He would care for us, and how we should not worry about tomorrow, what we should eat or drink. I reminded Him that was in His Bible. I asked God over and over again to make good on His promises. And guess what, son? I want you to guess."

"I don't know. What?"

"He always made good. Sometimes while in the middle of praying, I would get a knock on the door. A neighbor. An old friend. Somebody would stop by and bring me food. Much like a couple months ago when you and your wife came to my house with all those good home-cooked meals packaged up real nice and ready to eat. I had just got finished praying to God that day, too, when y'all showed up. And the food came exactly how I prayed: hearty, healthy, and pre-made. Ha Ha!" She clapped her hands. "You can't tell me my God isn't real! I've had people at the church, who didn't know my business, tell me that God impressed upon their hearts to give me a certain amount of cash. And it would be the exact amount of cash I needed to keep the heat on or water from getting turned off when you boys were growing up. No, I couldn't give you boys everything you wanted, but I gave you two all the love I had. And God provided for us. Prayer works, Paul. I'm a living witness, and I wouldn't lie to you."

"Momma, if God exists, why would He allow you to get Alzheimer's—I don't know a person on this earth who has served God more faithfully than you. How can you keep loving a God who would do this to you?"

"Why would He allow His righteous Son to die on the cross for my sins? You're a man of the law. How many men do you know who are sending their sons, their innocent sons, to the penitentiary or death penalty for someone else's crimes? How many?"

"No one."

"Yet, the God I serve and will serve to the day I die sent His only begotten Son to die for me and my ohhhhh so many transgressions. I know you look at me, Paul, and think I'm perfect because I'm your mother. And I was a good mother to both my boys. But especially you. But I'm not perfect by a long shot. I did many a thing I'm not proud of. But Jesus died for it all and my sins are covered under the blood He shed on my behalf. God said just how distant the east is from the west, that's how he would remove my sins from me. He placed my horrible sins into the depths of the sea, and I heard someone say he won't allow no fishin' there either. The Bible is true when it says he who is forgiven much, loves much. I love God so much because He forgave me for so much more. Think of it this way. We are a three part being. We are a spirit, we have a soul, and we live in a body. It is with the spirit that we worship and serve God. My mind, which has been hit by this Alzheimer's, is part of my soul-realm. Mind, will, and emotion. My body may get sick, like how I had to have a hip replacement, but this old feeble body has to die one day any way. From dust I came and unto dust shall I return. My spirit will live on forever, though. Just know that the God who allowed me to breathe my first breath will be there with me when I breathe my last breath. Ohhh, the old folks used to say, 'You can't make me doubt Him, I know too much a'bout Him.' Listen to your mother. Get to know God for yourself, Paul. Open the Bible and read it for yourself. Then one day you'll be able to pray for your wife. She needs a husband who knows the Lord, son. You hear me?"

"Yes, ma'am. I hear you."

Grateful for weekends because I couldn't fathom having to go in to work in my state of mind today, I dozed off again as Paul and his mother continued talking.

13

BACK TO THE BEGINNING

CHAMELEON

I felt like I was powered by a locomotive. I nearly took down the doorframe: hinges, doors, and all, as I fled the Healthy Women's Clinic. Thunderous sounds reverberated when I plunged my way out the front doors. The tailored Italian suit I wore did nothing to slow me down. My legs floated over manicured bushes and flower beds as if they were nonexistent. I continued my frenzied dash through the parking lot, down the street, and into the newest subdivision just around the corner. Never out of breath.

Before I left the premises of the clinic, I observed her. Red in the face and with a clenched mouth, the head nurse ran behind me swirling a stethoscope. A series of threats and insults slipped through her lips like wet spaghetti noodles.

"Come back here, you old pervert! You fraud you! I have something for you. Come . . . back . . . here." The nurse of twenty years was a short, pudgy, fiery redhead who was already out of breath, just running from the clinic onto the lawn.

"Not in my clinic, you won't!" Her screaming was overtaken by coughing and gasps for air. Like someone in desperate need of an inhaler. She bent over and steadied herself, placing her hands on her knees.

A cute little blonde-haired nurse in her early twenties came outside and placed her arm around the still coughing and wheezing head nurse.

"I just called the police! You won't get away with this one!"

Her voice faded as I made my way down the street and into the upscale neighborhood. It didn't matter, Whisperer had picked up where I left off.

I watched from behind a house as he drove into the subdivision. He stopped and spoke with a lady watering her flowers. While speaking with her, I saw an opportunity not to remain in one place for too long. I made a run for it.

He must've caught a glimpse of me because he sped off and jumped out of his car.

I watched his every move as I hid behind one house after another. Always two to three steps ahead of him, I observed as he removed a Taser from his hip holster and crept between houses. A German shepherd, rushed inside the backdoor by its owner, crashed into a barbecue grill, causing it to break apart on the concrete slab. He checked it out probably thinking it was me.

His head hung low as he walked to his car, putting away his Taser. He resumed looking around the area once he made it to his vehicle.

Peering from the side of a house, I observed as another officer pulled alongside him. They exchanged words before the subdivision was swarming with cops.

I hid in a covered hot tub in a fenced-in backyard. I could hear branches cracking and dirt crunching nearby. Someone even tugged on the top of the hot tub, but with my grip, they would've had to destroy the whole thing to even peek inside.

I watched as squad cars pulled off in every direction.

"He could be hiding in someone's home or garage," I heard him tell his chief.

"He very well might be, Paul, but we can't search inside every home. You know that. Maybe next time, son." His chief walked away.

"If it's okay with you, I'm just going to drive through the neighborhood a few more times."

"If that's what you need to do, I won't interfere. All I ask is that you remember your training."

"You got it, Chief."

I watched and listen from a house away.

When he returned to his vehicle, I remained safely behind the homes and walked several blocks away. Residents of the homes gathered together in small groups in front yards, driveways, and sidewalks.

Officer Paul Reese observed the neighborhood from his car when two men approached him. They talked for a moment. I figured I'd give him an opportunity to see me. Finally see me. I joined a group of children, fresh off a school bus crossing the street. Next, I heard the roaring of an engine and the screeching of tires. He jumped from his car, leaving the door open, and charged like a raging bull at me. Knowing his momentum was propelling him forward, I charged toward him. His hand reached out to grab me, but only grazed my sleeve as he flew past me in the opposite direction. Determination filled his eyes. I figured I might as well have a little fun with him. He repositioned himself to pursue me again. I could hear the quick tapping of rubber soles to pavement behind me. So I ran—just a tad bit faster. But he wouldn't quit. I decided to create some distance between us. Just so he would have a memory of who he was dealing with when he looked back on this moment.

I needed him to apprehend me. There were some important details I wanted to share with him, I *needed* to share. I figured I'd make it easy on him when I saw the two men approaching from a short distance. I turned to look at him, still approaching but quite a distance behind me now. Here was my opportunity. He was still watching. Still approaching.

Smack. The laws of physics are real. The three of us landed on the ground.

Here he was. Flying through the air like a grasshopper. He landed on top of me.

Officer Paul Reese gasped for air. "You, sir. Are under arrest. You have the right to remain silent."

With a gleam in his eye, he recited the Miranda Rights to me. He handcuffed me with a smile on his face.

"Bob, do you think you can pull your buddy out of the street and onto the sidewalk so he won't get run over by a vehicle."

"Oh, yeah, yeah. I can do that."

"I can see he's breathing. Let me get this one into the car, then I'll call an ambulance for you two."

Officer Paul Reese's voice was too cheerful for my liking.

"Rose! Are you there?"

"Unit 2372. Go ahead."

"10-15 on the seventy-year-old suspect."

"Excellent work, officer. Bring him in."

"On my way."

I wouldn't bring him back to the reality of the situation until he purposely focused his attention on me. Then, through the rearview mirror, it happened. His eyes met mine.

"You know, if those two had not been in my path, you would have never caught me, right?"

As he ran after me, I incrementally increased the distance between us. He knew it. And he knew I knew it. An old man, with gray hair and wrinkles, had beat him. Would've continued to beat him too. I just wanted him to be reminded. To never forget.

"Who are you?"

"You have me handcuffed in the back of your squad car, and you don't know who I am? Let me out of this car!" I knew what he meant. But it wasn't the time for me to reveal much about who I was.

"I don't know your legal name, but you are known as Chameleon."

"I've been told."

"You've been told by whom?"

"By your kind. Officers of the law."

"So, tell me. Why would you knock out a doctor, assume his identity, and hurt his patients?" "I was just handling all those assigned to me."

"Who assigned them to you?"

"The better question is, why are you so interested in me, Mr. Officer Paul Reese, of 1223 Eagle Way Drive, Champaign, Illinois? On the police force for exactly one year, four months, one week, and three days. Husband for two years, nine months, three weeks, and five days to a very pretty wife named Jenesis Marie."

I really struck a nerve when I mentioned his wife. My head hit the side of the door when he jerked the car to the side of the road before jumping out. Fist drawn back and trembling. His mouth quivering. Sweat dripping everywhere. Veins popping out of his arms. He meant business.

"If you even so much as think about visiting my wife in her dreams, I will hunt you down and execute my own personalized justice on you."

"Now, now, Officer Reese, you're supposed to be the one who upholds the law. You see how easy it is to break it for a cause you believe in? You and I are similar." I kept my tone neutral and gentle. Wanted to make him think about what I was saying. Hear my words.

"I am nothing like you."

"You don't even know me."

"I know enough about you, to know that we're nothing alike. You're a career criminal who preys on innocent people in the worst ways."

"Officer Reese. Sir. You know nothing."

"Okay, well, tell me who you are and why you do what you do. And how in the world do you know where I live?"

"I will tell you who I am, and why I do what I do, but first, let's talk about the five cases that you and your partner chose to investigate that are related to me."

"What five cases?"

"Oh, you know exactly what five cases I'm talking about. But I'll explain since you want to play coy. There are 489 cases attributed to me, but only 425 of those cases are actually mine. I know this for sure because I put a special mark on all of mine."

"You're admitting to branding your victims!"

"Some may look at it as a type of branding, but that's not really what it is. It's just for identification purposes."

"Pathetic!"

People hear what they want to hear.

"Of those 489 cases, you and your partner, Officer Jeff Hughes," I looked at the clock, "who happens to be at the high school right now doing some community outreach, selected five local cases to build your investigation around. You two selected these cases because you wanted to sit down with the victims, look into their eyes, and see if you could better understand me through them. If I may be so bold, it's a great batch."

"I'll ask again, how do you know this information? Have you been snooping around the station? Wait! No. You've partnered with some of the officers, haven't you? There is no way you could know this classified information otherwise. Unless, of course, you have some eyes, ears, or wiretaps at the station. Many of my colleagues say you're former CIA. But you don't fit CIA."

I would eventually tell him all my secrets. But not now.

"Come on. How did you get into the station? Was it Johnson? Sergeant Stevens? No, wait. I'm willing to bet it was Officer Prince. The money you're stealing from these clinics, are you splitting it with them?"

"You and your partner selected five of my all-time favorites for your investigation. Let's see, you chose Maria."

"So, who did you previously work for? Your reputation as an expert master-of-disguise precedes you. I hear you're the best of the best. That's how you've evaded us or escaped capture all these years. Huh. How do you do it?"

I understood exactly what he was attempting. He was using all types of tactics to get me to open up and talk. Whateva he was servin', I wasn't havin'. "And then you have Nancy. You were able to find Tamika. Though she was an easy one to find. Now, Abbarane and Beatriz were a little more hesitant before you could get them to comply, but your perseverance in persuading them both really paid off for you, huh?"

"Do you understand that you have some serious charges brought against you? The severity of your crimes is no casual matter. You're looking at two life sentences just in this region alone. Similar crimes were reported in St. Louis, Chicago, and other nearby smaller communities. Been traveling a little, have you?"

"They're all my favorites, really. But Abbarane is definitely at the top of my list. God . . . it was God who told me to do it."

"Now, that's enough, old man! It's bad enough that you have favorite victims in the first place, but to blame God for your sick behavior is just too much. Take some personal responsibility!"

"But you haven't even heard what I have to say, and you're already passing judgment on me." I learned that sometimes you can tell the truth, but people still can't hear it.

"I've been investigating you for four months now, and one thing I know for sure. You're really twisted, old man."

"Every person I—uh—how do you all phrase it in your reports? Oh yes, violated. Every person that I 'violated' was done so with perfection."

"What kind of a sick pervert are you?"

"I helped them. Every one of them is better because of what I've done. The world would be a darker, emptier, more grief-stricken place had I not done all that I have for those people."

"I have, at one time or another, tracked every single person that I encountered at a clinic. I like to keep tabs on them. Especially my favorites." Truth is they're all my favorite. Some just left a greater impression.

"What is your problem?"

"Abby."

"Who is Abby?"

"Abbarane. I call her Abby for short."

"Abbarane is your problem?"

"No, she is *not* my problem. She is my favorite."

"Just be quiet, now. We'll get your statement down at the station."

"Oh, where was I?" I could tell I was irritating him. "Oh, yes . . ."

"Oh, no!" Rush hour traffic caused the speedometer to rest at fifteen miles per hour.

"Abby was only fifteen at the time."

"Sick. Just sick."

"Listen. Abby, even at just fifteen, was stunning to look at."

"You old geezer! Do you remember your right to remain silent? Why don't you do that! Preferably until we get to the station."

"Many a young men at her school was captivated by her beauty and personality. She was popular among all her peers—girls and boys alike. That's how she ended up as a sophomore snagging the attention of that handsome boyfriend and popular senior class president, seventeen-year-old, Chad Evans. They dated for several months."

"How do you know all of this?"

"Oh, Paul, they don't call me the Chameleon for nothing."

"You know what? It really doesn't matter how you know what you know. With all the charges against you, you will never see the light of day again. Right now, I'm just satisfied that I have done the impossible by capturing you once and for all."

"Have you captured me? Once and for all?"

14

CHAMELEON ON BEATRIZ AND SON

PAUL

We finally arrived at the station after enduring what seemed like the slowest commute in history.

I pushed the button on the dispatch device attached to my uniform. "Rose, I need some assistance with transporting the suspect into the station."

"I have two officers on their way out. Over," Rose replied.

My heart pounded as I waited in the car with the Chameleon. This was the most surreal thing I had ever experienced.

The Chameleon interrupted my thoughts. "You're going to learn a lot today, son."

"I sure hope so." I stepped out as the chief and another officer approached.

"Look at you, Paul. You've done it again. Let's get him inside and processed." The chief assisted me with getting the Chameleon out of the car. Both the chief and I walked on either side of the Chameleon while the other officer followed closely behind. The Chameleon remained silent throughout the transport.

Once inside, I asked the officer at the counter if I could do the fingerprinting. He agreed to let me do it the old way, but he would re-do it with the scanning machine. Afterward, I examined each print to ensure there were no smears or other problems. The chief, smiling proud, observed. We took several mug shots that showed up on the computer screen. I had the booking officer to print copies and place in a file.

Taking what might seem like over-the-top precautions, I asked the chief for assistance with transporting the Chameleon to the interrogation room. Once inside, I handcuffed him to the table. I, then, requested two officers stand at the door at all times in case of an attempted escape.

"Chief, I know I am making a lot of requests right now, but I don't want to leave the Chameleon alone for even a minute if I can help it." Standing between the interrogation room and the hallway, I said, "Would you please send someone up to my desk to bring my files on him? They're in a brown accordion folder locked in the bottom right desk drawer. Here's the key."

"Sure thing, Reese. I'll send someone up now."

I sat next to the Chameleon and could hardly believe that the moment I'd been waiting for had finally arrived. Only a blank notepad and an ink pen was on the table before me. I couldn't decide where to begin with the questioning. I took in a deep breath to still myself. The chief observed through the glass window of the interrogation room.

"Would you like something to drink?"

The Chameleon, looking calm and polite, answered, "No, thank you, Paul."

"What is your real name?" I said.

"I am not at liberty to say," the Chameleon answered.

"Why not?"

"I'm just not." The Chameleon looked at me and chills ran up my spine.

I shrugged them off and continued. "Have you been going around to abortion clinics impersonating doctors?"

"Yes, I have."

"Why?" I was intrigued by his frankness.

"Because the unborn babies were assigned to me. I already told you this in the car."

"Who assigned the unborn babies to you?"

"My boss."

"And who do you work for?"

"I told you this already, also," the Chameleon said with confidence. "God."

There was a buzz at the door. An officer handed me the accordion file. I took a moment to look through the files, arranging my thoughts. I pulled out a picture of a much younger Mrs. Beatriz Barros. I placed the picture on the table in front of the Chameleon.

"Do you know this lady?"

The Chameleon glanced at the picture and smiled. "Yes, that's Beatriz. Beatriz Barros. She resides at 1211 Winchester Place in this city. It's been years since I've seen Beatriz. But I know she's fine—now."

"When were you last in the presence of Beatriz Barros?"

The Chameleon did not hesitate. "It was March 19, 1996, at the Healthy Women's Health Center."

I shuffled through my notes on Mrs. Barros, and discovered that this was the exact date and location of her intended abortion.

"Do you take pleasure in harming women who are already going through a devastating set of circumstances? Why fondle them? Why make them believe they had an abortion when you're doing . . . God only knows what . . . to them? What kind of sick pervert are you?" I was allowing my emotions to get the best of me.

"Let's get one thing straight, Officer-Paul-Reese, before we continue. I will say this one time, and one time only, because I do not have a lot of time before I have to go—"

"Go?" I interrupted him and glanced at the transparent glass where I knew the chief would be standing. "Sir, you're not going anywhere." I hit my fist against the table and glared at him.

The Chameleon acted as if I'd said nothing. "I am *not* some sick pervert as you just called me. I have never fondled anyone. Please add *that* to your handwritten notes. But you are right about one thing: only God knows what I have done to those women who were faced with all types of devastating circumstances that led them to seek an abortion."

I regained my composure and asked, "So, what did you do to the women who paid to have abortions?"

"I stopped the abortions."

"But nurses and patients said you worked on them in some manner. What were you doing to them?"

"Oh, that. I did two things."

I leaned in.

I had to make it seem as if they were having an abortion, so they would not become suspicious. So, I made a few non-harmful, superficial wounds to retrieve and leave small traces of blood. Then, I placed the letter *A* on all those assigned to me."

"Why the letter *A*?"

"During the time when the doctor would normally be performing the abortion, I wasted time and created superficial wounds on the mother's body, used suction machines to ensure the procedure appeared legitimate, and very carefully placed the letter *A* on the babies assigned to me."

"But why the letter *A*? I don't understand."

"The letter *A* stands for *Almost*, as in *Almost Aborted*. I marked all the babies assigned to me. To this day, they all have an *A* somewhere on their bodies. Each and every one of them."

"So, you branded your victims?"

"Branded sounds so harsh. I saved them, and marked them in the process."

"But why? Why go into these clinics and stop abortions by pretending to be the doctor, and then pretending to perform the abortions? Did someone hire you to do this?"

"Every baby that I intercepted from an abortion had to be born. Each one had a purpose to fulfill in this world that could only be accomplished by them, no one else. Let's look at Beatriz here." The Chameleon picked up the same picture I had placed on the table before him moments earlier. He steadied the picture on the table in an upright position. "Sure. She and her husband Anthony already had seven children and felt like they couldn't provide for another one. Yes, they were struggling to feed the mouths they already had. And I understand they both agreed that the best thing to do for their entire family was to terminate this pregnancy. I was there both days when they came into the Healthy Women's Health Center. I intervened. I stopped the abortion."

"That was her choice to make, not yours!"

"Have you met her son? The one I saved from the abortion, Officer Reese?"

"No, I haven't." My curiosity grew.

"Her son's name is Victor Barros, but you may know him as Victor B."

"Victor Bee . . . Victor Bee . . . Why would I know him? Oh, Victor B! You're not talking about that teenager who's a famous pop singer, are you?"

"That's exactly who I'm referencing, Officer Reese. Victor B. is the Barros' eighth child. He was born with a gift to sing. He came out of the womb knowing his purpose was to sing. As a little kid, he was a driven, smart, and gifted singer. Did you know that he made his first million at the age of nine?"

I tore a piece of paper out of my notepad and jotted a note. "And you know this how?"

"I just know, Officer Reese." The Chameleon flashed a smile.

I folded the paper, and then folded it again. I raised it over my head and looked in the direction of the chief who said he would remain on the other side of the two-way mirror. I stood and walked toward the door. It buzzed and another officer took the note from me before the heavy door made a loud clanking sound as it closed.

"So, you just know, huh? Do you stalk your victims also?"

"My job was complete when I stopped the abortion. It's just exciting to see what the children who were almost aborted become in life. In Victor's case, the world would be duller because nations of people wouldn't experience his music, and uplifting music is something the world needs more of. And his best work hasn't even been created yet.

"When I stopped that abortion, Victor Barros became an answer to his parents' prayers. Beatriz and Anthony wanted to abort Victor because they were in very bad shape financially, and couldn't afford to support the children they already had. Once Victor made his first million at the age of nine, his parents never had to work another day in their lives. Even if we don't consider the money aspect, let's look at what would have happened had I never stopped Beatriz from having an abortion on that day.

"Do you know she would've ended up in a mental institution because of the overwhelming depression brought on by the guilt of the abortion? As a result, the family would have suffered more by not having a mother at home. If she had aborted Victor, the struggle for the Barros family would have been greater, and even more devastating, than before she became pregnant with him."

"And you expect me to believe that you know what the Barros' lives would have been like if Victor had never been born?"

"Officer Reese"—the Chameleon adjusted his chair before looking me directly in the eyes—"would the Barros family be wealthy today or still struggling to make ends meet if their eight child had been aborted?"

Before I could answer, there was a buzz at the door, and a uniformed officer stood in the doorway waiting for me to come to him. "This is a note from the chief," the officer whispered.

The note read:

Researched and confirmed as requested. It is true what the Chameleon said. Victor B. made his first million at the age of nine. He is also the sole financial support of his parents.

—Chief

I quickly folded the note, and placed it in the accordion folder.

The child they'd wanted to abort during a moment of weakness became the biggest blessing of their life.

15

CHAMELEON ON MARIA AND JOSHUA

PAUL

"How do you know all of this?"

"I'll tell you before I leave, Officer Reese."

"Leave? What's this mess 'before you leave'?" I leaned in and whispered to the Chameleon, "Are you working with someone here?"

The Chameleon leaned in and whispered back, "Yes. I am, Officer Reese."

My heart skipped a couple of beats. I swallowed hard and waited to hear the names of the officers who were assisting him.

"I'm working with you, Officer Reese."

I sighed. "Keep talking, and I'll make sure your pillows are extra soft in your cell for the next eighty-five years."

I reached into the accordion file and pulled out another picture along with my hand-written notes from the interview. I positioned the picture on the table in front of the Chameleon and placed Beatriz Barros' picture back into the accordion file.

"Do you recognize this woman?"

"Yes. I certainly do, Officer Reese."

"What's her name?"

"That's Maria Herrera."

"How do you know Maria?"

"She came into the clinic to have an abortion."

"When did you first meet Maria?"

"I met her for the first time when she came into the clinic in preparation for her abortion."

"When she laid on the table thinking she was going to have an abortion, what did you do to her?"

"The exact same thing I did to Beatriz Barros and every other woman with a progressed pregnancy. Instead of inserting laminaria sticks, I inserted something harmless that resembled laminaria into their cervix. Nurses and other staff members at these clinics usually explained to the patients what to expect during the procedure. I simply performed acts that made them believe what had been explained to them had been done. When they returned on day two to have the laminaria removed, that's when I created superficial wounds in the cervix area. These women were told to expect some bleeding and spotting after the abortion, so I had to make sure that is exactly what they experienced. I had to ensure that nothing I did would cause these women to realize that they were still pregnant before they reached either the stage of viability or seven months of pregnancy.

"Why seven months?"

"Because it's against the law to terminate a pregnancy at seven months, and there's no way a doctor could fudge the data, though that hasn't stopped some of them from trying. Also, more times than not, by the time a mother reaches her seventh month of pregnancy, in conjunction with whatever remorse or guilt she may have felt after believing she had successfully aborted, she is usually relieved to know that the abortion failed. So, there is little chance that a mother will attempt a second abortion for the same pregnancy once she makes it to the seventh month and learns that the baby survived."

"So, why did you stop Maria's abortion? She, of all the victims you violated, had a right to an abortion after what happened to her."

"What happened to Maria was horrible. Sickening really. I understand that. But had she successfully aborted her son, Joshua, Maria would be a different person from the woman you met. She would a bitter, hard-to-get-along with, mean-spirited woman. She would hate God, still. Because I stopped Joshua from being aborted, Maria's granddaughter is alive today. Maria Herrera has a better understanding of God's sovereignty.

"Joshua, well, his life path involved being adopted by a physician whose wife was unable to bear children. Because he was adopted by this doctor, he was naturally encouraged to pursue medicine. Just as God shaped his cells, created his skin, connected his bones, and joined them to his ligaments and muscles, He also ordained Joshua's life's purpose. All right there in his mother's womb. He had to be born. He was the answer to someone's prayer—to thousands of someone else's prayers about their premature babies. From my vantage point, it's interesting, Officer

Reese. People often say, if there is a loving God why won't He stop this bad thing or that bad thing from happening. At the same time people are so contradictory. They want to be able to do whatever they want to do, and whenever they want to do it. Everyone seems to have a different idea about what is considered good or bad. Moral or immoral. What should or should not be stopped. People don't have a clue about all the bad that God stops and they'll never know because . . . well, He stopped it. Even further, there are certain plans God had in motion to stop certain things from ever occurring. His plan was to use people to stop those catastrophic events from ever taking place. However, the people He planned on being born were aborted. Because they were aborted, a domino effect occurred and certain events that were not supposed to happen, happened anyway. Why? Because of human meddling in a divine plan."

The Chameleon cleared his throat. "Let's look at Joshua, for instance. Because Joshua was born, he has saved a total of twenty-five babies' lives through his unique ability to perform open heart surgery on the world's smallest and sickest infants. He was born with a special, rare gift. His hands and his mind. As a preemie heart surgeon, he will touch many lives by doing what some in the cardiac medical community consider impossible. He is the only person in the world who can do what he does, the way he does it, with such precision and the steadiest of hands. At this very moment, this world would have twenty-five fewer people in it if Joshua had been aborted. That includes his niece, Maria. By the time his work is finished and his purpose is fulfilled on this earth, he would have saved a total of 4,789 babies' lives. God purposed for Joshua to be born. Because God has a plan—a mission—an assignment for Joshua's life that Joshua, and only Joshua, can fulfill. Families across the world would be grief-stricken if that abortion had been successful, Officer Reese."

I felt like someone had laid a three-hundred-pound weight of top secret information on the upper half of my body. *Snap out of it man. Don't allow this psychopath to do a number on your mind. You're smarter than to fall for his sack of shenanigans.*

"How do you know all of this?"

"I'll tell you before I leave today."

I felt anger rise at the thought of the Chameleon taunting me about escaping. If it was not for the fact that the Chameleon had escaped every single time before, I would've otherwise not reacted. Instead, the Chameleon's words caused me to change my line of questioning.

"So, how do you plan on escaping from here today, Chameleon?"

"Oh, Officer Reese." He flashed his signature charming smiled. "I plan on walking right out the front door."

"And how will you do that?"

"I'm just going to do it."

"Will you have any help?"

"Yeah, but not really."

"What does that mean?"

"Let's just say my help will come from someone you don't really know yet."

"Who?"

"I'm not at liberty to say, Officer Reese."

"What time do you plan on leaving?"

The Chameleon paused briefly. "Now, why would I tell you the precise time, Officer Reese? Ha! No, sir."

As I was about to speak, the chief spoke to me through the intercom system.

"I'm sending some information in to you, Reese." The door buzzed open before the chief could finish speaking.

One of the officers who was guarding the door stepped inside to hand me a file. The file contained recent pictures and older newspaper clippings of the abortion doctor that the Chameleon was presently still impersonating. There was a note in the file from the chief that read:

We just retrieved these pictures of Dr. Forrest off the Internet. Officer Mint verified with Dr. Forrest that these are photographs of him. Mint just met with the doctor at his clinic. He gave Mint these extra newspaper clippings. As you can see, the Chameleon looks just like him. Also, based on the fingerprints you just obtained from the Chameleon, the fingerprint database is indicating that the fingerprints are a match for Dr. Roger Forrest. We're investigating further.

—Chief Lewis

I considered myself a mentally sharp young man, but this case was becoming more bizarre by the minute. I was developing a slight headache.

"How . . . do . . . you . . . do . . . it?" It was all I could think to say as I, one by one, laid all the pictures and newspaper clippings of Dr. Forrest in front of the Chameleon. Rather than reply, the Chameleon shook his head.

"Let me see your hand." I grabbed his right hand and meticulously examined it. In a move uncharacteristic of me, I scratched at the Chameleon's fingertips in hopes that I would peel a substance off. When nothing on his hand changed, I stood up. I'm not proud of what I did next. How else would I know? I attempted to take the Chameleon's face off. He had to be wearing a prosthetic mask. Or thick layers of make-up.

"Ouch!" With his free hand, the Chameleon pushed me. It caused me to fall into my chair and slide clear across the room, past the long table, and to the door.

I stood and repositioned the chair at the table. I hit the table with my fist, causing the clippings and papers to bounce and land disorganized. "Explain to me how you are able to look just like another man right now. Better yet . . . Is your name Dr. Roger Forrest?"

"No, it's not."

"Who are you then?" I straightened the clippings and papers. I figured what I couldn't get from the Chameleon by force, I would gently coerce out of him.

"I go by Chameleon, Officer Reese. It's what I prefer. Thank you."

I muffled my face in both hands, closed my eyes, and let out a miniature scream. "This does not make any sense. Make this make sense for me, man."

"It will one day, Officer Reese. It's just today is not that day."

I stared at the Chameleon. I'm not typically a nail biter, but I bit my thumb nail to the quick, stopping only once it began to bleed.

16

CHAMELEON ON ABBY, "HIS FAVORITE"

PAUL

Reaching into the accordion folder, I pulled out Abbarane's file. There was no picture included.

"How do you know Abbarane Chaikin?"

"It's Abbarane Chaikin-Bachman, now."

"Yes. I know."

"I prefer to call her Abby. Remember?"

"Yes. Now, how do you know her?"

"Abby is probably my favorite of all the women I've encountered."

I thought, perhaps, just maybe, I could get the Chameleon to confess something sinister he'd done to Abby. I held still and waited.

"Yes, I remember you saying that in the car. Why was Abby your favorite?"

"Abby was a beautiful fifteen-year-old girl who had young teenage boys drooling over her."

"Did she cause you to drool over her also?"

"No, never!"

"Well, why was a beautiful, fifteen-year-old teenage girl your favorite?"

"Because that teenage girl had the heart of a warrior. Life wasn't easy for her by any stretch of the imagination, but she persevered. Abby never wanted an abortion. As you already know, Officer Reese, she was forced into it by her mother and by the mother of her boyfriend at that time. I was there when Abby's mother forced her to go through with everything. Abby was distraught leading up to the procedure. Her mother requested that we sedate her, and we obliged. Poor girl. It was difficult to watch the anguish that Abby found herself in. She really loved her mother, and wanted very much to please her. But Abby had a love for her unborn child that was slightly greater. She respected her mother, but not at the expense of her child. I found the most pleasure in doing what I do when it came to Abby."

"So, you're admitting to fondling her?"

"Why would I admit to doing something I never did, Officer Reese? You're so blind by who you think I am you still can't see the truth when it's staring you in the face. But you will come to know the truth. And you will fully understand it. I promise."

"All this talk about finding the most pleasure you ever had when it came to Abby, I just thought . . ."

"Don't think. Just listen for now. I found the most pleasure when it came to Abby because I know her heart was broken when she went under sedation. And her heart was even more broken when she awoke from her procedure. My pleasure was in knowing that if she could hold on just for a little while, she would receive the fullness of her joy restored to her as a result of what I had done . . . or not done, depending on how you look at it. That, Officer Reese, is what brought me the most pleasure. Do you understand?"

"Are you saying that Abby told you she did not want an abortion?"

"Abby told everyone, including her own mother, that she did not want an abortion."

"Is that why you took her money and pretended like you were performing an abortion."

"No. But it helped. And about the money. Since you brought it up. I always donate the abortion money I take to full-time residential living facilities for unwed mothers. Just like the one Abby went to. They provide much of what's needed to bring a baby into the world when the support of family is nonexistent."

"Why not just tell Abby and her mother to leave since the patient did not want the abortion?"

"Her mother would have just taken her somewhere else. My assignment was to stop the abortion. I completed my assignment."

"Who told you to stop Abby's abortion?"

"All of my assignments come from God. I keep telling you that."

"Why do you keep blaming God for choices you made to infringe upon other people's lives?"

"I would never blame God for a choice I made. But I will give Him all the credit for a life He assigned me to save."

"So, let me hear it. Why do you think you were supposed to save the life of Abby's child?"

"His name is Chad. And Chad, like all the babies I saved, has a purpose to fulfill on this earth that only Chad can fulfill."

"So, what was Chad's purpose?"

"If the abortion that Abby's and Chad's mother planned had been successful like they hoped for, on the one-year anniversary of that abortion, Abby would have taken her own life. So, the day that I saved baby Chad's life, I simultaneously saved Abby's life also."

"So, that was his life's purpose? To save his mother from taking her life because she didn't take his life?"

"That's one part of his purpose. You do know that a person can have multiple purposes to fulfill in life, right?"

"What's the other reason Chad had to be born? I'm curious to hear this fairytale. By the way, do you make these up as you go? Or have you been working on these for a while."

"Chad," the Chameleon continued as if I had never insulted him, "went to the University of Pennsylvania and Yale and got several degrees which helped propel him into his current profession. Today he is a medical scientist. He's also an epidemiologist—someone who studies diseases. Do you know why this is important, Officer Reese?"

"Do I know why it is important for someone to study diseases?" I was confused.

"No, sir. Do you know why it is important that Chad's profession is epidemiology?"

"No, I can't say that I do." I wondered what type of yellow brick road he was trying to take me down now.

"Some people live an entire lifetime and never learn why they were born. They never walk in their purpose for existing. Not Chad. He felt pulled toward epidemiology.

He had professors and girlfriends, roommates and buddies to tell him he was too smart to become some mad scientist. People attempted to convince him to become a physician or a lawyer. But that was never his life purpose. Not why he was created. He stayed true to the things he felt passionate about, which was medical science and eventually the study of disease."

His handcuffed wrist prohibited him from leaning in toward me too much.

"Now hear me, Officer Reese. This is important. The day will come when there will be a contagious disease that breaks out in the United States and across several continents. This contagious disease will be spread through saliva. Such as when people sneeze and the airborne moisture from the sneeze travels and is inhaled by others. Yes. The contagious disease will be deadly to anyone and everyone who comes in direct contact with it, and it will kill people within approximately twenty-four hours of first becoming exposed to it. It will result in pandemonium. It will certainly become an epidemic, and people will be afraid to leave their own homes. It will affect adults, babies, teenagers, and the elderly. It will affect everyone. Entire families and in some instances, entire companies and communities will die as a result of this disease. Hundreds of thousands of people will die from it. In a short span of time. But one man. Hear me. One man will make a major medical breakthrough in a laboratory. That one man will find the only cure for this deadly disease. That one man is Mr. Chad Chaikin. Officer Reese, rather you believe me or not, Chad had to be born. He has an assignment in life that only he can fulfill."

"And, what is this deadly disease that is supposed to breakout in the distant future?"

"Oh, don't worry. You will be alive when it breaks out. You will see the day when Chad is credited all over the news for being the one who develops the vaccination and subsequent oral medication to combat this deadly disease. Mock me today, if you wish. I am okay with that. But you will recall the words I speak to you on today. And you will witness on the television, Internet, and on magazine and newspaper covers that Chad Chaikin receives a Nobel Prize as a result of a failed abortion combined with fulfilled purpose."

I clapped and the sound echoed throughout the room. "You deserve some sort of an award."

I twisted and turned in my chair, hearing my stiff joints pop.

I was convinced that the Chameleon was crazy, and saddened that he might not spend a lifetime in prison after all. He would spend the rest of his life in a mental institution.

17

CHAMELEON ON TAMIKA AND TYRONE

PAUL

A jolt of cleverness came over me as I pulled the file on the next set of victims from the accordion folder. I pulled out several pictures of Tyrone, Tamika Jackson's son, and laid them in front of the Chameleon. But they weren't just any pictures, they were mugshots of him from the many times he'd been arrested.

I smiled for the first time since the interview began. *I want to see him get out of this.* "Do you know who this criminal is?"

"Of course. It's my job to know who he is."

"Well, who is it?" I was looking to throw the Chameleon off his square with all this talk about babies being saved from abortions to fulfill a purpose in life.

"That's Tyrone. Tyrone Jackson." The Chameleon let out a soft chuckle. "You remind me why Tyrone is also one of my most favorite babies that I saved."

"Why would you boast about a convicted criminal being a favorite baby of yours worth saving?"

"Tyrone was a bad kid. He was a real nightmare." The Chameleon shook his head and laughed. "You know a child is bad when his own mother gives up on him. Tyrone. He's a favorite of mine because he represents what God's grace and mercy can do for a person. Officer Reese, you and I both know that Tyrone started out as a criminal, but we also know that he gave up that lifestyle a long time ago. You've attempted to convinced yourself, Officer Reese, that God is not real. But deep, down inside, you know that God, and only God, delivered Tyrone from that lifestyle. There are some people that only God can help. And Tyrone was one of them. What I like about Tyrone is that he was 100 percent dedicated to being a terror and doing wrong. When he chose to live for the same God who chose to die for him, Tyrone then took his same tenacity, his same energy, and became 100 percent dedicated to being an ambassador for Christ Jesus. Well, you know his story. You met with him and his mother not that long ago."

My hand throbbed after I smacked the table. "Who are you working with at this station?"

With his usual resolve, the Chameleon kept right on talking about Tyrone as if I'd never asked a question, which infuriated me even more.

"His mother, Tamika, wanted an abortion and she did not care who knew it. She felt like she was carrying Satan's offspring. When Tyrone started acting out as a child, she couldn't understand how he had survived the abortion, and she wasn't happy about it. But, Officer Reese, as odd as it may sound to you, Tyrone had to be born too. He has a purpose in this life that is as great as everyone else that I've told you about. Tyrone has an idea about what his purpose in life is, but he doesn't fully understand the degree of his impact. Following his passion and opening a gym for inner city youth is much bigger than he knows. No one has a clue. But I will share with you something that neither Tyrone nor his own mother knows about him. Tyrone is a life-saver."

"Let me guess. He saved someone from drowning in his swimming pool, huh?" I was fed up with hearing the Chameleon's tales.

"Not quite, but give me a chance to explain, please. When Tyrone got out of prison, he changed his life around for God, got his GED, a business degree, and a seminary degree. He went back to the streets where he grew up, and opened a gym. You were there. So, you saw that the gym gives youth access to boxing, track and field, basketball, football, tutoring sessions, GED classes, business classes, Bible studies, and a barber school for young men who are prone to mischief and gang activity due to absentee fathers. What I like about Tyrone is his transparency.

"He has already touched hundreds of young black boys' and men's lives motivating them to stay in school, graduate, go off to college, open their own businesses, stay out of jail, stay out of gangs, stay off drugs, and avoid an early grave. He, by opening this gym and mentoring, has transformed many young men from becoming a menace to society to being an asset instead. The lives of many would have been so much worse off had he never been born."

"Okay, so he's helped some young men who were okay at sports to become better. Great!"

"No, Officer Reese, no." The Chameleon attempted to move closer to me, but again, the handcuffs restricted his movement. "You're missing it."

"What am I missing?"

"I need for you to use your imagination for me. You're a police officer, so this should be relatively easy. Let's say, for instance, the abortion attempt to end Tyrone's life had been successful, okay? So, there is no Tyrone Jackson in this world. If there is no Tyrone Jackson, then there is no Better You Gym. If there is no Better You Gym, there are no top-rated coaches volunteering their services to the underprivileged here. Young black males are not going to that gym. But they are going somewhere. They're in gangs. They are doing something with all their free time because nobody is hiring them. They're selling drugs. They're car-jacking. They're doing drive-by shootings. They are not going off to college, because they don't know they even have certain abilities, wits, and talents. They don't know they have these certain talents because no one is available to encourage them to think or to try all kinds of sports until they find their niche. They are not learning to love themselves or love God, because Tyrone is not there to point them in the direction of God. They are not getting their GEDs because no one else is encouraging them to do so. They're not starting their own businesses, because there is no one else in this city who had a vision to help young black men the way a non-aborted Tyrone would have. So, these particular young black men do what comes easiest to them in their underprivileged lives and neighborhoods, and that's get into trouble."

He had my attention. Clever.

"The trouble some of these young men would have gotten into had Tyrone been aborted would have been murder, Officer Reese. What neither Tyrone nor his mother knows is that because Tyrone was born, he has changed the course of these young black men's lives, and their destinies. By directly changing the course of their lives, he has indirectly saved the lives of others.

"For example, there is a young black man by the name of Jerry Dotts. He's a defensive player on the collegiate level today because of Tyrone's encouragement and ability to pinpoint Jerry's gift in football. If Tyrone had been aborted, Jerry Dotts would be serving a life sentence in prison today for murdering the district attorney during a carjacking at a nearby gas station. Tyrone's involvement in Jerry's life is the sole reason he's in college today, and not prison. Eddie is a barber today, and not dead. Why? Because Tyrone was born. Charles is heading to the NBA next year instead of being paralyzed and confined to a wheelchair due to a drug deal gone wrong. Why? Because Tyrone was born. Ramone will be the first person in his family, on both sides, to go to college, instead of getting strung out on drugs. Why, Officer Reese? Because Tyrone was not aborted. Judge Minny F. Hasselbeck, here in this city, will not be shot and killed just outside the courthouse by an enraged Eric Brown who would have blamed her for injustice. Because Tyrone was born, he was able to minister to Eric Brown, and reassure him that God is the Judge of judges. Even judges have to answer to God, Officer Reese. So, Eric Brown today is a minister instead of a murderer. Why? Because Tyrone was born."

"I want you to write down the names of everyone you said Tyrone has influenced. First and last names. And . . .

and I want you to write down what they're doing in life today." I was determined to prove that the Chameleon was crazy. Yet, I was beginning to wonder if there was some truth to what the Chameleon claimed.

"Sure. I just need for you to uncuff me," the Chameleon replied.

"Oh, no sir. You're gonna have to write while you're cuffed."

"How about I tell you the names and their professions, and you write it down, Officer Reese?"

"I have it all on tape. I'll retrieve the names later." I was ready to move on.

18

NANCY, NATASHA, AND
AN EXPLANATION

PAUL

I swept up all the pictures of Tyrone in a single motion and laid a new picture on the table. "Who is this?"

"Nancy. Nancy Smith, mother of Natasha Carmichael."

"So, why did you interfere with this woman's rights and violate her body? Because that's exactly what you did."

"I interfered with Nancy's rights because of Natasha. If Natasha's life had ended in the womb, a multitude of people would have blamed God for not stopping a mass murderer years later. Why? He used her, and she stopped one. God purposed for certain people to be born so certain things would not happen. But when human interference removes a life, it leaves a void that causes a domino effect, which sets into motion some events that should have never occurred. Events that would not have occurred had that person been allowed to be born to fulfill their purpose. She was the answer to prayers that people had not prayed yet.

"Officer Reese, Natasha befriended a potential shooting-spree mass-murderer who would have certainly snapped had she not been born. While in high school, there was a young male student who was being bullied. Each and every one of his days at school were miserable because of the constant emotional, physical, and psychological abuse he endured from a group of mean-spirited, popular boys who viewed it as sport. To them, it was fun and games. But they inflicted an enormous amount of hurt onto an already damaged soul. You see, this young man had no father or mother because they'd both died in a car accident. He lived with his elderly grandmother who was on a fixed income. She could not afford the best of anything. But he was not a problem for her. He was a good kid who was just hurting inside. He just wanted the opportunity to go to school, get good grades, make his parents proud, and give back to his grandmother who had given so much to him. But these privileged, rich kids, who had too much, would never understand his level of suffering, stemming from a young age, and wouldn't stop inflicting pain on his already fragile soul. But God. God looked through the telescope of time. He saw this young man's hurt. He became acquainted with his broken heart. He heard his nighttime cries of grief. He felt the anguish in his spirit.

"And God. Yes, God! Sent an answer to this young man's prayer. This young man prayed the simplest prayer that anyone could ever pray. Sometimes it is the only prayer that some can find the strength to pray. This young man, out of his pain, suffering, and brokenness, cried out and prayed, 'God, help me!' God ordained that his help was on the way. He manifested this help when He commanded that I stop that abortion. His help was in the form of a hot-headed, outspoken, move to the beat of her own drum, young lady who was tired of people bullying this young man. She felt an overwhelming need to stand up for her classmate. It drove her. She felt a great sense of peace, of pleasure, after she stood up for him. It's a moment that she rarely speaks of, but it's one she'll never forget. Why? Because it's one of the main reasons she was created. It was written in the book of her life before she was formed in her mother's belly. She was the answer to not only that young man's prayer, but she was the answer to the prayers of protection that many parents prayed each morning before they sent their children off to school. Natasha befriended a fragile soul and stood up for him when he could not stand up for himself.

"On the right day, standing in the right place, at the right moment, Natasha and all her feistiness confronted six of the school's most popular brats who mistreated and humiliated a young man in the school hallway near his locker. They attempted to stuff this young man into his locker as they had done once before. And he was at his wits' end. Natasha stopped the humiliation once and for all. In that moment, she changed his life forever. She became his best friend and helped to shape and change his destiny. Had she not been born, he would have had no one to intervene on his behalf. What no one other than that young man knows is that he had several rounds of ammunition and firearms in his locker. On that very day, he would have taken the lives of all of those who repeatedly mentally and physically harmed him, as well as innocent bystanders, and then he would have taken his own life. She had to be born even though her life seems insignificant and many would never understand the full value of her life through a simple act of kindness. Many, including her, will never know that by her mere existence, she saved thirty-eight lives in a single day. She will never invent anything. She will never become a doctor. She didn't graduate at the top of her class. Her name will never be mentioned in a magazine or newspaper for anything significant. She will never go down in the history books for being some great influential or historical figure. But her life's work is as great as any famous person you can name. In fact, her life's purpose is greater than most who are famous today. She has value.

"You see, Officer Reese, she was assigned to me. I have never lost one assigned to me. She had to be born. And I had to make sure that abortion was *almost* an abortion, but not an *actual* abortion. Officer Reese, this case is named *Operation Almost*, not because I've almost been captured, but because these young, important, precious lives were *almost* aborted.

"The person's whose life she saved is now a huge advocate of bully prevention. His name is Officer Jeff Hughes. His fiancée, whom you have yet to meet, is Natasha. She's the one who was almost aborted."

19

CHAMELEON

PAUL

I tilted the chair backward and rested my head in my interlocked hands. I found it difficult to comprehend what the Chameleon had just revealed to me. I didn't know whether to believe him, or to consider him an insane lunatic and request a psychologist. I was stunned and paralyzed by this recent information. Furthermore, I didn't have the facts of how the Chameleon knew about Jeff's passion for the bullying prevention campaign. Most perplexing of all was how he knew that I'd never met Jeff's fiancée. But, against everything in me, I started to believe the Chameleon had insight into the things he spoke about that went beyond the obvious. I just wasn't sure how he knew what he knew.

"Who are you? And how do you know these things?" I finally spoke after a period of silence.

"I know these things, Officer Reese, because... I'm an angel."

I snapped back to reality. I had no belief in God, so I certainly didn't believe in angels. But if I was a believer in God, the Chameleon was almost convincing. As a mentally sharp agent of the law, I had a duty to let him know that his con wasn't working on me. "If you're an angel, then I'm King David, Moses, and Noah all in one."

Consistent. He remained unfazed by my dismissal of who he claimed to be.

"As an angel sent by God, my job is to stop specific abortions. There are other angels too. One such angel is the Whisperer. His job is to whisper into the ears of mothers at clinics preparing to go through with abortions. That angel whispers into a mother's ear until the word grips her heart. He tells her to leave. Leave before the abortion doctor could perform the procedure. He's pretty successful also. There are many children who are alive today because of the Whisperer."

I was intrigued by the Chameleon. By now, I had been in the interrogation room with him for nearly three hours. I had drunk a cup of cappuccino this morning, a couple bottles of water, and a sixty-four-ounce slushy lemonade. I hated to leave the room, but I was fighting a losing battle. I walked over to the door and motioned with my hand. There was a buzzing sound, and then the door opened. I stepped out of the interrogation room and into the hallway where the two officers were still standing.

"I'm stepping away for a quick moment. Please, do not let anyone in and certainly don't allow the suspect out."

I walked over to the chief who had left the observatory room and met me in the hallway. "I'm heading to the front desk and restroom. I'll be right back. I asked Hodges and Parker not to open the interrogation room for anyone."

"I'll go with you," Chief Lewis said.

We walked down the hall and made a quick stop at the restroom before heading to the front desk.

"Chief, did you hear the Chameleon claim he was an angel?"

"Yeah, I heard."

"What do you think about that?"

"I thought it was very interesting." Chief's right eyebrow attempted to meet his receding hairline.

"Should we have a psychiatrist come evaluate him?"

"Officer Reese, you're the lead on this. I would not object if that's something you believe is necessary."

We stopped at the front counter and I filled out the *Request for Psychiatric Evaluation Form for Suspect or Inmate.*

"Do you know if the psychiatrist is available?"

"I don't know, but I can call up to the office and see." Alice picked up the phone.

(CHAMELEON)

There were no windows to the outside world in the interrogation room. Just concrete walls on every side and a reflective observatory glass. I knelt on the floor underneath the table as if I'd dropped something and attempted to pick it up with my one free hand. The other hand, my left one, was still handcuffed to the table. When I got off my knee, I'd changed my appearance. Just like that. Then, using my free hand, I simply thumped the handcuffs once, and they opened. After I removed my bound hand, I laid the handcuffs neatly on the table. I stood, and adjusted the police uniform pants that I was now wearing as I walked to the door. When I motioned with my hands, the door buzzed open and I walked right out as the door shut behind me. The two officers watching the door were completely caught off guard.

"Officer Reese, I never saw you go back into the room. How did you do that? Did you see when he went back in?" Officer Hodges asked Officer Parker.

"You fellas better keep your eyes wide open. What are you doing out here—sleeping?" Under the appearance of Officer Paul Reese, I walked right down the hallway and past the real Officer Paul Reese, who stood at the counter filling out a psychiatric request form for me while he talked to the chief.

I walked right out the front door of the police station. A couple of officers, believing I was really Paul, gave me a hard time. I just smiled and walked into the parking lot where the officers parked their personal vehicles. I disappeared out of sight.

(PAUL)

As I completed the psychiatric request form, Alice informed me that she'd spoken with the psychiatrist who was on duty, and she was on her way down to review my request form.

"She should be able to evaluate your suspect within thirty minutes, Officer Reese."

"Alice, just one more request before we go." The chief smiled.

"Anything for you, Chief," Alice replied with a big grin on her face.

"Will you please give Officer Reese a confession form?"

"Sure thing!" She walked over to the file cabinet and pulled out a double-sided confession form. "Here it is. Can I get anything else for you, gentlemen?"

"No, Alice. You have been very helpful." The chief winked and grabbed a mini candy bar.

"Take as many as you'd like, I sure don't need any." Alice took the lid back off the jar and angled it in our direction. We each grabbed two more, then headed back toward the interrogation room.

"Now that you've talked to the Chameleon for several hours, Paul, what do you think of him?"

"He's nothing like I imagined him. I thought he would've had the demeanor of a former CIA or FBI agent. You know, kind of arrogant toward me since I'm a local cop. But he's almost childlike in the sense that I honestly believe *he* believes his own lies. I kind of feel sorry for him in a way, Chief."

"So, what do you make of his ability to transform himself to look like other people?" We were nearly to the interrogation room.

"Now, that I can't figure out. I'll revisit that line of questioning now."

I waited in front of the door for the chief to buzz me in. The door opened and my heart froze. The room magnified, then shrunk before me. My heart resumed a rapid thumping before I felt it weighing down my chest cavity.

The room was empty.

I never allowed the door to close. With my foot holding the door open, I yelled at the two rookie officers who were responsible for guarding the door.

"Parker and Hodges! Get in here now!" My voice shocked me as it embodied the sound of thunder.

They jumped from their seats and entered the interrogation room.

"Why is my interrogation room empty while a pair of handcuffs sits on that table right there?"

Open, empty mouths were all they could offer me.

Hodges finally managed a few words. "The only person who came and went out of this room was you, Officer Reese."

"He's absolutely right. You're the only person who has passed through this door since we've been here."

"Well, if I'm the only person who's passed through this door since the two of you have been sitting here, and I left the Chameleon in this room, then please tell me where in this room can I find the Chameleon?"

"Your guess is as good as ours, Officer Reese," Officer Parker said.

"Wrong answer! No one just disappears!" I tried to calm my voice. "I left to go to the restroom for one moment. Just one moment. And in less than ten minutes, the two of you cannot guard a man handcuffed in a locked room? Then you want me to believe that he just disappeared into thin air? Worthless, I tell you. You are both . . . worth-less."

Back and forth I walked. *Breathe. Breathe. Breathe in. Hold it.* While standing in the threshold of the interrogation room, I heard the voice of the very last person I'd hoped to hear.

"What's the matter, Reesie? Did you lose something? Or should I say *someone*? How, Reese? How'd you lose a full-grown man that you knew had a history of escaping? How'd that happen, genius?"

Something snapped in me. I charged Officer Prince, grabbing his uniform collar and gathering it into knots. "If I find out that you assisted the Chameleon in escaping on my watch, you will rot in a prison cell next to him, you worthless piece of—"

"That's enough, Reese!" The chief hurried from the observation room. "Follow me. Now!"

Officer Prince pushed me off only after I relaxed my fingers. The chief walked back into the observation room. Inside, the room was dark and the panel with all the controls for the cameras and the locked door were backlit in blue.

I followed the chief, jittery and unfocused. I couldn't shift my thoughts away from pounding in Officer Prince's head.

Suddenly, my mind clear and I blabbered, "I want to see the video of the interrogation room. I want to see what happened while I stepped away. I hope you're willing to arrest any and every officer who shows up on the video as helping the Chameleon escape, Chief. This is ridiculous!"

"Sit down, Paul!"

I flopped into one of the many chairs that lined the room.

"Pull your chair a little closer. Here, near the television screen. I need you to watch the last fifteen minutes of the recording."

The chief hit rewind and watched as the device stopped at 3:15:44. He pressed the play button. The video showed me sitting near the table talking to the Chameleon. It showed when I stood, walked toward the door, and motioned for the chief to open it, and I walked out. We focused our attention on another screen that showed all five different camera angles at once. We wanted to see if the door closed behind me. And it did. The chief resumed play. We turned our attention back to the screen that showed a view directly facing the Chameleon. For several minutes, the Chameleon just sat doing nothing. After seven minutes passed, the chief and I watched as the Chameleon knelt on the floor. He was underneath the table for thirty-three seconds.

"What in the world is he doing under there?" I asked.

Just as I finished speaking, the Chameleon arose from under the table. I sprang up and walked within inches of the screen. "No, way! What? Chief, what is this?"

"This is the video surveillance of the interrogation room, Officer Reese."

"What . . . how . . . I don't understand. Why does . . . ? How did . . . ?"

Back and forth I paced.

"How did the Chameleon kneel under that table, but come up looking exactly like me, Chief?"

"That's a good question, Paul. How do you think he did it?"

"Wait a minute. I was with *you* the entire time that I was not with him. So, I hope you are not insinuating that I assisted the Chameleon with his escape."

"No one is accusing you of anything, Paul." Chief Lewis didn't seem rattled by what we'd just seen.

"Well, how do *you* explain the Chameleon looking like me on this video?"

"Let's finish watching what happened."

The chief pushed play. The Chameleon, looking exactly like me, tapped the handcuffs one time, and he simply took them off and laid them on the table. He walked toward the door, it opened, and he walked out.

"Can you play it from another angle? Zoom in underneath the table before, during, and after he knelt down." I sat down. I stood back up. "We need to go check out the interrogation room. Maybe the clothes he had on are in there underneath the table. I can go check."

"Paul!" Just as the chief was trying to calm me down, the psychiatrist, escorted by Officer Prince, entered the room.

"Hello, Officer Reese." Dr. Langley looked at the request form that I'd filled out. "I see here that you put a rush on the form for me to interview one of your suspects. Where can I find him?"

"You won't be finding him here, that's for sure." Officer Prince laughed. "But you might want to go ahead and do that psych eval on Officer Reese though. I've never seen a black man get that pale before."

"You don't have an off switch!" I lunged toward him, prepared to escort him out of the room. The chief grabbed me before I could make contact.

"That's it, Reese. You're out of here! Go home. Now!"

"But, Chief, you heard him provoking me."

"I will handle Officer Prince. But you . . . you've had a long day. Go home to your wife. Sleep it off. Take tomorrow off . . . with pay. I'll see you on Thursday."

"But, Chief—"

"Go home, Reese! I'm not asking you." Chief pointed to the door.

I turned, walked out the door and down the hallway.

"Officer Prince, I need a word with you," I could hear the chief yell.

I drove home. Bewildered.

20

TOO MUCH

PAUL

I pulled into my garage, attempting to make sense of the day. "Could there be any truth to what he said?"

"Paul?" Jenesis opened the kitchen door that led to the garage. "What are you doing just sitting out here in the car alone? I need your help."

"I'm coming, I'm coming."

"I called you like four times. You were supposed to be home by four o'clock. Did something happen?"

"I just captured the Chameleon. That's all."

"Who is the Chameleon again?"

My mouth dropped open, and I just looked at her.

"I'm kidding. You haven't stopped talking about him since you volunteered for this case. But I need you to help me with your mother. She's wilding out and I can't calm her down."

"Fill me in."

"First off, you're going to need someone here with her until you get off work. I can barely take care of myself; I can't take care of her too."

"Okay. I'll get on it tomorrow."

"Wait!" She pressed her hands into my chest and pushed me a few feet away from the door of my mother's room. "I had to."

"You had to what?" I had a sudden, sinking feeling.

"I had to put her in restraints and give her a sleeping pill just for her to calm down."

I pushed passed my wife and my heart fluttered at what I saw. "Help me get these off her, please!" Two cloth restraints on her wrists and two on her ankles. It made the tearing sound that Velcro makes when pulled apart. *My mother was nobody's prisoner. And she wouldn't be one in my home!*

"I'm sorry, Paul. I had to do it. Otherwise, she would've hurt—"

Mom awakened. "How was school today, Mark?" Her words slurred like someone failing a roadside sobriety test.

"Momma." I stroked her hand. "It's me. Paul. Not Mark."

"Who are you? I don't know you. Please leave my house before I have to call the police."

"I'm your son. And I *am* the police."

"You're not my son. I only have one son, and he's six years old. Get outta here!" Though weak from the medicine, she pushed me away and tried to get out of the bed.

"No, Momma. You have to stay in the bed so you won't hurt yourself."

"Don't you tell me no, boy! I do as I please." The top of my hand and other arm stung as she dug her nails into me as I tried to lay her back into her bed.

Jenesis sat in the chair watching.

"Will you help me get these back on her?"

"Sure."

"Ahhh! Stop it! Stop it!" Momma thrashed with greater strength now.

As I left the room, panting for air, my feet felt like they were made of concrete blocks.

"Let me outta here! Let me out! My husband will be home soon. Then you'll get it!"

"I'll stay with her. Why don't you call someone?"

An hour later, a home health nurse arrived and got Momma settled for the night. My mind was fried, my body exhausted. And now this. I replayed my mother's words. Whenever she was rational, she had a lot to say that I yearned to hear, even if it was about God and prayer. And that's all she talked about now-a-days.

For dinner we made sandwiches and afterward, all I wanted to do was hit the sack. For the first time in my adult life, I knelt next to my bed and I prayed. For my mother. For Jenesis. For myself.

"God, if You're real like my mother says You are, I need You to reveal Yourself to me. Help my mother. Help my wife. Help me."

It was only nine o'clock, but I crawled into bed and turned off the light.

The next morning, I woke up at six like I would for a work day. I couldn't have slept in if I'd wanted to. I had the Chameleon and all that I'd witnessed on my mind. I wished the warm water from the showerhead would wash all my troubles down the drain. *Snap out of it.* Putting on a pair of knee length shorts, I prepared to shave. I had everything I needed laid out on the bathroom counter: shaving cream, a hand-held close-up mirror, an electric razor, a straight razor, and some aftershave. The white foam filled my hand from the can and I smeared a thick white beard and mustache across my face. I started with the straight razor. Stopping every so often, I picked up the close-up mirror to make sure I didn't miss a spot, even though I stood in front of the large mirror mounted on the wall.

Jenesis, just waking up, joined me in the bathroom. A smile escaped me. It'd been months since she'd focused on anything other than her infertility.

She yawned and curled a piece of hair between her fingers. "Good morning, Mr. Reese."

"Good morning, Jen." I stopped shaving for a moment, and planted a foamy kiss on her lips before resuming.

She walked behind me as I shaved and wrapped her arms around my bare chest. She leaned the side of her face into my back and remained very still as I shaved. She remained like that for several seconds.

"Please, let me know when it's safe for me to move. I don't want to be the cause of you cutting yourself."

I finished shaving the area just above my lip. "You can move now if you'd like."

Jenesis unwrapped her arms. Hands caressing my back used to be a common occurrence. I closed my eyes and relished the moment. Then she did that thing with her finger that always sent chills up my spine no matter where she touched. Ever so slightly, she ran a single finger across my back and over my shoulders.

"You have a great physique, Mr. Cop." She chuckled at her own morning time silliness.

She looked as beautiful to me as the day we exchanged vows. A single finger of hers continued across my body as I attempted to shave.

"I never noticed your birthmark. I love it! But it's in the most remote place, you know."

"What birthmark?"

"You probably can't see it because of where it is, almost underneath your armpit."

I continued to shave.

"It looks like an upside-down capital letter *A*."

My hand lost its grip and I dropped my electric shaver as it hit the mirror on its way to the floor. The floor resembled a booby trap.

"Paul! Breathe!"

I could feel my eyes roll to the top of my head as the room begin to spin. I staggered to the right. Jenesis held me up.

I bent down.

"What are you doing?"

"I need to see." I picked up the biggest broken piece of glass and angled it in the bathroom mirror to see this letter *A*.

"Sit down, Paul!"

"I see it!" It was just as Jenesis had described. My mind was back in the interrogation room. Then in the car. Then back to the interrogation room. The Chameleon had confessed. This very thing. About marking his victims. With the letter *A*. Though the air conditioner was in full effect, and I kept the house cool in the humid springtime, sweat covered my body as if I'd just taken a shower.

"Honey. Honey. Paul!"

"I need to have a word with my mother."

"Have a seat here on the toilet. You don't look well. Does anything hurt? She slapped her hand on my forehead. "Should I drive you to the doctor?"

I shook my head and blinked a few times. "No. No, I'm okay." I blinked a few more times and stabilized my vision. "I'm just a little dizzy, but I'll be okay."

Holding on to the railing, I went down the stairs by twos.

Let her be lucid. Let her be lucid.

"Paul, are you kidding me? You're moving too fast!" Jenesis trailed behind.

"Momma!" I said from the kitchen on my way into her room.

"Shhhhh!" The home health nurse hissed at me. "I just got her settled down five minutes ago, and I have this mess she created to clean up. If you wake her up, you're on your own, and I'm outta here."

Well, that's that!

"I need to go to the station."

Jenesis had the home health nurse take a look at me. She recommended that I go to a quick in-and-out convenient care clinic. I refused. Jenesis retaliated by refusing to allow me to leave the house.

"You heard the nurse. You nearly blacked out. You're in no shape to drive, Paul. Thank goodness this was your day off anyway. If you're looking stable as the day progresses, maybe I'll let you go back to work tomorrow."

Meanwhile, my mother remained incoherent.

21

ALMOST SPECIAL FORCES

PAUL

The next day, I arrived at work a half hour early. I waited in the hallway next to the chief's locked door. Lost in my thoughts, I didn't see him approach until he was a few feet in front of me.

"Can't believe I'm saying this, but you saw that I almost had him, Chief. Been flippin' it over in my mind from every angle. But I still I don't understand how he did that Houdini magic thing. Do you have any news on him?"

"No, son. I don't. Paul?" He wrestled with his keys. "You don't look good. Do you need another day off?"

"No, sir. I'm fine." *Shoulders back. Stomach in. Head up.* "I just want to know how the Chameleon escaped."

"I've been the chief around here for a long time. Write up your report on the Chameleon, then get busy doing something else. Otherwise, this case will drive you crazy. I want you and Hughes to keep a close eye on Main Street National Bank over on Hickory Street. There have been several bank robberies in that general area. It's the only one that hasn't been hit yet, and we think they might be next. Remember your training."

"Yes, sir." I headed to my desk to wait for my shift to start, and for Jeff to arrive.

"Hey, partner, I heard that you had the Chameleon on lockdown for almost four hours. So, what did I miss?"

Looking at Jeff, his mouth still moving, all that played in my mind was what the Chameleon had said about my partner.

"Jeff, why are you so active in anti-bullying campaigns in all the schools across this city?"

"What does this have to do with the question I just asked you? Though I'm glad to see you're interested in my efforts. When I was a freshman in high school, I was the victim of constant bullying by a group of popular jerks. They made my life a living nightmare. It took years for me to get over it. I just want to help others who might be getting bullied, because I know what it's like. No one should have to endure that."

"Well, for what it's worth. I think you're doing a great job." It was the sanest thought I'd had in two days.

"Thanks, Paul. That means a lot. You should come at least once to see what it's all about."

"I will. In fact, I would love to."

We left to patrol the streets of Champaign. I was happy to get out of the station. I didn't want to run into any of the other officers who had previously been on the *Operation Almost* case. Yet, even out of the office, my mind was spinning.

"Jeff, you can drive." I tossed him the key.

"You feeling okay?" I'd never relinquished the driver's seat to anyone. For any reason.

"I'm fine."

I was lost in my thoughts throughout our field duty. We monitored speed limits, responded to a few calls, monitored the bank, and even brought some order to a pro-life/pro-choice protest that was taking place in front of the Lafayette Women's Clinic.

As we got out of the patrol car to set up some perimeters and guidelines meant to keep the protest safe for both sides, I noticed the woman whose life I'd saved a year earlier was a part of the protest—on the pro-choice side. I got closer.

When Sarah Davis yelled out, "A woman's body, a woman's choice," I saw it. A small, barely noticeable, capital letter *A* just along her jawline. *I'm losing my mind, but how ironic.* Frozen in my steps, I was lost deep in my thoughts. I wondered if it was possible for a person who was pro-choice to be one of the Chameleon's almost aborted babies. How a person who had almost been aborted herself, but saved, could be pro-choice at all. *Wonder if she would still be pro-choice if she knew she was almost aborted. Maybe I'm starting to believe the words of a crazy man, and I shouldn't. Maybe I'm crazy!*

"Officer Reese? Paul!" Jeff elbowed me as I stared at the letter *A* on Sarah Davis' face.

"Yeah, man. What?"

"You okay? I called your name like ten times. Mostly everyone around us turned to look at me except you." Wrinkles gathered between Jeff's eyes as he spoke. "Let's just go."

"I'm sorry. I didn't hear you." I felt bad knowing that if it had been a serious situation, I would've put my partner, myself, and innocent people in jeopardy.

"It's lunchtime anyway." Jeff drove us back to the station.

I sat at my desk eating the lunch that I'd become accustomed to fixing for myself. Alice from the front desk called my phone. "Officer Reese, there is a gentleman down here insisting that he delivers this package to you and only you."

"Thanks, Alice. I'm on my way down now."

I took the steps to the main level. There was a tall, dark-haired, handsome young man in his late thirties standing in the lobby with a manila envelope. As I approached the counter, the man walked over to me, and without uttering a word, slapped the folder in my hand. I glanced down at the folder, and by the time I looked up to question the man, he was already approaching the door.

"Sir. Sir, wait!" It was too late. He'd walked out of the station.

I ripped open the envelope. Inside was a letter and a file. The letter encouraged me to read the contents of the file in private. I hurried back to my desk and sat down. When I pulled the file out, I noticed it was on our station's reporting paper, yellowed with age. An *Operation Almost* file. One of the numbered files that was missing from the stack of files Jeff and I had looked through.

The date of the attempted abortion for the victim at First Street Clinic was several months before my date of birth. When I flipped through the papers, into my lap fell a picture of . . . my very own mother. I felt numb. As I read through the report and tried to make sense of what I was reading, I fought back tears with all my manhood. It read just like all the other *Operation Almost* cases that I'd spent months studying and investigating. Like many others, this report was written by an officer whom I'd never met. The officer who wrote the report dated it May 3, 2002. I had been twelve years old. Highlighted was the officer's interview with the Chameleon.

> *Mrs. Deborah Reese was forced by her drunkard husband to have an abortion against her wishes. I stopped her abortion because her son had to be born. There are criminals in this world who will only be captured because Paul Reese was born. Because he will capture certain criminals, many lives will be unharmed or saved that otherwise would have been destroyed. He was assigned to me. I fulfilled my assignment, so that he can fulfill his life's purpose.*

I bolted from my seat. With everything else that had transpired, my mind couldn't handle this news. I had no doubt that the file was real. All I could think to do was go home. I'd never had an asthma attack, but the way I struggled for breath, I figured that's what one felt like. When I stood, I swayed as the room blurred. I pushed through several sets of doors and got to the staircase to make my way to the first floor. My uniform dampened with sweat. On my way down the stairs, I ran into the last person I needed to see at a moment like this—Officer Prince.

"You okay there, Reesie?" Officer Prince asked.

The words of the Chameleon, the letter *A* on me, the missing file, Jeff's confession of being bullied, an inability to breathe, a racing heart . . . all this pressure churned inside me like high winds of the perfect storm. Without warning, I swooned and the world went black.

When I came to, I was lying on a bench in the locker room full of other officers. As the haze lifted, I could hear lots of side chatter going on, but I couldn't make out what anyone was saying. My head and neck ached. I sat up on the bench and tried to shake off the dizziness. All the chatter stopped as everyone focused their attention on me. I looked around the locker room, offended by who I saw. It was all the officers who'd tried to convince me not to take the case.

"What is this?" Straddling the bench, I stood. My legs wobbled before I collapsed.

"We tried to tell you not to take this case, but you wouldn't listen," Officer Rodriguez yelled out.

"Don't do that," Sergeant Stevens interjected.

"Yeah, let's not be too hard on him. Besides, that's not why we're here," Officer Bond said.

"Reese, all jokes aside," Officer Prince said, dropping to sit next to me, "you're not losing your mind, although I'm sure you feel like you are."

It was the sincerest I'd ever heard Officer Prince be.

"Officer Prince is right," Officer Johnson said. "In fact, you didn't choose this case. This case chose you."

"Now, it's not a lot of us, but at some point in our career, this case chose each person in this room. We call ourselves *Almost Special Forces*," Sergeant Stevens said. "Because everyone you see in this room was almost aborted, but saved by the Chameleon. Like the Chameleon confessed, he placed the letter *A* somewhere on the body of everyone he saved. Everyone in this room bears the mark, courtesy of the Chameleon, somewhere on his body."

With that, they each began to either roll up their sleeves, pull up their shirt, take off their shoe, or pull up their pants legs to show me the letter *A* on their bodies.

Officer Bond stood in front of me starting to unbuckle his pants.

"Man, what are you doing?" I asked.

"I'm about to show you my letter *A* like everyone else did."

"Uh, . . . I believe you."

Everyone laughed.

"Well, at least Officer Reese is returning back to his normal sarcastic self," Officer Prince said.

"Man, my *A* is on my upper thigh. I don't know what you were thinking," Officer Bond said defensively, trying to clear up any misconceptions.

All the officers surrounded me, giving me words of encouragement, followed by a group hug.

"So,"—I cleared my throat—"are you all telling me that each of you personally met the Chameleon?"

"That's exactly what we're telling you," Officer Mint said.

"He pulled that whole 'transforming into a replica of you' routine just before he escaped on each of us too," Officer Johnson said.

"Don't ask us how, but he hand-delivered each of our files to us personally. I take it that's what sent you over the top, Reese?" Officer Bond asked.

"Yeah."

"Well, just know that we're all here for you, Reese. Including Officer Michelle White who's off work today. As far as we know, we are the only Almost Special Forces officers. The mystery around here is whether the chief is one of us too. He has never admitted to it, but he sure is overly tolerant of the Chameleon and our inability to capture him," Sergeant Stevens said.

"But make no mistake," Officer Rodriguez said, "Chief puts on a good front in our meetings."

Officer Prince stood up. "Man, I know I gave you the hardest time of us all, but I knew this day would come. It came for each of us. I'm not making any excuses or trying to undo any of the love circulating this room for you right now, but you were just so cocky! And it was irritating."

"Yeah."

"He's right!"

"I agree."

"Sure were."

"And on top of being a jerk, you accused each of us in here of being crooked cops that you were going to find pleasure locking away," Officer Rodriguez said.

"He said that?" someone asked.

"Yeah he did."

"We had secret meetings regarding needing to teach you a lesson or two in camaraderie," Sergeant Stevens said.

"Had to!" Officer Johnson said.

"Now, some of these guys took it a little too far," Sergeant Stevens said.

"Even though you were a hundred percent right that all of us was hiding something and not being forthcoming with you, you were, obviously now, wrong about what we were hiding. But Officer Reese, if you're honest, you were rough, also in how you handled us. You were blinded by your own ambitions," Sargent Stevens said.

"We still wanted to have a little fun with you before all the fun ended. So, on top of teaching you a string of lessons in humility, I was mostly just having fun with you. I hope you understand." Officer Prince extended his fist to me. I met his fist bump.

"I think Reese gets the award for taking this case the most serious of anyone in here. What do y'all think?" Officer Johnson asked.

In unison, everyone said, "Yes!"

"He was about to have us all locked up. But, me, he was going to have me put under the jail," Officer Prince chimed in as we all burst out in laughter.

I remembered when the chief told me the day would come when I would need to lean on them for support. I didn't understand what the chief meant then, but I understood now.

There was a call over the transmitters.

"Well, as much as I would love to stay and party with you, Officer Reese, duty calls. If you need anything, I'm here for you man." Officer Bond shook my hand before darting out.

One by one, each of the officers did the same. Officer Prince and Sargent Stevens were the last to leave.

"Sarg! Officer Prince!" I called them back into the locker room just before the door shut on their way out. "I'm sorry I said you were crooked cops and wanted to lock you up. I didn't know." I had never swallowed my pride the way I did at that very moment.

"You're a good cop, Officer Reese. I know that. We all know that," Sargent Stevens said.

"If ever you need to talk outside of work about all of this, I'll leave my cell phone number on your desk. I'm here for you, just like those guys were here for me when I found out," Officer Prince said.

They gave me a pat on the shoulder and left the locker room.

I felt a resurgence of strength. I decided to use this energy to write up my report on the Chameleon. I knew Jeff would be looking for me because I was more than forty-five minutes missing in action.

When I made it to the office I shared with Jeff, my partner was sitting at his desk with a lady sitting in a nearby chair.

"Paul, where have you been, man? I've been waiting for almost an hour to introduce you to my fiancée, Nattie. Well, her real name is Natasha."

I walked over to Natasha and shook her hand. "It's a real pleasure to finally meet you, Natasha. We were starting to believe that you were a figment of Jeff's imagination. But you are as beautiful as he said you were. Jeff is a good guy."

"Thank you, Paul. Jeff has had much to say about you as well. He's really happy to have you as his partner. He says there's never a dull moment with you around."

We all laughed. Jeff walked Natasha out to her car. I sat down and wrote up my report on the Chameleon. I ended my report with the famous final words: *I almost had him, but he escaped.*

I drove home that evening, praying that my mother was in her right mind because she was the only one who could fill in the holes about my *almost* abortion and I needed answers.

For the second time in my adult life, I prayed. "God, my mother said that you hear and answer prayers. If you are real, show me by allowing my mother to be in her right mind when I get home, so I can get the answers I need from her about this letter *A*. In Jesus' name. Amen."

I arrived home with my *Operation Almost* file in my hand. My mother was sitting in a chair in her room.

"Momma, we need to talk."

She reached for the file. "I've been wondering when this day would come."

Thank You, God, she's in her right mind. "Tell me it's not true!" I buried my face in her lap like the little boy in me did whenever I'd had a rough day at school.

She flipped through the folder, reading a little here and there. "Yes. Oh. Yes, I remember. Paul, everything in here is accurate. This is your story. My story. Our story."

I sat on the edge of her bed. *My sweet mother.* She couldn't have almost done this. *Not my kind, loving, good to me, mother.* I needed to see her face as she explained this painful truth to me.

"Your father was a bright man. Had two degrees. One in civil engineering the other in computer science. He had a good job. Making good money over at the university where your wife works now. We never wanted for anything. But your father was an alcoholic. They paid for him to get treatment. The university did. The first time it helped for a little while. After that, he went to work drunk one time too many, and they let him go. We lost everything. He never took responsibility for anything. Blamed me. Blamed your brother. Then, when I became pregnant with you, he blamed you. He gave me an ultimatum. Abort you or lose him and tear our family apart. He was a pleasant man when he wasn't drinking. I loved him dearly. I had been a homemaker my whole life, and I didn't want to lose him or you." She reached for my hand, and I extended it to her. "I wanted my whole family! Many times. Many, many times I told him no to the abortion. He only hit me when he was drunk though. He was trying to beat you out of me. Things went from bad to worse. I thought by agreeing to his wishes, everything would go back to normal. He made me believe that's what it would take. But I've also known how to pray ever since I was a little girl.

"Every time I look at you, Paul, it's a reminder of why I love God so much. You are a miracle! God not only forgave me for all my other sins, but He stopped me from taking your life."

"So, you met the Chameleon?"

"Apparently so. There's no other explanation why your abortion failed. God sent an angel to make sure you lived. I serve God, and worship Him as deeply and unapologetically as I do because of you."

I understood.

As the weeks and months passed, my mother had few coherent moments after that day. The Alzheimer's seemed to have won, but not before she had done the impossible. That day, she led me to Christ.

The lessons I had recently learned from my mother about prayer, faith in God, forgiveness, and grace and mercy could not have come at a better time in my life. As Jenesis struggled with her faith in God due to her continuous struggles with infertility, I learned to cover my wife in prayer and love. That, coupled with her seeing a Christian therapist, is how she's able to cope from one day to the next.

I have not become hopeless in our desire to conceive a child together. If God could stop me from being aborted, surely He can open my wife's barren womb. My Bible tells me He did it for Hannah, and Rachel, too. But if God never does it for us, I will serve Him until the day I die, as my mother's words have now become my own: "You can't make me doubt Him, 'cause I know too much about Him."

EPILOGUE

NEW ROOKIES VOLUNTEER FOR *ALMOST* CASE

PAUL

A little over a year had passed since I'd been on the *Operation Almost* case. We were in our weekly staff meeting. The third shift overlapped with ours by a half hour, allowing some officers to remain on duty. Chief briefed everyone on current issues in the city and state. He informed us about new laws and procedures, and passed out flyers on missing persons. Then he assigned cases. First, to volunteers. Then, to voluntolds. After several officers volunteered for most of the cases, the chief picked a box off the floor and plopped it down on the table in the front of the room.

"We need a volunteer for this forty-five-years, bundle of cases."

"Oh, Chief! Please, tell us this is not the *Operation Almost* case again," Officer Rodriguez yelled out.

"Yeah, Chief," Officer Mint added. "Not this again."

"Yes, this again! The Chameleon has hit another clinic, so he's back doing what he does best, and we need a set of partners to volunteer to capture the old fart."

"Chief, we all know that nobody is ever going to catch this guy!" someone yelled from the back of the room.

"Yeah, Chief, I don't think anyone in here is ready to endure what all the *Operation Almost* case brings with it," Officer Bond said from the front row.

An ambitious, rookie officer by the name of Dallas Wilson, who looked to prove himself, spoke up. "I'll volunteer, Chief. I mean, my partner and I will take on this *Operation Almost* case, whatever it is."

"Man, since you don't know what the *Operation Almost* case is, why don't you just leave it alone and volunteer for a case that you have more knowledge about," Officer Prince said.

Dallas, a tall, blond-haired, blue-eyed, young man was as good-looking and charming as Officer Prince. "Well, Mr. Prince, I'm taking this case, your highness."

Chuckles filled the room.

"Don't do it, Dallas! Run while you have a chance. Just walk away from this case. Walk. Away. You've been warned," I chimed in.

"Warned? Are you threatening me? Chief, did he just threaten me? What are you all trying to hide? Why are y'all so determined to get me not to take this case?" He straightened his back as he spoke.

"Who does he sound just like?" Sergeant Stevens asked.

Those who'd been in the room a year earlier laughed.

"Chief, please, sign us up for the *Operation Almost* case. We'll take it," Officer Dallas Wilson yelled out over all the laughter.

Once the staff meeting ended, the rookie walked through the parking lot with his partner. I ran behind them. "Officer Wilson, may I have a word with you in private, sir?"

His partner got the hint and walked off.

"How may I help you, officer?"

"I just wanted to tell you, when you start to feel as if you are losing your mind because of this case, here's my cell phone number, give me a call. Any time. Day or night. I'm here for you."

"I won't be feeling like I'm losing my mind, Officer Reese." He tore up my phone number and dropped it on the ground. "Just because you almost caught the Chameleon and failed, don't mean I will fail. Yeah, don't look shocked! I've already started the investigation. Just know, I will report any crooked cops in the process." He poked his finger in my chest as he spoke.

Understanding what Dallas was about to endure, I placed my hand on his shoulder. "Rookie, when you come to understand that you can grasp at it, but you can't catch the wind either, then, you'll understand fully."

POSTSCRIPT
ALMOST . . . BUT

Chameleon

Shoulders passing. Quick glimpses. Forgotten momentary eye contact. Rude interactions. Polite gestures. Passersby. In grocery stores. Up and down the world's busiest streets. Quiet strolls in parks. Strangers encounter one another every day. Tens. Hundreds. Thousands. In corporate America. Airports. Train stations. Bus terminals. During morning and evening rush hours. Hundreds of thousands over a lifetime. Unacquainted, people zoom right by one another, driving on busy highways. Pass each other in crowded hallways at school. Across university campuses. Technology: gives new access to millions through the click of a button. Professors. Veterans. Mechanics. Physicians. Accountants. Police officers. Criminals. Plumbers. Active-duty Military. Blue collar. White collar. Construction workers. Postal workers. Attorneys. Nurses. Judges. Architects. Cashiers. Journalists. Janitors. Government Officials. Welfare recipients. News Reporters. Principals. Prisoners. Stay-at-home moms. Actors and actresses. Cafeteria workers. Singers and performers. Pharmacists. Street pharmacists. Secretaries. Athletes. CEOs. High school dropouts. Valedictorians. Preachers. Teachers. Entrepreneurs. Coaches. Bank presidents. Supervisors. Self-made millionaires. Angry folk. Happy folk. Sad folk. Mad folk. Married folk. Single folk. Only child. One of many children. Male. Female. Young. Old. Babies. Teenagers. Young adults. Acquainted. Unacquainted. Pro-lifers. Pro-choicers. Asian. Indian. American. French. Jewish. European. African. White. Black. Hispanic. Loved. Seemingly unlovable. People.

A small percentage: almost. Some don't know their own stories. Others do. Unless they tell you their story, you may never know they exist. They do. These are a few of their stories. In a twin-city region in Illinois, there are a small percentage of people who had to be. They represent a small number of some very special individuals living in small towns and big cities across the United States. Throughout the world. They are the "Almost" bunch. Almost . . . but God.

My name is Chameleon, and I am still at large.